INTO THE
DARK

by

CINDY
MCDONALD

Into the Dark

For information call: 304-995-1295
or Email: cindys.mcdonald@gmail.com

Designed by Acorn Book Services

Publication Managed by McWriter Books
http://www.cindymcwriter.com

Cover designed by Dawne Dominique

ISBN-10:0991368045
ISBN-13:978-0-9913680-4-4

Printed in the United States of America

Into the Dark is dedicated to my dear friend, Pam Coladonato. She passed away during the writing of this book. Pam was a talented and vibrant woman taken away too soon. I had the privilege to work under her direction, choreographing fourteen musicals. During that time, I was honored by the friendship that grew and flourished. I will miss Pam. Her memory will live forever in my heart.

ACKNOWLEDGMENTS

There are many people I wish to thank who had a hand in the publishing and pre-publishing process of To the Breaking Pointe. My dear friend and confidant, Linda Taylor, who always reads my manuscripts before they go to my editor—thank you for all of those wonderful "suggestions" of yours—I don't know what I'd do without them! I wish to thank my wonderful publishing manager, good friend, and fellow author, Lauren Carr, for her constant support and insightful editorial reviews of all my books. I'd like to thank my editor and proofreader, Colleen McSpirit and Sherri Good, and the creative genius behind this fabulous cover, Dawne Dominique. Last but certainly never least; I want to thank my husband, Saint Bill, your love and support always takes my breath away—you are my everything.

Cover design: Dawne Dominique

Editorial Review: Lauren Carr

1st Edit: Colleen McSpirit

Proofreader: Silver Lining Editing & Proofreading

TABLE OF CONTENTS

Into The
DARK

BOOK THREE

People are made of flesh and blood and a miracle fiber called courage.

~Mignon McLaughlin
The Neurotic's Notebook, 196

Only in the agony of parting do we look into the depths of love.

~George Eliot

PROLOGUE

Amazonian Valley, Peru

Luis Chaves watched Esteban Rojas gasp for breath. He gestured for two of his Peruvian guerilla fighters to yank the battered wooden chair that he was bound to an upright position. They ripped the thin piece of fabric from his face. Puddles of water surrounded the chair. Water rippled from Esteban's hair, down his face, through his rough thick beard, and over his saturated clothing. He shivered even though cloying heat consumed the hut. Vomit spewed from his mouth, while he blinked his eyes trying to focus. Luis had come into his camp with guns blazing to take over his operation. Most of Esteban's men were dead, and those who were alive had promptly vowed their allegiance to Chaves' cause.

Luis was once Esteban's confidante, but friends quickly become backstabbing enemies in the Amazonian Valley where drugs, weapons, and human trafficking rule the region. Luis grabbed a handful of Esteban's dark hair to yank his head upward.

He was nose-to-nose with Esteban. "You are weak. Your face is a pitiful bloody pulp from the beatings, and I will continue with the water board-ing until you tell me! Where is it, Esteban?"

"I ... I t-told you, I no l-longer have it."

Luis backhanded him. Blood spewed from Esteban's nose, washing over his already bloodied face. "It was valuable evidence, why would you not have it? You must! We were friends, but you have not been a useful ally for over a year. I did not want to do this ..." He turned to a man guarding the opening of the hut and nodded. The man left for a moment, and then returned with a little girl in his grip. A large gap split the top of her lip extending to the base of her nose to form a cleft lip. The gap was crooked and red. Her face was filthy from be-ing drug out of her village and through the brush of the Amazon. Her large inky eyes were filled with terror. Esteban struggled to focus on the young girl. Once he recognized her, he dropped his chin to his chest in defeat.

Luis waved a hand at the guard. He pulled the girl away, closing the door, and then Luis told

Esteban, "I will shoot your daughter if you do not tell me."

He knew that Esteban had no relationship with his daughter. He had decided years ago to leave the impoverished village that he and the girl's mother lived in to follow Luis. He had returned to the village only a handful of times, only to be turned away by the child's mother.

Yet for the sake of the woman that he once cared for and had created a less than perfect child with, Luis was confident that Esteban would give him the information that he needed.

Esteban struggled to speak. "P ... Patrizia has nothing to do with this." He spit watery mucus to the floor. Through a cough he insisted, "Let her go. I will tell you where it is, but you will not be able to get to it. It is no longer in Peru. It is in America with a woman who was my hostage."

"What are you talking about?"

"I knew this day would come. I knew your friendship was a temporary arrangement. When I got my hands on the evidence, I knew that I had to find a secure place to hide it. You trusted me to keep it safe, but what would become of me when you had no use for my services anymore? I hid it inside the American woman. I thought she would be mine for a long time. I was wrong."

Luis narrowed his eyes. He was uncertain if he should believe Esteban's words. "What is her name?"

"Dr. Rayne Lee. It is on a sub dermal microchip in her neck. She knows nothing of it. We drugged her when we put it in. We kept her drugged for days. We killed her husband, Matthew Lee. Her daughter, Sierra, was killed too. She was only four—collateral damage." He dragged in another ragged breath. Pressing through a rasping cough, he said, "The doctor was very beautiful so I kept her as my slave for months until a squad came and rescued her. They were well-trained soldiers—Americano. She is back in America. You will never be able to touch her."

Luis' gun exploded.

"Take this mess out of here and bring me the girl," Luis instructed the guards.

They picked up the chair that held what remained of Esteban Rojas and carried it out of the hut, leaving a wide trail of blood in the soil. A moment later, the guard at the door brought Esteban's estranged daughter in as he was instructed. Luis turned to the small girl with long dark hair and caramel skin that was interrupted by the ugly birth defect beneath her nose.

Esteban was of no use to him and neither was his pitiful little daughter. His hand hovered over the knife tucked in the sheath on his belt. He should slit her throat and dispose of her. She was just another child living in poverty in a dinky hut. He would be doing her a favor. He would be sparing her a life of drugs or slavery or worse—especially because of her wretched appearance.

With thoughts of murder in his mind, he made his way toward the girl cowering in the guard's steely grip. And then Esteban's words came back to him, "*We killed her husband, Matthew Lee, and her little daughter, Sierra. She was only four ...*"

Yes, he remembered the attack. He remembered Esteban bragging about killing everyone in the camp, including Senator Billings and Dr. Matthew Lee.

He also remembered Esteban telling him how he had taken a beautiful American woman as a sex slave—it was Lee's wife. Yes, now he remembered. If he was correct, the attack took place approximately four years ago.

Yes ... yes, and then Esteban's obligations started to slip almost two years afterward. Esteban said that the woman had a little daughter—Sierra. His eyes swept over Patrizia, who appeared to be about the age that Lee's child would be now if she'd been spared. Perhaps the trembling child before him would be of more use to him than he originally thought. He crossed his arms over his chest, studying her more closely now.

Luis' dark eyes were harsh and narrowed. His skin was ruddy and hard. His voice was laced with malice. "I did not have my men kill your mother when they took you away, but I will have them kill her just like I killed your father if you do not do as you are told! Do you understand?"

Tears saturated Patrizia's flushed face forming fleshy rivers down her cheeks through the dirt and grime. Trembling with fright, she said, "*Si*."

"Do you speak English?" he demanded in the only language that he knew, Spanish.

"Si, my mother teaches it in our village," Patrizia explained.

"That's right your mother is a teacher. Repeat after me in English," he demanded. "I am Sierra Lee."

The girl shrunk away, not understanding what he wanted from her. He bellowed, "Say it! I am Sierra Lee!"

Shaking with trepidation, Patrizia repeated the words in English, "I … am … Sierra … Lee."

"No!" Luis growled. "You must say it without an accent! You must say it as if you are an Americano!"

Patrizia was so frightened that she could not move. She could not stifle the cries that spilled from her throat. She tried again, "I-I … am … S-Sierra … Lee."

Rage rushed through Luis' veins. Again his hand found its way to the knife. He did not speak English, but he knew how it was supposed to sound. She was of no use to him! He should kill the ugly little wretch and find another way to get to Dr. Lee. As he drew closer to the horrified child, he suddenly stopped. *Wait a minute ... her mother is the teacher in the village. She teaches English to the children.*

Whirling around, Luis hurried to the opening of the hut. He called to his guards. "Bring the child's mother to me, immediately!"

The guards leapt from a bench and hurried to their dusty decrepit Jeeps. The vehicles fishtailed down the rutted road, leaving a tornado of dirt in their wake.

From the doorway Luis watched the Jeeps disappear into the miasma of dust, and then he called out, "Renzo!" A short dark-haired man came to the door. After dialing in a number, Luis handed him a cell phone. "Call this number and tell this man who you are with, and then tell him to get me Dr. Rayne Lee's contact information. He has all the connections to do this. Tell him that I will contact him at a later date, and we will talk about what he can do for me, and in exchange, what I will not do to him."

"*Si*." Renzo agreed.

Pleased with himself and the plan that was hatching in his mind, Luis nodded to the guard to release the child from his grasp. They stepped out of the hut.

Patrizia could hear him instructing the guard to stand watch over the hut. Her stomach lurched. She had botched the test that this horrible man had thrust upon her. A fresh spade of fear pierced through her—she was certain that they would kill her mother for her failure! She collapsed to the floor, weeping.

"Forgive me, Mama, forgive me."

CHAPTER ONE

Clutching Sierra to her breast, she had just made it inside the hut. She could hear the sound of running feet passing the tiny hut, the desperate pleas of women begging for mercy, and rapid gunfire filling the heat of the afternoon. Her four-year-old child wailed in horror. Setting Sierra aside, she yelled over the chaos, "Lay down on the floor!" And then she pushed the insignificant thatched door closed, hoping that the guerillas who were attacking the village would pass them by.

She crawled across the dirt to flip the old scarred wooden table on its side so that she and Sierra could hide behind it. Glasses, plates, and a pitcher of water shattered over the dirt. The table would provide scarce cover against the high-powered weapons that exploded all around them, but it was the only option at hand.

She cradled her child in her lap while they huddled between a chair and the table. Where's Matt? She wondered. *She had gone outside to see if he was tending to a patient when all hell had erupted.*

Men with dark hoods over their faces had stormed the village, shooting anything that was moving— women, children, and of course every man they saw, but she had made it to the hut! Oh God, oh God, what if Matt is dead? What if Senator Billings is dead?

The door to the hut whipped open, and even though her ears stung from the explosion of gunfire, she could hear the sound of combat boots shuffling over the dirt floor. In one swift move, the table was jerked away. Now she was looking into the barrel of a gun, and behind it was a pair of dark steely eyes peering out from behind a dirty sweaty scarf. She pulled Sierra tighter to her chest, closed her eyes, and whispered a desperate prayer...

Unable to breathe, Dr. Rayne Lee sat up in her bed, clutching the sheets. Sweat dripped down her face. Her saturated hair clung to her cheeks. Her chest heaved in and out, trying to take in air. Her wild wide eyes searched the room, looking for the ghastly intruder, but he had vanished into the dark crevasses of the past.

Taking slow deep breaths, Rayne willed herself to calm down. She glanced at the clock on the nightstand—it was 4:30AM. No, she was not going to frantically reach for the light like she used to do when the memories were fresh wounds that oozed habitual nightmares. She raked her fingers through her long dark hair to push it back, and then she dabbed her face with the sheets. She hadn't had a dream in more than a year, and she hadn't had to visit with Dr. Lockhart in a year and a half. She thought it was over—for the most part, anyway.

Frustration beat inside her chest. She punched the fluff of the comforter bunched between her legs. Why now? She had struggled through two years of intense therapy to regain her sanity. She'd needed the therapy after the guerillas attacked the village where she and Matt had gone with Senator Billings to provide humanitarian health aide. Matt had gone to the Amazon Valley in Peru several times without a hitch and had felt safe enough to bring her and Sierra along. But then Esteban Rojas and his militia attacked and killed everyone in the camp, except for Rayne. She became his slave for seven months—seven horrid months during which she prayed for death every day. And then Uncle Walt and his team known as First Force came to rescue her.

That was four years ago. No, she would never forget her husband, Dr. Matthew Lee, who she loved so dearly, and her beautiful daughter, Sierra, who she yearned to hold and kiss every day. Yes, her life was back on track, as well as could be expected. Rayne was the head medic for her uncle's international security firm, First Force. Her uncle's team consisted of ex-military Special Forces. She lived at First Force Headquarters, a Georgian mansion where she provided medical care for the team or any clients who may have been injured during a mission. First Force provided rescue missions for the private sector and every now and then for the government on a "don't ask, don't tell" basis.

She used to live at the mansion alone. For the past year Jack Haliday, an ex-Navy SEAL, and his daughter, Lil, lived in the west wing. After Jack's wife was brutally murdered, he became a member of First Force and brought his daughter to live at the mansion.

Over the past year she'd become very close with Lil and, if she were honest, with Jack as well. No, nothing romantic had happened between them—neither of them was ready for that—but Jack was easy to live with, easy going and, yes, easy on the eyes.

So what had brought on the dream?

Refusing to allow the dark demons back into her head, Rayne laid down against the pillow, performing an exercise that Dr. Lockhart had used during therapy sessions—exhaling the bad feelings, and then trying to inhale better ones. No, not necessarily good feelings—most times that was impossible. Therefore, Dr. Lockhart encouraged just better ones.

September's beautiful full harvest moon beamed through the window, blessing her with a natural night light only the good Lord could provide. She'd spent a lot of time over the past four years being angry with God. Nowadays she was finding ways to make peace with him. It was a slow but positive process.

Rolling over, her eyes fell upon the framed photograph that sat next to the clock on her night-stand. She had been in therapy for a long time before she could display the picture. She picked it up. By the pearly light of the moon she looked at the picture of Matt holding Sierra on his hip with his arm around her.

They looked so happy.

They were happy.

The photo had been taken by Uncle Walt at his Georgian mansion that his grandmother had left him—along with her fortune. Walt had taken the picture right before he drove them to the airport to leave for Peru. Little did she know that it would be the last family photograph ever taken.

She held the photograph to her chest, closed her eyes, and continued the breathing exercise she used to do on a daily basis.

* * * * *

Rayne woke with a jolt when Tickles, Lil's fluffy tabby kitten, jumped onto her stomach. Letting out a relieved breath, she lowered her head back to the pillow while stroking the kitty's ears.

"Well good morning, Tickles," Rayne whispered, her voice coming out raspy from sleep.

A pleasing breeze blew the curtains out into fat billows, and then sucked them back against the screen. Rayne was surprised that she'd fallen back asleep after her early morning fright. An errant strand of her hair wisped across her cheek on the brisk but pleasant September morning, reminding her that every day is a new day—a new opportunity for sanity.

The kitten purred, pressing her head against the picture frame that Rayne was still holding to her chest. Just then a little voice called through the slight gap Rayne always left in the doorway of the sitting room that led into her bedroom.

"Dr. Rayne, Daddy's making breakfast. He's got your oatmeal on the stove. You'd better come out. He's not too good at cooking it. It always boils over when he does it," Lil Haliday warned.

Rayne smiled. Yep, Jack Haliday was easy to live with, but the man simply could not prepare a bowl of oatmeal correctly to save his life. "Okay, I'll be right out, sweetie. Can you come get Tickles off my belly?"

Now the sound of Lil's giggles could be heard, along with the sound of her slippers hurrying through the sitting room. A nanosecond later, the curly haired scamp trotted through the bedroom door and stood at Rayne's bedside.

"Sorry," Lil said, gathering the kitten into her arms. "She must'a slipped passed me when I came to the door."

Rayne placed the photo back on the nightstand, and then hitched up on her elbow to rest her cheek in the palm of her hand. "Only a few more days until kindergarten starts. Are you excited?"

Smiling down at the kitty that was batting at one of the curls dangling down over her face, Lil shrugged. "I dunno. I guess so." She looked up at Rayne through her long lashes, concern filling her eyes. "What if the kids don't like me?"

"Are you kidding me? What's not to like? They're gonna love you. You'll have all kinds of new friends. Just think of all the birthday parties and sleepovers you'll be invited to."

Lil didn't seem too convinced. "I hope so. We'd better hurry, Dr. Rayne, or your oatmeal's gonna be yucky," the little girl advised with a crinkle in her nose.

Rayne tossed the blankets aside with a whoosh. "You're right. Let me throw on some sweats, and then I'll be right in."

"Okay," Lil said. She hurried to the bedroom door, but before she stepped through, she stopped and turned. "Are you sure the kids are gonna like me?"

"As sure as the sun comes up every morning."

Lil smiled and trotted out of the bedroom through the sitting room. Rayne could hear her slippers tapping against the marble floors in the corridor. She understood Lil's concern. The fact was that Lil's birthday was past the cut-off date to get into kindergarten, but Rayne had convinced Jack to have her tested. Lil was extremely intelligent and could read at a first-grade level. Rayne felt she would thrive in school—not to mention the interaction with other children would be beneficial as well.

Lil had spent a year in preschool. The school was very small, and there had been only ten students in her class—seven of whom were boys. The three girls in the class spent more time defending themselves than interacting. It wasn't exactly the preschool experience that Rayne or Lil's grandmother had had in mind, but they made it work. No one was surprised when Lil passed the test for early entry into kindergarten with no trouble at all and was accepted without question.

The First Force Headquarters was located in a very bucolic area of Harverton, Pennsylvania. Uncle Walt used to use the mansion as a safe house, but about a year prior he had converted it into their headquarters. That's when Jack and Lil had moved into the west wing. Over that time, Lil's only real companions had been her father, Rayne, Walt, her grandmother, Dale Martin; and the team members of First Force. They were all terrific influences, but they weren't children. Lil needed to mingle with her peers.

Wearing a pair of navy blue sweats and flip-flops, Rayne caught a glimpse of herself in the vanity mirror as she passed it. Her long dark hair was askew from the tossing and turning she'd done in her bed. She grabbed the brush, raked it through her hair a few times to smooth it, and then shuffled down the corridor toward the kitchen.

Lil sat at the breakfast bar eating scrambled eggs with a glop of melted cheddar cheese on top, or, as Jack liked to refer to them as, "cheesy eggs." Jack sat on the next stool. His thick nest of dark hair was a bit bed-tossed. He hadn't shaved yet, so he had a dark shadow of whiskers covering his jaw. When Rayne entered the room, he sat up very straight, flashed his thousand-megawatt smile, while presenting a bowl of perfectly cooked oatmeal sitting on the bar. Much to her surprise, he'd formed a happy face atop the cereal with fresh blueberries.

Rayne couldn't help but smile at the adorable grin staring up at her from her breakfast bowl, not to mention Jack's antics—he was pumping his eyebrows up and down. She clapped her hands. Laughing, Lil joined in.

"Very well done, Mr. Haliday."

"Practice makes perfect—we SEALs aim to please."

Rayne scooped up a spoonful of oatmeal to taste it. "Mmmm, it's not burnt. It's good."

"You had doubts?" Jack asked as if he were truly affronted.

"I'm afraid so."

"Okay, can't say I blame ya." Jack chuckled. "I'm going for a run, wanna come? Lil can ride her bike," he suggested.

Looking up from her oatmeal, Rayne shrugged. "I don't run."

"Ah, c'mon, I won't be too hard on ya. We'll only do a couple miles," Jack cajoled.

The left corner of her lip lifted. "Let me put it this way: I don't like running, and I never run. I guess I figure that I'm saving it up for that moment when I have to run for my life—then I should be able to run like hell."

"Hmmm, I can't afford that attitude. It's a good possibility that I'll have to run for my life every time I leave on a mission," Jack pointed out.

"That's very true."

"I don't mind running. It's good for you." He beat on his chest with his fist. "Good heart health and all that stuff."

"Actually, studies show that runners tend to have more coronary plaque buildup, not to mention chondromalacia patella," Rayne added and then stuffed a spoonful of oatmeal into her mouth. She opted not to inform him that women were more susceptible to chondromalacia patella than men. She was enjoying Jack's baffled expression at the big word she had thrown at him too much to spoil the fun. Around a mouthful of oatmeal, she clarified, "*Chondromalacia patella*—otherwise known as runner's knee."

Leaning a hip against the breakfast counter, Jack folded his arms across his chest. "So you're saying that running is basically bad for me?"

Rayne shrugged. "No. I'm saying that running, just like anything else, is good when done in moderation. I'm sure that a daily five or six mile run is perfectly fine. But if you were doing, say, fifteen or twenty miles per day, that would be overkill and not *necessarily* good for you."

"Ahhh, doctors—vague as usual. I'm going for a run."

Smiling, she peeked at him through her lashes. "Be my guest."

Jack tossed her an ornery grin and a wink on his way out the kitchen door. He'd definitely caught on. It didn't matter. Picking up her chamomile tea, Rayne decided to enjoy the view of his firm buttocks beneath the gray sweatpants and his broad muscled shoulders spilling out of the sleeveless sweatshirt that he wore.

After he slammed the door and the sound of his footsteps faded from the porch, she casually made her way to the window to watch him jog down the driveway. Oh, yes indeed, Jack Haliday was nothing but pure eye candy.

"Daddy's been going on a lot of runs lately," Lil's voice broke through her muse.

"I suppose…" Rayne said, turning. Her eyes flicked to the calendar on the refrigerator, and she noted the date.

It was the day.

One year ago…this day.

How could she have not noticed the date?

How could she have let it slip by?

Her heart sank. She studied Lil for a moment. The little girl was deep in thought, and yet Rayne didn't think that she was aware of the date—not really. Perhaps she knew it was close because the events had happened directly after her fourth birthday, and they had just celebrated her fifth over the weekend. Rayne took a long sip of her tea.

One year ago, a biker gang had attacked Jack's home in Rosemount. Jack had been critically shot, and his wife, Laura, had been killed right in front of him.

Rayne gazed across the breakfast bar at Lil, who was drinking the last of her chocolate milk. She was such a brave soul. Walt had carried her out of their burning home that day. Closing her eyes, Rayne could still see Grant Ketchum, a member of First Force, carrying Lil into the medical unit in the lower level of the mansion. Soot covered her face.

She clutched a purple unicorn pillow pet. Her lovely brown eyes filled with despair.

Rayne watched Lil lift the cup to her lips and drink down the last few gulps of milk. She remembered one of the first moments she'd spent with this beautiful little girl. She'd just finished surgery on Jack and had come upstairs to check on the girl's condition. Certain that the little one must have been hungry; she had made Lil a peanut butter and jelly sandwich. Surprisingly, Lil had eaten it, so she went to the pantry to retrieve a package of Oreo cookies—they had been her daughter Sierra's favorite, so she always kept some on hand. She remembered their conversation so vividly…

Rayne had asked Lil, "How many cookies does your mommy allow you to have?"

"Two," Lil said.

"Two it is," Rayne replied. She placed the cookies on Lil's plate. "These cookies are really good if you dip—" *her voice fell away. Lil's eyes were beautiful, big brown eyes with tiny gold flecks, full of wonder even during the horrific circumstances.*

Lil took the cookie between her fingers and dipped it into the milk. She held it carefully above the glass, allowing the excess to dribble off. Lil said, "I wonder if they dip Oreos in milk in Heaven."

Rayne managed to say, "I—I'll bet they do."

"Jesus probably likes it, so the angels probably do too. That's good. Cuz Mommy likes to dip her Oreos in milk."

Even now, Rayne sucked in a ragged breath at the memory of Lil's words. Though an entire year had passed, the image that Lil had managed to contrive of her mother dipping cookies in milk in the presence of Jesus and the angels had the same powerful effect on Rayne. This brave little innocent had found a way to cope with her mother's death, and yet four years after Sierra's demise, Rayne still struggled to cope, still struggled to conjure an image of Sierra dipping cookies in milk in the presence of angels in Heaven. The only image that she saw was the one of her child being ripped from her arms. She figured that the reason Lil was able to imagine soothing similes was because she hadn't actually witnessed her mother's death. Thank God.

Finishing her milk, Lil carried her cup and her plate to the sink. Rayne wiped a tear from her eye. Lil's mother, Laura, was missing so much—just like she had been robbed of the opportunity to see Sierra grow and flourish. Laura would miss Lil's first day of kindergarten. Rayne was determined to put Lil's mind at ease about going to school—not just for Lil, but also for Laura.

"Hey, I'm going to the mall after lunch, want to come along?" Rayne asked.

"Sure," Lil said. "I got a gift card from Little Big Man for my birthday for the book store, can we go there?"

Rayne smiled. "Little Big Man" was Lil's pet name for Stewart Little—the team's pilot. He was a huge man who rarely smiled. As a matter of fact, a grimace was considered Little's default expression. Why Lil didn't run in the other direction screaming when Little was around was a mystery to all of them. Instead she adored the irritable man and had dubbed him "Little Big Man" because he was so big, yet his name was Little.

Lil found his name most interesting. Little found it most annoying—or at least he pretended to. The truth was that he liked the small girl very much.

"I'd be happy to make a stop at the book store," Rayne said.

"Do you think Daddy could come with us? I don't want him to be alone on Mommy's death day."

CHAPTER TWO

Amazonian Valley

Bibiana Vasquez wrapped her arms around her body as if it was thirty degrees outside, and yet the sweat poured down her temples in the merciless heat. Her dark eyes were trained on the thatched door of the hut that Esteban's soldiers had dragged her into, shoved her into a chair, and told her to wait.

What could Esteban possibly want from Patrizia? What could he want from her? She had not seen or heard from him in years, yet they came in the drape of darkness last night to drag Patrizia away, and now they came for her as well. They had nothing to offer him. They had no money. No information on drug runners or weapons dealers.

And so she waited and worried …

What had become of her daughter, Patrizia? She wiped her watery eyes, and raked her harried fingers through her long black hair. It wasn't so long ago that Esteban Rojas lived in her village. He was a handsome man, and she was so very taken with him. He would come to her hut and they would go for a walk, hand in hand. Esteban was so charming, so full of life. Soon their feelings ignited into kissing, and the kissing exploded into a passion that neither of them could deny.

They would leave the village to find stolen moments of sultry pleasure. Beneath the Mauritia palms on an old scratchy blanket, she yearned to feel the sizzle and burn of his heated skin sliding over hers—to feel him climb to the top of his desire at the moment that she did, and then to lie close, holding each other's moist, naked bodies. They were young and didn't mind the heat—it only added to their pleasure. Bibiana had fallen hopelessly in love with Esteban, and he said that he loved her, too.

They planned to be married, until Luis Chaves came to the village looking for young men who wanted more than the poverty that resided there. He came with his promises of adventure and glory and more money than a young man like Esteban had ever dreamed of. Luis did a lot of talking, and Esteban did a lot of listening.

Soon their starlit walks became fewer and their nights of frenzied passion less. Bibiana realized that she'd become pregnant and when she told Esteban, he informed her that he was leaving the village to join Luis' militia. He left her behind to have the baby alone. Her heart was broken and her love for Esteban shattered.

When he would return to the village, he expected nights of reckless pleasure, but she would not. He did not force himself on her. For that she was thankful. After a while, he stopped coming to the village—until last night. She buried her face in her trembling hands.

Why?

She was not sure how long she'd been sitting in the chair waiting for Esteban to make his appearance. Her throat was dry and her mind was weary with worry. She prayed that he had not harmed Patrizia. Her daughter was all she had in this world.

Although Patrizia was deformed, she was a sweet child, intelligent, compassionate, and loving. Esteban would have nothing to do with her. He was disgusted by her face. He never came to know what a dear child she was. Bibiana pitied him for everything that he'd lost after he'd allowed himself to be dragged into the thick mire of greed and violence that Luis offered up on a golden platter of lies and deceit.

Bibiana was jerked from her thoughts when the door whipped open. Her eyes widened and her mouth dropped when Luis Chaves stepped into the hut with Patrizia in his strong grip. Jumping to her feet, her eyes met his sour stare.

"Mama!" Patrizia cried out, reaching with stretched fingertips toward her.

Luis bellowed, "*Silencio!*" He pulled his knife from the sheath and pointed it at Bibiana. His dark eyes were filled with malevolence. His voice was low and concise. "You will do as you are told, or I will kill your daughter and sell you into slavery."

"What do you want, Luis? Where is Esteban?" Bibiana demanded.

"I killed him." He relished in Bibiana's sickened expression, and then he continued, "I do not tolerate those who do not fulfill their obligations, and so you will fulfill yours or your daughter will die and you will pay with your freedom."

"There is no freedom in poverty, but it does not surprise me that you kill a friend when they no longer suit your needs," Bibiana bit out.

Luis smiled, his rotted teeth peeking out from his dry cracked lips. "Then you understand my capabilities. I want you to teach Patrizia to speak English."

"Patrizia knows how to speak English," Bibiana stated.

"No—not just the words, I want her to speak as if she were an Americano. I don't want an accent—you have two days to do this, Bibiana, or I will kill you both! Begin!" With that Luis marched out of the hut, closing the door behind him. Bibiana could hear him give instructions to a guard beyond the door to keep watch.

Relieved that the vile man had gone, Patrizia rushed into her mother's arms and wept into her bosom. "Oh, Mama, I am so sorry! I tried to say the words the way he wanted me to, but I could not! I was afraid that he would kill you!" The child's words came out in a panicked garble. Bibiana could barely understand what she was saying. All she knew was that her little girl had been frightened and bullied, and now the task at hand was not only impossible but ridiculous as well. How could she teach a child to speak without an accent in merely two days? She would have to try. She would have to be stern with Patrizia in order to save her life.

Being stern would prove to be a challenge. Bibiana was most gentle with Patrizia because of the cruel structure of her face. The world was a malicious place, unforgiving of such ugly appearances. The children in the village knew how to be nasty, and so Bibiana tried to show her daughter only tenderness, only love when she entered their home. For the next two days she would not be able to be tender—not if she wanted her daughter to see the third.

She grabbed Patrizia by the shoulder and looked into her eyes. "Calm down now, Patrizia. I need to know what Luis asked you to say."

Patrizia gulped in short hiccups of air, trying to pull together some composure. She was only eight, but she understood the dire situation that they were in. She understood that this time failure would prove to be fatal—not only for herself, but for her mother, too.

Bibiana looked around the hut. A grimy pitcher filled with water sat on an old table. She hadn't noticed it before, but then again, she was too busy fretting to notice much. She took her daughter by the hand and led her to the chair that she'd been sitting in waiting for Esteban to arrive. She sat the girl down, brushed back several stray strands of hair from her face, and then she poured a small amount of water into a dusty glass and gave it to Patrizia.

Kneeling down in front of the child, she pressed the glass into her hand. "Drink this, and tell me what Luis wanted you to say."

Patrizia took a sip of the water. Bibiana felt bad that the water was warm but it was wet, and she was certain that the child's throat had been dry for a long time. The girl cleared her throat before she spoke. "He wanted me to say that I was another little girl. He wanted me to say that my name is Sierra Lee.

I didn't know this girl. I didn't know anyone with that name in our village. Did you?"

Thoughtfully, Bibiana stood. Patrizia was speaking in the past tense, as if the girl no longer existed. She made her way across the table to another chair and sat down. "No," she replied. "I don't know anyone with that name. It is not a Peruvian name. It sounds American. Who could this little girl be and why does he want you to say that you are her?"

"Mama …" Patrizia whispered, and then she dropped her chin into her chest. Another round of tears fell from her eyes.

"What is it, Patrizia?"

Slowly, Patrizia lifted her gaze to meet her mother's. "They shot a man. This man, Luis, said he was my father. His name was Esteban. Is it true? Was he my father?"

Agony clutched Bibiana's heart. She cupped her hand over her mouth to stifle the gasp that threatened to burst through her lips, and then drew it into a fist. They had killed Esteban in front of Patrizia. What a horrible thing for a child to witness—an execution. Even though Patrizia never knew her father, she should not have been exposed to such a horrid display. Luis Chaves was an animal!

She placed her hands over Patrizia's and squeezed, trying to transfer what little strength she could offer. She murmured, "Yes, Esteban Rojas was your father, but he was not always like this. He was once a good and decent man. You must try to forget what you have seen. You my beautiful child are good and decent and compassionate—never forget that."

Patrizia wiped the tears from her face. "I was outside the hut. But I could hear everything they were saying. This man, Esteban Rojas, knew who this girl was, Mama. My father knew her. The girl is dead. Her mother is in America. They want something from her, and I think that is why they want me to say that I am this girl, Sierra Lee."

"What do they want from this woman?"

"I don't know—something that my father put inside her. I don't want to help them, Mama."

Bibiana looked to the floor not really seeing it. The information that her daughter just gave her was not surprising. These men were wretched creatures. They took what they wanted or needed from people and left the rest to rot in the Amazon wilderness. She did not want to aide them in any way either, but their choices were nonexistent. They either helped Luis Chaves or he would kill them—it was as simple as that.

Two days—she had a mere two days to teach Patrizia to speak without an accent, and like it or not, she would try like hell to accomplish that task.

* * * * *

Harverton, Pennsylvania

Lil's eyes were wide with anticipation. She ran her fingers along the line of books on the shelves at the Calico Cat Bookstore. The new books' covers were shiny, and the pages weren't folded or creased from reading them over and over again, like the ones that were stacked on the shelf in her bedroom.

Little Big Man had given her a gift certificate for as many as four books. Her heart swelled at the thought of Dr. Rayne or her father snuggled up next to her in bed at night to read one chapter from a Ramona book by Beverly Cleary before she went to sleep. Oh how she adored Ramona! She seemed to have a lot in common with her—other than Ramona had a mommy and she did not. Tickles always perched herself up on the pillow above Lil's head to listen along.

In the year's time that she and her father had been living at the mansion they had read almost all of the Ramona books—only one or two remained, so Lil planned to purchase those and some Henry Huggins books, too. Henry was a character that was sometimes featured in the Ramona stories. He seemed like a very interesting fellow, and Lil decided that this was a good time to learn more about him.

Her fingers came to a halt when she touched the books that she was hunting. Carefully, she drew them from the row and placed them in the basket that the nice bookstore lady, Amelia, gave her on the way in, and then her finger went back to perusing the long column of Beverly Cleary books for a Henry Huggins story.

"This one!" Lil exclaimed. The curls gathered by a yellow bow into a wild ponytail on top of her head danced as she turned to show her father. "Henry Huggins—he finds a puppy in this one!"

The corners of Jack's lips curled. "Looks like a good story, baby. How many books do you have in your basket?"

"Three, I've got enough money for four—but if you buy the Henry Huggins book then I could save the rest for later, and see if I want another Henry Huggins book, or something else."

Jack hesitated. She was playing him—the little scamp. At this point he knew exactly what Laura's reaction would be. "If you want four books, use your gift card to buy them. Otherwise, save back some to buy the fourth book at a later date."

"But, Daddy …"

"Lil …"

She made a face. Finally, after some thought, she accepted her father's advice and kept only three books in her basket. "Oh, all right," she muttered under her breath.

Whew! He got through that.

"Very wise decision," Jack put in. Lil was so much like her mother, and he hoped that she would turn out as Laura would have wanted. He hoped that he was doing everything in his power to bring her up in the best possible way.

"I'm gonna show Little Big Man this one. Maybe he'll read a chapter or two to me," Lil said with a smile in her voice.

"Little *reads* to you?"

She shrugged. "Sometimes I take a book down to the garage when he's working on the helicopter. He'll read a chapter, but he's not as good at it as you and Dr. Rayne are. He doesn't put any emphasis in his reading."

"Imagine my surprise," Jack said. "Well, whip that gift card out, and we'll meet Doc Rayne at the coffee shop, as promised."

Lil placed her basket on the counter and dug through her pink Hello Kitty purse to produce the tiny red envelope containing the precious gift card.

"Are you staying for story time today, Lil?" Amelia asked as she ran the books through the scanner.

"I'm afraid not, we don't have time today," Jack stated just as Rayne stepped into the shop.

"Oh, that's too bad. There are several girls in the story area that will probably be in your kindergarten class," Amelia said, nodding toward the small area with a big blue rug that children were starting to gather on.

Lil took a step backward. "Daddy's right, we don't have time for a story today, Miss Amelia."

Rayne could see the hesitation that bordered on trepidation in Lil's eyes. Perhaps Lil wasn't ready for kindergarten. Was she pushing her too hard? Guilt began to spill into her chest. Perhaps this was too soon after all. Just as the bad feelings of doubt were starting to simmer, it seemed like something was pressing her forward, a voice whispering in her ear, and she spoke up as if the voice was speaking for her, "Nonsense. We have time. C'mon, Lil, let's have a seat and listen for a while. Maybe you'll meet some of your classmates."

Handing Jack her package, she took Lil by the hand and led her into the story area, making sure that Lil was next to a girl who looked to be about five. Lil was pale. Again, Rayne felt a hand in the middle of her back, and she knew that somehow Laura was giving her the "go ahead."

Rayne touched a little blonde girl on the shoulder. "Hi, this is Lil. What's your name, sweetie?"

The little girl smiled and said, "Maggie." She held up a shopping bag from JC Penney. "I got some school clothes. I'm going to kindergarten in two more days." The girl displayed two little fingers. Her blue eyes were beaming with eagerness to unlock the mystery of school buses, lunch boxes, backpacks with pockets and zippers, and secret compartments.

"How nice! Lil's going to kindergarten, too. Is Mrs. Bower your teacher?"

Maggie smiled brightly. "Yes! Is she your teacher, Lil?"

Not sure what to make of the girl, Lil managed a nod. Rayne helped along. "Why don't you sit next to Maggie, and listen to the story? Your daddy and I will be along the wall with the other adults. Okay?"

Maggie put her hand out to Lil, inviting her to sit down, but Lil just stared at her not knowing how to respond.

Miss Amelia called out, "C'mon everyone, take a seat, I'm about to start the story!"

"Go ahead, Lil … sit down," Rayne cajoled, slipping the bag of books from her hand.

Lil eased herself onto the rug next to the blonde girl named Maggie, forcing a smile for her classmate. Feeling ill at ease, Rayne quietly backed away toward the wall where Jack was standing.

"I dunno, Rayne. She seems super uncomfortable. Do you really think she's ready for kindergarten?" he whispered, uncertainty and concern filling his tone.

"She's going to be just fine," Rayne managed, seeming to know that it was the correct response.

With a svelte smile on his lips, Jack put in, "You're so confident about these things. Laura was that way."

Jack rarely spoke of his late wife. Perhaps it was the day—the one year anniversary of Laura's brutal demise. Leaning against the wall, Rayne thought, *she certainly was.*

After story time ended, Lil managed a stiff good-bye to Maggie and her mother. Hand in hand, with Lil in between, Jack and Rayne made their way to the coffee shop where they served Lil's favorite chocolate chip cookies.

Entering the shop, they took a seat at a table, piling their packages in the center, while Jack went to the counter to order a coffee, tea for Rayne, and the cookies.

"Well," Rayne began, "Did you like Maggie?"

Lil lifted a shoulder. "She seems okay."

"Okay? I thought she was very friendly. I'll bet you become very good friends," Rayne assured.

"Maybe," Lil muttered. She pulled the Henry Huggins book from the bag and began thumbing through the pages.

Rayne grabbed a bag from the table. She pulled out a small silver box, and then held it out toward Lil. "Open this, I bought it just for you," she explained.

Putting Henry Huggins aside, Lil opened the box. Her eyes brightened. Her lips curled. Inside the box was a delicate strand of saltwater pearls. Lil took in a breath. "They're beautiful, Dr. Rayne."

Rayne took the box from her hand, removing the necklace, and clasping it around Lil's neck. She said, "This is what is known as a 'bravery necklace.' My mom gave me one a long time ago when I was afraid to walk down a very long aisle at my Aunt

Susan's wedding. She said that if I got scared to just touch the necklace, and it will help me to be brave. So, I thought maybe you might need one for kindergarten."

Lil threw her arms around Rayne, hugging her as tightly as she could. "Thank you, Dr. Rayne. I love you," she said.

Rayne could feel the tears welling in her eyes. It had been so long since a little girl had spoken those words to her. She hugged Lil back, trying not to let any tears escape. She failed.

"What's this all about?" Jack asked, setting a tray of steaming cups and warm cookies on the table.

"Look, Daddy! Look at my bravery necklace! Two more days until kindergarten and I already know someone," Lil told him, while she fingered the lovely necklace about her throat.

"Wow, it sure is beautiful, baby," Jack smiled at Rayne. With a wink, he said, "Have a cookie, Doc."

Rayne grinned at him. Yep, much to her surprise, she was grinning. She simply couldn't stop herself. She was feeling an inner peace that she hadn't felt in a long time. It was okay to love Lil back, and she found herself thinking that it might even be okay to fall for Jack Haliday.

* * * * *

When they returned to the mansion, they found Walt Wabash's SUV parked out front. Rayne's stomach instantly tensed—a mission. Yes, Uncle Walt sometimes drove from his residence in Rosemount to visit, but it was a little late in the day for that. She glanced across the cab to see Jack's eyes narrow—his jaw tightened. She could see that he too suspected that Walt's visit was business.

They pulled up to the house just as Walt was getting out of the vehicle with his briefcase in his fist, and then two more vehicles pulled through the huge wrought iron security gate at the end of the driveway—Grant Ketchum's red Camaro, and Smitty's charcoal gray Terrain rolled to a stop behind Jack's black Grand Jeep Cherokee.

Eyebrows raised, Jack pulled his cell phone from his jacket to check his text messages. "Wonder what's going on," he muttered.

Hitching her chin toward Jack's cell, Rayne asked, "Has the team been called up?"

"I didn't get an alert. Let's check it out," Jack said.

When they entered the house, Walt was already in his office to the left of the grand foyer, setting his briefcase on his desk. Grant and his new wife, Silja, walked up the front steps with Jack and Rayne, while Smitty hung back with Lil, admiring the books that she'd just purchased with her gift card and, of course, the bravery necklace Rayne had given her.

"Good job, Doc," Smitty called to Rayne, referring to the necklace, as the men filed into Walt's office, closing the door behind them. They were now in the "situation room" or as Rayne oftentimes referred to it as the "bat cave."

Rayne turned to Silja. "I'll make some coffee. Do you know what this is all about?"

"Not really," Silja replied. "But it must not be a very hot mission. Only Grant and Smitty were called in. Unless they're in some kind of deep do-do, and if anyone was in said do-do, it would *definitely* be those two," she giggled.

* * * * *

Ex-Marine Grant Ketchum from West Virginia, Will "Smitty" Smith who served as a field medic for the Army's Special Forces, and ex-Navy SEAL Jack Haliday took seats in the large office where their boss, retired CIA agent, Walt Wabash conducted meetings and planned missions for team First Force.

In his mid-fifties, Walt was an attractive man with a spatter of gray through his once dark hair. He kept in very good shape and stood at about six-foot-three. He leaned back in his chair, folding his hands across his wide chest.

"I wish all of our missions were as easy as this one," Walt began. "As you know, the President will be nominating Judge Alejandro Pérez to the

Supreme Court within a week or so. The judge was born in Peru, but became an American citizen at the young age of ten. Over the years, Judge Pérez has overseen some very controversial cases, and has handed down some controversial sentences—especially when it came to drugs and weapons trafficking. That said the Secret Service has asked me to provide two men to shadow Judge Pérez within his home." Pausing, Walt scrubbed a weary hand over his chin.

He reached into his open briefcase to retrieve two envelopes, tossing one to Grant and the other to Smitty. "Here are your plane tickets to D.C. You'll leave tomorrow at 06:00 hours. You'll be picked up at Dulles by Secret Service and briefed. Hopefully, this will go smooth as silk—a cakewalk. Once Justice Pérez's appointment is announced and confirmed, they'll assign him permanent security and you'll be free to return. I'm thinking not more than two weeks, hopefully."

"Why only two men, Walt?" Jack inquired.

"They would've taken the entire team, but I don't like for everyone to be gone in case we get a mission—especially for the length of time that Grant and Smitty are needed. Believe me, I'm not the only private agency they've called in on this one. The Secret Service has been taking a lot of hits lately over their competency. They want this to be a non-event, so their calling in all the stops from former agents and security connections."

"Good enough," Smitty said. "We'll be ready to bug out in the morning."

"Good," Walt said. "And boys ... stop somewhere and get a haircut on the way home, please."

Jack chuckled. Puzzled, Smitty and Grant ran a hand over their heads. Both men felt that their hair was a just length, but they would do as Walt had instructed. Smitty held the door open for Grant, shrugging when his friend and colleague tossed him a baffled look.

Smitty turned before leaving the room. Holding up his plane tickets, he said, "Hey, Haliday, sure you don't want this assignment?"

Jack snorted, while raking his fingers through his dark thick tresses, he replied, "Naw, I like my purdy hair."

"Bastard," Smitty said as he stepped out of the room, closing the door behind him. Jack chuckled.

"The haircuts are probably gonna be the hardest part of this assignment," Walt noted with a smirk.

CHAPTER THREE

Walking hand in hand along the stony dirt road lined with thatched huts, Mauritia palms, large leafy foliage, and succulents Sierra counted to twenty in Spanish, "Dieciocho, diecinueve, veinte!"

"Very good! What a smart girl you are!" she praised the child.

The road was busy with villagers, nodding at her and her daughter as they passed. Some called out greetings. Sierra was only too happy to reply in the villager's native tongue. They would smile at the child through the maize of dust that seemed to constantly cling in the thick air and cloying heat.

The basket on her arm pinched her skin as they made their way to the hut at the edge of the village where Matt was seeing patients. Searching her mind, she couldn't recall why she was not in the hut with him giving vaccinations or tending a Peruvian child with a sore throat. Funny, she was usually at Matt's side. After all, she was a doctor, too. Swiping a delinquent strand of hair from her face back toward the French braid twisted in her hair, she looked into the sapphire sky and scorching sun.

Perhaps she was running late. Perhaps Matt had let her sleep in, although it seemed like mid-afternoon. Usually at this time of day, Sierra would be with the babysitter, learning to count in Spanish or learning simple Spanish pleasantries. Yet here they were walking along as if she didn't have a place in the world to be.

Sierra broke through her contemplation, "Mommy, who are they?"

She turned toward the west end of the village to see a cloud of dust rising over the huts like a furious tornado coiling into the town. Engines revved, men were yelling in Spanish, but she couldn't understand their words, and that's when the shooting started. Everyone on the street dropped their baskets and ran panicked in all directions. Shards of bark from the palms splintered into the air, while bamboo from the thatched huts spit into the street from random missed shots.

Three rusted out Jeeps rounded the bend filled with men wearing black scarves over their faces, shooting at everyone, anyone, including women, old decrepit men. Terrified children fell to the ground with bullet wounds in their bodies.

Sierra screamed.

She whipped Sierra into her arms and hurried into the bush, trying to find a way to safety. The shrieks and cries of horrified people and fast spitting gunfire filled the air. With her child pressed to her chest, she frantically rushed through the large leafed foliage, hitting her in the face, slicing the skin on her arms. Her heavy breaths boomed inside her head. Her heart pumped so hard that she thought it would burst through her chest. Sweat poured down her brow, stinging her eyes.

She came to a hut. She didn't know whose home it was, and she didn't care. She needed shelter—a place to hide and pray that the attackers would be satisfied with the kill on the street and not venture into the huts. These people had no money. They had nothing of value.

She grabbed the handle of the thatched door, except she was yanked backward by her braid. Landing on her back, she lay in the dust, coughing, trying to catch a breath, trying to see through the miasma of grime, when her daughter was snatched from her arms by a tall man wearing a black scarf. He dragged her, kicking and screaming, up the short steps into the hut ...

"Sierra!" Rayne shrieked into the dark. "Sierra! My God, Sierra!"

In frenzy, she jumped to her knees. With her fingers spread wide, Rayne swept her hands over the bed searching for her daughter when strong arms enveloped her. She couldn't breathe. She pulled, pushed, and punched to escape the grip of the horrible man who killed her daughter and husband and took her hostage, Esteban Rojas.

Then a voice spoke softly to her, pressing his mouth into her saturated hair, "Shhh, easy now," he said, rocking her to and fro. "Shhh, it's okay, Rayne. It's okay, you're with me, Jack."

She gasped in a long breath, as if she hadn't taken in oxygen for hours. Her fisted fingers slowly relaxed, opening against his hard warm chest. She could feel him breathing evenly in and out and the thrum of his strong heartbeat. He was real. He was completely calm. It was Jack.

Jack brushed the tangled hair from her face to look down into her flushed cheeks and troubled eyes. "You're okay," he whispered. "Lie back against the pillow, and take some slow deep breaths."

Between hiccups of tears and breathing, Rayne managed, "It was just one of my nightmares. I'm sorry I woke you." Worried, she pushed up to her elbows. "I didn't wake Lil, did I?"

"No …" he said with a chuckle in his voice. "That child could sleep through a bomb," lifting the blankets, he urged, "lie back, relax. C'mon, get under the covers, it's kinda chilly tonight."

Rayne let him cover her up. His silhouette against the window where the moon's light sifted through the curtains made for a sexy yet imposing figure. She said, "Again, I'm sorry I woke you. Poor man, you shouldn't have to be bothered with a frantic woman and her nightmares."

Jack turned on the lamp on the nightstand. Now he was no longer a shape in the dark. He was dressed in cozy gray lounging pants that rode low on his lean hips, smoothing down over long muscular legs.

"No worries," he said. "I'm pretty good at tending nightmares."

"Oh ... does Lil have them often?"

"From time to time. You both have been through a terrible ordeal and lost love ones. Nightmares are part of the package, I'm afraid."

"Do you still have nightmares?" she asked him.

Something snaked across his lips. She wasn't sure if it was a sad svelte smile or a quiver. He dropped his gaze to his bare feet. He said, "I'll be right back." With that he left the room leaving her alone with the bits and pieces that she could remember of the dream.

Again, Rayne couldn't figure what was triggering the dreams. Each dream was a different scenario of what took place that day. In fact, the ordeal didn't take place during the daylight—Esteban Rojas and his men attacked their camp in the middle of the night, and yet all of the dreams took place during the day. Truth was she couldn't remember the event in detail. It had been suggested to her by her physiologist that perhaps it was a defense mechanism that her mind wouldn't allow her to remember the horrifying specifics of her daughter's death.

She made no effort to not think about Sierra. She couldn't do that—nor had Dr. Lockhart ever encouraged her to. Sierra should always be a part of her memories. She found that she thought about her daughter far more often than she did her late husband, Matt. It wasn't that she loved Matt less; it probably was because Sierra was her child—she carried her in her womb for nine months, nursed her, cared for her when she was ill. Perhaps that was the difference.

Matt never seemed to make an appearance in her dreams. She almost felt blessed for that. She had enough on her mind with Sierra, let alone adding Matt to the mix.

What seemed like only moments later, Jack stepped through her bedroom door now wearing a white T-shirt with the word *NAVY* scrolled across the chest—it only accentuated his sculpted physique.

The mattress dipped when he sat down to give her a cup of hot tea. "Here, drink this," he urged quietly.

Rayne glanced at the cup with steam swirling above the rim, and then she lifted her eyes to meet his. Her left eyebrow arched, she muttered, "I don't need tended to."

Half smiling, Jack shrugged. "It wasn't too long ago that you tended to me, or don't you remember the gaping gunshot wound in my side?"

"I remember."

"Well, consider this payback."

"Payback? You don't owe me anything, Jack."

"I owe you everything."

"Don't be ridiculous," she said.

"Don't be stubborn," he said.

"It seems we're at an impasse," she pointed out.

"Okay ... let's compromise. I won't be ridiculous if you stop being stubborn. Now drink this." He lifted the cup closer toward her. An ornery curve formed on his lips, rendering her defenseless. He was too damned adorable, handsome, and yes, she had to admit he was freakin' sexy as sin. He was making it almost easy to forget the night terror that she'd just experienced. For that she was most thankful.

Her mouth betrayed her with a slight amused curl. Taking the cup from his hand, she took a whiff of the tea. "Mmmm ... chamomile ... my favorite."

"I'm ridiculously observant," Jack put in.

Pressing her eyes closed, Rayne took a sip, allowing the comforting warmth to slide down her throat. Jack Haliday was ridiculously alluring. "Thank you," she whispered.

"I'll stay as long as you need me to," Jack said, and then he took her face into his hands and pressed his lips to her forehead. His lips were warm and even when he pulled away, she could still feel the warmth lingering on her skin. She wanted him to crawl into her bed, take her into his arms and hold her through the night.

Her mind was racing with thoughts of how beautiful his body must be when stripped down and how good he would feel inside her. She hadn't been intimate with a man in four years, not since Matt. She hadn't even thought about the touch of a man, the scent of a man, in all that time, until Jack Haliday stepped into her life. She didn't want to think about it—not after the seven months of horror she'd experienced under the subjugation of Esteban Rojas. The nightly rapes—the way he pulled her hair, and how he would demand that she strip for him in front of his guards. No, she hadn't wanted to think about a man's touch.

Over the past year, Jack's gentle nature and keen sense of humor had brought her back to the land of the living. Now the touch of a man—Jack's touch was all she could think of. She was not going to allow Esteban Rojas destroy the rest of her life. She would fight for a life. Who knows? She just might take up jogging, except she couldn't tell Jack that—she couldn't say those things to him.

He'd kissed her on the forehead—on the forehead—not the lips. It could have been meant as a comforting kiss—nothing more. She wasn't sure if Jack was ready to move on after the loss of his wife. She wasn't sure if he was having nightmares of that awful day one year ago.

There was no way in the world she was going to make any crazy assumptions that Jack was into her. She wasn't going to say or do anything that would cause a huge misunderstanding and a shroud of awkwardness to blanket the house. No way in hell.

She swallowed back. "I'm fine now. Thanks so much, Jack … for everything."

"You're sure?"

She nodded.

"There's nothing I wouldn't do for you, Dr. Rayne Lee. You know that, right?"

Taking another sip of the tea for no other reason than to prevent her from saying something so audacious as: Then climb into my bed and stay the night. She simply nodded.

He adjusted the blankets over her and quietly left the room.

* * * * *

The marble floor felt chilled against his feet. Jack made his way down the corridor until he reached the west wing of the house. Gingerly, he opened Lil's bedroom door just a crack and peered through.

His daughter was cuddled with her kitten, safe and sound asleep. Just as carefully, he closed the door and returned to his own, slipping the T-shirt over his head, tossing it into a corner.

He felt badly that Rayne's night terrors had returned. He knew that it had been a long time since she'd had them, and he felt guilty for how he was feeling when he was holding her close to his bare chest. He wanted to comfort her, except he wanted to get into her bed, hold her until the bad memories dissipated, and then ever so gently make love to her. He wanted her to not only be comforted, but to know that he wanted to be the one who was always there to chase the demons away. He wanted her to know that she could always find reassurance and security within his embrace.

She was too vulnerable. Her eyes were bruised with anxiety, so he did the only thing that he could think of to show her how much he cared—he kissed her on the forehead. He wanted to kiss her lips, but he didn't want to frighten her or crowd her—he would die before he did such a thing.

Jack crawled into his bed, folding the covers over his body. Rayne had asked him if he still experienced nightmares. He managed to dodge the question, but not very gracefully. Draping his arm over his eyes, he prayed that the nightmares wouldn't come calling tonight. There was one sure-fire way to keep the dreams at bay—talk with Laura.

Sometimes if he discussed what was on his mind with her, the nightmares would not come. Not that Laura sent the nightmares—she would never do something as dastardly as that. Laura was good and kind and loving. She wasn't capable of such wickedness. No, rather he felt that if at all possible, she would do everything in her power to block bad feelings or dreams.

He hadn't talked to her in quite some time—a month or so, and he felt a deep yearning to talk with her tonight. He needed to tell her something and hoped that she would understand, although he had no doubts that she would.

Can one really talk to those whom they've lost? He wasn't absolutely sure. But it must be possible on some level. When he made visits to Laura's grave to place flowers for her birthday, Christmas, or plant her favorite flowers in the spring beneath her headstone, he would see many people standing over a grave site talking to whomever lie underneath. Some would sit on benches provided, while others stood with their heads bowed talking to a parent or a child or a spouse. He preferred to talk to Laura in private, at night, in his bed—like they used to have many talks. He missed those talks. He yearned for those moments. But he yearned to begin again, and that's what he needed to say to her tonight.

How do I start? C'mon, Haliday, Laura was a straight-shooter. She wouldn't want you to beat around the bush. Just speak your mind, that's the way she would want it to be.

"Laura …" he whispered into the dark. "I love you, and I will always love you. I've met a woman—extenuating circumstances brought us together and have grown into so much more." Pausing, he smiled. "She's a good woman—a very good woman, like you. Lil loves her, and she's so good to Lil. I think you'd like her. Anyway, I want to pursue a relationship with this woman—her name is Rayne. Yeah, like the rain that falls, but it isn't spelled that way.

"Please don't think that I've forgotten or ever will forget you—that just isn't possible. You're in Lil's eyes. You're in Lil's giggle, but most of all you are in my heart and you always will be."

Had he said enough? Had he explained in the right way? He hoped so. He would never want Laura to feel tossed aside, unloved, or forgotten. As he rolled over, he felt a peace fall over him.

Memories spilled into his heart: The warm sun against their skin as they lay on the beach in Hawaii on their honeymoon. The day that Lil was born—the smile on Laura's lips and the gleam in her eye as she cuddled the newborn, letting her suckle her breast for the first time. Lil's first birthday party at their house in Rosemount—Laura made sure that everything was perfect, and the vacation they took in Disneyland the summer before Laura died.

The memories warmed his heart, and somehow he knew that Laura understood. She approved. In some sage way, Laura was giving him her blessing.

Closing his eyes, he whispered, "Thank you ..." as he drifted to sleep, finding comfort in the memories and knowing that the nightmares would not come—at least not tonight.

* * * * *

Amazonian Valley

Patrizia was exhausted. Her mother had drilled her all afternoon with only a short break to eat when a guard delivered a meager meal of bread and hummus. The sun had set hours ago. It was early morning. Patrizia wanted nothing more than to lay her head down anywhere and sleep, but her mother was unrelenting.

"We must go over these phrases again, Patrizia. You must speak smoothly, without an accent. Now concentrate, and repeat: I am Sierra Lee," Bibiana insisted. She spoke in English. Since she had begun working with her daughter, she forbade Spanish to be spoken—the more Patrizia spoke the language of the Americano, the better she would become. At least Bibiana hoped.

Patrizia yawned. Her head bobbed down toward her chest and then back up again. Her eyes were half-lidded. She murmured, "I ... am ... Sierra ..." her voice trailed off. Her eyes closed. She had fallen asleep in mid-sentence. The poor child simply could not repeat another word, another phrase. Bibiana figured it to be around two a.m. She had been pushing Patrizia beyond the limits for many hours.

Dropping her weary head into her hands, a feeling of desperation crushed her. She felt gutted by it. Was Patrizia's speech sounding more American? At this late hour and in her fatigued condition, she really wasn't sure. She was absolutely certain of one thing, Luis would make good on his promise to slit her daughter's throat if they did not succeed in stripping her of a Peruvian accent. They only had one more day to complete the task.

Luis was a fool. How can you teach a child to speak in a different dialect than what they have spoken all of their life in just two days? Even if Patrizia moved to America, she would retain her accent for many years. Likewise, if a young child came to live in Peru, they would most likely pick up an accent rather quickly.

Bibiana's head was spinning. She would leave Patrizia to sleep until the morning light filtered into the hut, and then they would begin again. It was an extreme situation that they were in, but without rest, how could she expect Patrizia to learn or retain anything at all? Perhaps after she'd slept for five or six hours, she would feel a little rejuvenated, and they could continue with the lessons with more success.

Gathering her daughter from the chair into her arms, she looked into Patrizia's face. So many saw her as ugly, hideous, but she saw a wonderful girl with a beautiful spirit. She didn't have the money to pay for a fancy operation that would fix the disfigurement she was cursed with at birth. She had no idea how to get financial aid for an operation. Such a life altering procedure was something that only miracles were made of. There would be no miracles for Patrizia—there may not be a Wednesday in her future. Laying her cheek on the top of her child's head, she tried to push the terrifying thoughts from her mind and drift off to sleep. She too needed to rest if they were going to survive this nightmare.

* * * * *

The thatched door flung open. Bibiana woke with a start. The sun had not awakened her as she thought it would, instead Luis' voice boomed through the small space.

"Why are you sleeping, you lazy women! I want to hear the girl speak, and it had better be good! I am wasting my food and my time on your worthless souls!" Luis bellowed, grabbing Bibiana by the arm, hauling her out of the chair.

Patrizia cowered in her mother's arms. Instantly, Bibiana was filled with rage. She spit out an angry statement in Spanish, "We only speak English in this hut! If you don't speak the English, do not speak at all!"

Luis was taken aback by her daring. "You are in no position to tell me what to do! I will kill you where you stand, and be happy to have rid the world of such an unattractive woman. You will be of no use as a slave! No man will want to lie with you," he spit out a poisonous chuckle, "unless he is given a paper bag! Then again, you are big in the right places, huh." Luis pinched her right breast hard.

The guards near the door laughed. Flinching at the pain, and pulling away from his sickening touch, Bibiana dropped her gaze to the floor. It was true. Bibiana was not a beauty by any means. She was short—not quite five-foot-one inches; she was on the tubby side, and very well endowed.

Seeing her mother humiliated by a man not worth the air that he was sucking, Patrizia launched herself at him, hitting him in the stomach with her tiny fists, and kicking him in the shins.

"My mama is a beautiful woman!" she yelled in Spanish. "You are nothing but a pig!"

Luis laughed at the child's willful display, and then his face turned hard. He grabbed the child by the arm, and demanded, "Let me hear you speak the English! It had better be to my liking if you know what is good for you and your mother!" He shoved Patrizia into a chair. Tears of malevolent frustration saturated the girl's face.

Bibiana hugged her to her chest, whispering into her ear, "Calm down, my Patrizia. Calm down. You must do your best to speak the English or we are done for." She eased away from Patrizia, but the child could barely catch her breath. The tears would not cease, and the trembling would not relent.

Bibiana knelt down before her daughter. In as calm and tender a voice as she could muster, she said, "Repeat after me … My name is Sierra Lee."

Patrizia tried to form the sentence, but the words would not come out. Her distorted lip moved. It quivered, but no sound came from her mouth. Fear, frustration, anger, and hatred boiled to the surface. She burst into tears, unable to respond to her mother.

Luis booted Bibiana aside. With a yelp she fell into the dust. He grabbed Patrizia by the arm, jerking her from the chair. "You will say the words! Say them now! My name is Sierra Lee!"

Patrizia's eyes snapped around the room. The guards stared at her with scowls on their faces. Their weapons at the ready to execute any command that Luis gave them. Her mother's face was flushed with fear, and Luis' eyes burned into her like red-hot lasers. She hated him. She hated the village where no one would stand up to the guerillas when they drove

71

into town like a hurricane destroying everything in their path. She hated the children who taunted her because she wasn't born with a perfect face, but most of all, she hated what this man was asking her do. He wanted her to help him betray a woman into believing that her daughter still walked the Earth, so he could take from her some treasure that she possessed for an evil purpose, no doubt.

She didn't want Luis and his men to hurt her mother, but try as she might, the words would not pass through her mouth.

Luis shook her again. "What are you waiting for? Don't you know that I will kill your mother if you don't do as I say?"

"Please, Patrizia, please try to say the words," her mother begged.

Overwhelmed, Patrizia covered her face with her grubby hands. Luis pushed her into her mother's arms. "I should kill you now!" he yelled. "I should take my knife and gut you then leave you for the vultures! If I come tomorrow and she will not speak, perhaps I will not kill you. Maybe I will cut you, tie you to a log, and let the alligators in the river eat you alive!" He marched to the door, and then he turned back. Yanking his knife from its sheath, he pointed it at them, and exclaimed, "Tomorrow, Bibiana! Tomorrow!"

* * * * *

An ugly silence filled the hut after Luis slammed the door. Feeling the burn of defeat wash over her, Bibiana climbed into the chair. Tears streamed down her cheeks while she raked her fingers through her hair. There was no way out. Even if Patrizia spoke the words to Luis' expectations, would he kill them for sport after his use for her was over? There were no guarantees. She looked down at Patrizia on the floor. She was not crying, rather she sat perfectly still staring into the dirt. Undoubtedly, she was disgusted by her failure.

Bibiana wondered if she would be able to perform the task tomorrow. Squeezing her eyes closed, she raised her face to the ceiling, dreading Luis' rage and what would come afterward if Patrizia did not rise to his demands tomorrow.

With the heels of her hands, she wiped her tears away. In a weary voice, Bibiana called to her daughter in English, "Come to the table, Patrizia. We must practice."

CHAPTER FOUR

Whistling a tune, Jack mopped his brow while he made his way up the stairs from the gym into the kitchen. Being an early riser, he was self-appointed to breakfast duty, while leaving dinner detail to Rayne. He was fairly talented at making eggs and bacon, but felt it was a safer bet to leave things like chicken parmesan to the more experienced cook in the house.

When he opened the door to step into the kitchen, he was most surprised to find Lil sitting at the breakfast bar. Her curls looked like they'd been put through a blender and her eyes were still droopy with sleep. Jack checked his watch, 07:00 hours. Usually Lil wandered into the kitchen closer to 08:00. Her early appearance actually worked because tomorrow was the first day of kindergarten, and for the rest of the year she would most likely need to be up by this time anyway.

"You're up early," Jack pointed out. "Would you like some cereal?"

Around a wide yawn, Lil replied, "Sure. Are you taking me to the bus tomorrow morning?"

"Wouldn't miss it."

"Is Dr. Rayne coming, too?"

"I'll bet she is. Are you getting excited?" he asked, hoping for a positive response.

Thoughtfully, Lil fingered the saltwater pearls around her neck, and then smiling, she said, "Yes."

"Good deal," Jack said, just as his cell phone buzzed with a text message. After glancing at the screen, he said, "Hey, Grandma Dale wants to take you shopping today to buy some school clothes."

"But Dr. Rayne already got me some."

Pouring cereal into a *Princess Aurora* bowl, Jack put in, "Well, my understanding is that girls can never have too many clothes … or shoes," he mused while adding the milk, and then setting the bowl in front of her. "Besides, this gives you and Grandma a chance for some time together—you always enjoy that."

"Hey! Maybe we'll bump into Maggie at the mall," Lil said, pushing her hair from her face.

"Maybe," Jack replied. He had his doubts, but he was willing to go along with anything that would promote a positive attitude toward kindergarten.

The truth was that Jack had called Dale the day before about Lil's hesitations because she was a teacher in the district that they used to live in. Immediately, Dale asked if Lil had a backpack. Jack had no idea that she needed a backpack. Dale was thrilled to offer to take Lil shopping for one, and said she would send a text in the morning with a time she would pick up Lil. The text indicated ten a.m. and that she would have her home by dinner. Glancing at his daughter, Jack was relieved that he had plenty of time to get Lil to take a shower and do something with those out of control curls.

* * * * *

Waving goodbye to Dale and Lil as they pulled out of the driveway, Jack closed the heavy Mahogany and beveled glass front door. When he turned, he almost bumped into Rayne. "Hey … you're getting up late. How are you this morning?"

"Oh … um … I'm fine. I had some emails to catch up on," Rayne said. She was dressed in a red tunic sweater with a fall floral scarf wrapped around her neck, and a pair of skinny jeans tucked inside a pair of tall leather riding boots. She left her long dark hair cascade over her shoulders. Pushing the leather strap of a small purse further up her shoulder, she added, "I'm on my way out. I'll catch up with you later."

As Rayne attempted to step passed him, he gently grabbed her arm. "This isn't about last night, is it?

I'm sorry if I made you feel uncomfortable. I was just trying to help."

Uncomfortable? This man made her feel anything but uncomfortable. He drew out feelings that she hadn't experienced in a very long time. She was more concerned for his comfort level. She didn't want him to feel responsible or obligated to her in any way. Again, she was more than contented with their living arrangements, and she didn't want to do anything to compromise what they had.

The corners of her plump lips curled slightly. "I am in no way uncomfortable, Jack. I told you … I had some emails to catch up on. That's all. I'm on my way into Harverton. I want to go to the farmer's market for some pumpkins and mums, and I know Lil likes the fudge that I buy there, so I thought—"

"Mind if I tag along?" Jack asked. "I haven't been to a farmers' market in a long time. My mom used to drag my brother and me there every Saturday morning. We hated it, but somehow I think walking through one with you might be a little more enjoyable."

Rayne was taken aback. Scratch that, she wasn't taken aback, she was stunned that Jack wanted to walk through a farmer's market—with her. Did she mind if he tagged along? Hell no—she would be thrilled to death, but of course she wouldn't let on. Releasing a sigh, she said, "No … I don't mind if you come—"

"Great! Give me a few minutes to change out of these sweats," he said as he hurried toward the west wing of the house. "I'll be right back."

After watching Jack round the corner out of sight, Rayne fell against the door. *Hokay ... what just happened?*

* * * * *

Harverton, Pennsylvania was a quaint small town. The streets were constructed of brick and the shops that lined the sidewalks wore awnings of every color and shape. Several coffee shops and restaurants provided wrought iron tables and chairs outside of their establishments, and they were very busy with the farmer's market in town.

The traffic was heavier than usual and the cross-walks were bustling with women pushing strollers amid several small children keeping in step behind them. This would be the last week that the market would see so many youngsters as school would be in session starting tomorrow morning. The young mothers would have fewer children to keep track of among the many booths that lined the town square located across the street from the courthouse. The poor dears would have a less stressed look about them, while they perused the mother-load of fresh produce.

As Rayne carefully steered her red Ford Explorer along the busy street, Jack spotted an aged Cadillac pulling out of a parking space in front of the Korean War Memorial—directly across from the market. It wasn't a free parking space like the garage next to the courthouse, but that was most likely packed. Not willing to let the grand opportunity pass, Rayne eased her vehicle into the space. It would be a shorter distance to lug pumpkins, and with Jack along, she figured she could buy more than one—possibly three.

After dropping four quarters into the meter, Jack and Rayne made their way across the street into the market. This was Rayne's favorite time of year—when the trees began to show a strong yearning to bare their branches with just a tinge of yellow and orange. The breeze was warm and welcoming, but it held a crisp warning that one should not be so taken in for summer was close to drawing her last breath. The flaps on the rows of tents that housed different farms' produce snapped in the breeze as if to announce: McMurray's Apple Farm! Buy your fudge here! Walnut Creek Produce! Oh yes, she intended to visit all of them and then some.

Rayne was pulled away from her thoughts of the delightful September day by the sight of women passing by with sultry gleams in their eyes, and a sensuous lift to their lips. At first she was baffled, and then she realized that they were sizing up one Mr. Jack Haliday. She had to chuckle to herself.

Yep, he was an eyeful of man candy, and he was with her. Hands off, ladies.

"Hey look at this!" Jack called to her. Rayne stopped. She hadn't realized that she'd walked at least fifteen feet ahead of him. She turned to see Jack holding up an oddly shaped squash. She'd seen the squashes many times at the market, but she didn't really know what they were called or what they were used for. Jack seemed tickled by his find, so she moseyed back to have a look.

"I haven't seen one of these in years," Jack went on, holding up a golden bell-shaped squash for her to see.

"What kind of squash is that?" she asked.

"It's called a golden patty pan squash. My mom used to buy them all the time," Jack told her.

"I've seen them around. What are they used for?"

That ornery, sexy, adorable smile that she'd become so accustomed to but never took for granted, snaked across his lips. He was enjoying the fact that he had the doctor bemused. He asked, "Have you got sugar, brown sugar, cinnamon, and vanilla at the house?"

"Sure, I've got all kinds of baking supplies. Why?"

"When we get back, I'm gonna make you the best damned apple pie you've ever tasted," he declared, while holding up two of the squashes for the young girl tending the stand. Captivated by the overtly handsome man, she jumped from the stool that she was perched upon behind the bins of assorted squash and apples to wait on him. With bedroom eyes and her tongue practically dragging on the grass, she bagged the squash and took Jack's money. Rayne couldn't blame her. Her tongue had been dragging on the ground all morning, too.

"Sooo, you're going to bake me an apple pie with those funny looking things when we get home?" Rayne inquired in a teasing manner.

"You bet," Jack retorted with a cool confidence.

"I can't wait."

After several hours of walking, talking, and perusing, they packed Rayne's SUV with an impressive haul: two one gallon jugs of cider, three butternut squash, two golden patty pan squash, one Granny Smith apple, one Honey Crisp apple, one pot of yellow mums, one pot of burgundy mums, and three pounds of assorted fudge from the fudge lady who was delighted to let Jack sample to his heart's content. They had to make a second trip to carry the pumpkins to the vehicle.

Jack managed the two largest pumpkins through the crowds in the market and across the crosswalk, while Rayne carried the smaller one. He loaded his pumpkins into the back of the SUV, and when she transferred her pumpkin from her arms to his, their hands brushed. They both hesitated, feeling the heat that rushed through them. It was undeniable when their eyes met.

Rayne's throat was suddenly dry. She licked her lips unable to cast her gaze away from his mouth, and then he smiled. Oh yeah, it was *that* smile—the one that drove her crazy every day since the man stepped foot into the mansion, every day that she sat across from him at the breakfast bar, and every evening that she ate dinner with him.

She let go of the pumpkin too soon. Jack didn't have a good hold. It fell, splattering between them, yet neither of them moved, neither of them flinched—they both just stood there like two goofy teenagers at their first high school dance, trying to figure out where to put their hands for a slow dance.

Jack blinked back into the moment. Clearing his throat, he asked, "Are you ready for some kick-ass apple pie?"

Rayne smiled. With a rasp in her voice, she said, "Very."

They got into the Explorer, leaving the broken pumpkin behind.

As Rayne drove slowly toward the end of town, Jack asked her to make a quick stop at Shuster's Grocery. It was a little store located almost at the last traffic light in Harverton. The owner, Sam Shuster, was a Vietnam veteran. He also served as the interim pastor at the Presbyterian Church on Sixth Street when Pastor Jordan was sick or out of town. Sam was about sixty-five and walked with a severe limp.

The guys from the team always did their shopping in Shuster's Grocery to support a fellow vet, not to mention that they enjoyed Sam's quick wit.

When Jack jumped back into the vehicle, he showed Rayne his purchase: a package of frozen pie crusts. Rayne widened her eyes and dropped her jaw open as if she were appalled. "You're going to use *frozen* pie crusts for your *kick-ass* apple pie?"

"Hey, these are great baking time savers, and they taste pretty good too." He raised his hands in surrender. "I know, I know, some may consider it cheating—"

"Whoa, you're just one surprise after another, Mr. Haliday. First I find out that you can bake, and now I'm finding out there's some cheating involved."

"Just drive, woman. You'll take it all back when you bite into my tasty masterpiece."

"No doubt," Rayne muttered.

* * * * *

The pleasant breeze had transformed into a gusty wind by the time they arrived home. The leaves that were weak and simply couldn't hold on whipped passed the large arched kitchen window, while Rayne sat at the breakfast bar, sipping tea, watching Jack gather the baking supplies needed to make his special recipe.

While Jack peeled and sliced the apples and the squash, he told Rayne how he grew up in Texas and joined the Navy with high hopes of becoming a SEAL. He even let Rayne into his private world by telling her how he met Laura at a nightclub while he was on leave, and how they were married within the year.

"Wow," Rayne commented. "You must believe in love at first sight. One year is a short time to know someone to make a commitment like marriage."

Tossing a heaping handful of flour onto the counter, Jack said, "When you know it's right—it's right. I knew Laura was the one for me the moment I laid eyes on her." He looked up at Rayne, his hazel gaze burning into her brown eyes. They seemed to be smiling at her and tempting her at the same time when he said, "I've always known what I want when I see it, and I've always been pretty lucky at being right." Carefully, he pulled one of the thawed pie crusts from the package, unwrapped it, and then laid the rolled up dough on the flour-covered surface. "Hey, are you just gonna sit there sipping that tea, or are you gonna make yourself useful?"

"What do you want me to do?"

"How about roll out this crust for me?" he said, holding the wooden rolling pin out to her.

Rayne hesitated. "Um … I'm not very good at rolling pie crust. It always rips, and I wouldn't want to ruin your masterpiece."

Jack chuckled. "It rips, you say? Well, you must not be doing it correctly."

Rayne cocked her head to the side. "Apparently not."

He wiggled his pointer finger at her to come closer. Rayne pushed off the stool to stand next to him, but Jack shuffled her to stand in front of him to face the counter, while he imprisoned her between his arms. Her tummy tightened. Gently, he used his chin to move her hair away from her ear, and then he whispered, "Grab some flour with your fingers and smooth it over the roller."

Trying not to show how fired up she was, she took in a steadying breath, and then reached into the canister on the counter to gather a fistful of flour. Unerringly, she rubbed the flour over the roller.

Jack whispered, "Now take a firm hold of the handles …" Rayne complied. Jack placed his hands over hers. "Nice and easy, roll it over the dough, using just enough force to stretch it out." His hands guided her through the task, while he murmured in her ear, "That's right … now add some flour to the dough to keep it supple …"

She could feel the stiff column of his erection against her buttocks. He adjusted his stance slightly to hide his excitement. Everything feminine in Rayne clenched. Feeling the wetness forming between her legs, she moved toward him to allow the bulge to brush up against her. With every stroke of the roller, the warmth of his strong hands atop of hers, and his breath feathering her skin was driving her crazy. A heat crept up her spine. She could feel the flush on her cheeks.

"Looking good. Now lay the crust across the pan," he instructed. His voice had changed from calm and patient to raspy and husky.

Gingerly, she lifted the crust from the counter and laid it across the pie pan. Leaning into her, Jack reached for the bowl of sliced apples and squash smothered in sugar and cinnamon. Missing the touch of his hands, Rayne took hold of the bowl, too and helped him pour the mixture into the crust. He placed the second roll of dough onto the floured space.

"Are you ready to go solo, or do you still need assistance with the roller?"

Rayne swallowed hard. "Oh, I'm not sure I quite have it yet, and like I said, I wouldn't want to ruin your work of art."

Jack smiled against her neck. "I aim to please," he whispered. Slowly he ran his hands across her hips, up her ribs, and down her arms until his hands covered hers already grasping the handles of the roller. "Let's review ... forward ... then back—"

"Just enough force to stretch it out," Rayne put in.

"You're a quick study, Dr. Rayne."

Picking up the dough, she murmured, "Now gently lay it across the pan."

"Gently?"

She lifted a shoulder. "Well, not necessarily."

Together they worked the dough around the rim of the pan to form a curvy crust. Jack said, "Press it together, gently—or not." He picked up a knife and cut into the top crust. "Now vents to let the steam escape."

"Are you sure we want that to happen?" Rayne questioned, breathless.

"Not really."

Rayne thought she would burst. Tossing any inhibitions she may have earlier had, she turned around taking his face into her flour-covered hands to pull him into a heated kiss. He swallowed her into his arms, pressing deeper into her lips, savoring the passion.

When she finally released him, Jack teasingly asked, "Are you trying to seduce me?"

Rayne liked it. She freely admitted, "I am."

"It's working."

Rayne inquired, "How long does it have to bake?"

"About an hour."

Twisting one of his dark locks in her fingers, Rayne posed, "Is that enough time?"

"Gawd, I hope not."

"You'd better put it in," Rayne told him.

"It's definitely ready."

"Absolutely," she agreed.

Without hesitation, Jack swept up the pie and placed it in the oven, setting the timer for sixty minutes.

Rayne leaned against the wall, crossing her arms under her breasts to admire his tight rear as he bent over to place the pie in the oven. When he straightened, she couldn't stop the desire that was driving the curl of her lips. She reached her hand out to him. Accepting her hand, he pulled her into his arms, kissing her neck, her right ear lobe, nibbling his way across her delicate jaw to her lips. Spellbound, she hopped up, wrapping her legs around his torso, pressing her tongue into his mouth, wanting nothing more than to be as close to this man as she could possibly get.

In a silky voice, she whispered, "I want you, Jack. I want you now."

As he carried her through the house toward his bedroom, her frantic fingers unbuttoned his shirt. She pushed it from his shoulders to sweep her mouth over his throat, shoulders, and chest. When they arrived in his room, Jack laid her across his bed. Quickly he shimmied out of the shirt that was dangling from his elbows, allowing it to fall to the floor, and then he made quick work of her riding boots, tossing each over his shoulder after he pulled them from her feet.

Before he could touch any more of her clothing, Rayne sat up to grab the button on his Levis, unzipping him with unerring speed, pulling the jeans and briefs to his knees in one haul, letting his erection spring free. She ran her tongue up the length of the shaft. Jack's stomach contracted, his head fell back, letting out a growl of pleasure that was almost her undoing. His body was as gorgeous as she had imagined and more. Her tongue continued to explore his sex until his hands grabbed her shoulders, pushing her into the mattress.

"You have way too many clothes on, and I have way too little patience," he said in a husky tone. With cool endurance, he slipped her jeans and panties from her hips, down her long slender legs to the floor, and then he removed her scarf. "Arms up," he instructed. Rayne raised her arms to let him pull her sweater over her head, and soon her bra was dropping to the floor.

Her dusty pink nipples stood at attention. Jack slowly lowered his body to hover over hers. Closing her eyes, she arched her back upward to give him full access as his tongue licked, sucked, and nibbled at her nipples. Ever so slightly, he pumped his hips to let his penis caress her warm wet clit. She spread her legs farther apart. Every cell in her body was super sensitized, enjoying every sweet sensation that his body was offering hers.

He raked his fingers through her long dark hair. "You are so beautiful. Your hair, your body, you are a beautiful person, Rayne Lee, and I want to make love to you right now."

"Don't hold back, Jack, because I certainly won't be," she said, grabbing him by his taunt buttocks, pulling his hips and his erection closer to the heat of her desire.

He slid inside her. She let out a moan that she couldn't have called back if she tried. He filled her up, and he felt so incredibly good inside her as his heated body slid over hers in a rhythm that she'd forgotten about long ago. Their breathing accelerated almost to a pant as they climbed to a place where all their inhibitions couldn't survive only the touch, the feel, the ecstasy of passion driving them closer and closer to their flashpoint.

Jack's fingers tightened in the tangle of her hair as the spurts of his pleasure reached the top, while her fingers dug into his shoulders and her back arched higher into the pain and hunger of her longing. The world where their lives had been destroyed and then slowly painstakingly rebuilt melted around them. It was only the pinnacle of their rapture in each other's arms that mattered—only them and nothing or no one else.

Her body relaxed, exhausted, and replete. He kissed her cheeks, jaw, and throat. Carefully, he rolled down beside her, caressing her hair. She opened her eyes in search of what was in his, and she saw exactly what she wanted to see—what she needed to see—a man completely rapt in a woman that he'd just made love to. She favored him with a demure smile. He returned the favor, and then gently brushed his lips over hers. It wasn't necessarily a kiss—it was sexier than that. She thought it was his way of saying, I am so glad to be here with you. I wouldn't want to be with anyone else.

He lay back against the pillow, lifting her to lie upon his chest. Oh yeah, this man was everything she'd ever hoped he would be.

She lay against his wide chest, feeling it rise and fall with each sated breath. Her body was boneless—so completely at peace. She relished in the feel of his fingers lightly caressing her bare shoulder. No, there would be no awkwardness in the house. She knew that their lovemaking was pure of heart. Jack wasn't some horny womanizing pig looking for a quick booty call—Jack was a sincere man who loved his daughter, believed in family values, and she truly believed that he would come to love her as well—if he didn't already.

Rayne's heart swelled. He was so warm and safe and strong and loving. She was falling into those emotions that she hadn't felt in so very long—not since Matt. No, there would never be a replacement for Matt, but she knew that it was time to let the healing she'd already begun move her forward into another relationship, and give herself permission to do so. Carefree contentment enveloped her, lulling her into a deep sated sleep.

Jack flinched when the buzzer on the stove went off alerting them that an hour had passed and the pie was ready to come out of the oven. Damn, she could lie in this man's arms all day long and make love with him over and over again.

"Dang … I'd better get the pie before it burns. Wouldn't want to ruin my masterpiece," Jack said, while easing out of the bed, searching the floor for his boxer brief. The buzzer sounded again. Jumping on one foot, Jack hurried toward the bedroom door while trying to pull on his shorts.

Lord have mercy, Rayne couldn't take her eyes off the man. Nevertheless she couldn't suppress a giggle watching him jump around. She called after him, "I know whose making the pies for Thanksgiving!"

"Agreed, but only on one condition—we use the same baking technique as we did today," Jack called over his shoulder as he rushed down the corridor.

Rayne snuggled deeper into the blankets. The bed was warm where he'd been laying and his musky scent lingered on the pillow. "No problem, Mr. Haliday. No problem at all," she murmured.

CHAPTER FIVE

Washington D.C.

Grant and Smitty hit the ground running. Agents from the Secret Service picked them up at Dulles International Airport as Walt said. After receiving their assignments, they spent the morning in a large room at the Secret Service Headquarters with a crowd of security agents listening to countless briefings about Justice Alejandro Pérez—his background, his daily schedule, the court cases pending on his bench, who he had meetings with in the coming weeks, what restaurants he and his wife frequented, who he dined with, what time he usually left his office, and what time he arrived at his residence at the end of each day. The judge was consistent if nothing else.

Loosening his tie, Smitty muttered to Grant, "I wonder what time we can expect the judge's next bowel movement." Grant let out a weary chuckle at his friend's comment. They were on their way out of a meeting for a twenty-minute break until the next began.

They pushed through the doors into the sunshine for some fresh air. Grant almost plowed into Smitty when he came to an abrupt halt. "Hey," Smitty said over his shoulder. "Isn't that Peyton Mattock—that guy who was in charge of the mission in Russia back in March?"

Grant looked passed Smitty's shoulder. He didn't need for him to point or gesture in any way toward the man whom he was talking about. Peyton Mattock stood out from the crowd. The man was well built and about six-foot-three, but that wasn't what set him aside from the rest—many of the agents were tall and well-muscled. Peyton wore his long dark hair in dreadlocks pulled away from his face in a ponytail. Even during the evening, he wore a pair of Oakley sunglasses. Leaning against the building, Peyton watched the agents file out, while sipping a cup of coffee. He was sporting a well-tailored gray suit with the tie completely un-done, both ends were dangling loose around his neck, and his white shirt was unfastened down to the third button.

"That's him all right," Grant said. "Not too many ops look like that. How the hell did he get into this assignment with that freakin' hair?"

"I dunno, but I'm sure as hell gonna ask him," Smitty retorted, while running a hand over his fresh buzz cut. They made their way through the throng of agents toward the man that they'd teamed up with in Russia to rescue Grant's new wife, Silja.

Peyton didn't look up at them when they approached. He simply took another sip of his coffee and said, "Hey, boys, I see you drew the short shitty end of the stick, too."

Grant offered his hand. "Good to see you, Peyton. They dragged your ass all the way from Russia for this assignment?"

With a cool grin, Peyton shook Grant's hand. "Like I said, I came out on the losing end of things." He looked passed them. "Just the two of you? Nobody else from your team?"

Dropping his chin to his chest, Smitty snorted. He knew that Peyton was referring to their colleague, Casey Rhodes—the very attractive dark-haired, leggy, First Force sniper. He said, "No, just us, I'm afraid. Sooo, no haircut for you on this one, Mattock?"

Peyton drew his Oakley's to edge of his nose to peer over the top at Smitty and Grant's short hair. Pushing them back into place, he let out an ornery chuckle. "Nope. They dragged me kicking and screaming across an ocean for this dog and pony show—I wasn't cutting my hair. I'm working the lawn and garden detail anyway—I'll be wearing a jumpsuit with my assumed name on it. I think they think that the dreads will make me more *believable*—not that the Secret Service would ever use stereo types or anything like that."

"Lucky you," Smitty said around a snort at Peyton's sarcasm.

"Damn straight," Peyton added, tossing his cup into a nearby trashcan. "What have you been assigned to?"

"We're on twelve hour shifts on the first floor of the house, 17:00 hours to 05:00 hours," Smitty explained.

Peyton fingered the lapel of Smitty's suit. "You'll be wearing the strait jackets even during the wee hours of the morning?"

"Abso-freakin-lutely," Smitty groused. Hitching his chin, he said, "C'mon, we'd better get back in there. I just can't wait to find out if ol' Alejandro has any hemorrhoids."

"I'm on the edge of my seat," Grant put in, as the three men made their way toward the doors. Peyton was quickly buttoning his shirt and trying to do up his tie without a mirror.

* * * * *

After taking out the French braid, Rayne ran her fingers through her hair to loosen it from her scalp. She tossed her robe over the foot post of her bed, and crawled between the sheets. Laying her head against the pillow, she wished that she and Jack had made love in her bed, perhaps the scent of his cologne would still linger on the pillowcase.

Closing her eyes, she took in a long gratifying breath, trying to relive the day in her mind's eye— the crisp breeze blowing through the rows of booths at the farmer's market, Jack's easy going smile, how excited he was when he came upon the golden patty pan squash, and mmm, the wonderful flavor of the apple pie that he'd baked with the squash and a few well-chosen apples.

She giggled to herself—the lesson in rolling out pie dough was an exercise in oh la la, and surprisingly enough, the frozen pie crust was pretty darn good, too. But the best part of the day was lying beneath that man, feeling him move inside of her, kissing his lips in the heat of the rhythm, and then falling asleep beside him in the warmth of his embrace.

When Lil arrived home, they had dinner and pie and laughter. After Lil dressed for bed, they gathered on the couch with the curly haired scamp tucked between them. Jack slipped in a DVD, and they all cuddled under a fleece blanket that Jack's mom had sent him for Christmas to watch *Brave*.

This was not an unusual evening for them. Many nights they sat together to watch a Disney flick, but tonight was different. She and Jack had forged a relationship, and movie time felt more like family time than any other night before.

During the movie, Rayne caught Jack peeking at her askance over Lil's head many times. She hoped that he was thinking what she was thinking: *Oh yes, this could be a family. This could grow and flourish into so many wonderful things. This could be just the beginning of the healing that all of us so desperately need.* There was no doubt in her mind that God had his hand in this day.

Whatta day!

Snuggling down into her bed, she felt warmth rising inside her. This was the start of something good. She felt sure that she had the strength and the yearning to begin again—with Jack, and now she had no reservations that he was feeling the same thing, too.

Her thoughts were interrupted by a tap at the door of the sitting room just beyond her bedroom. Pushing up to her elbows, she called, "Yes …"

"There are two pieces of pie left, want some?" Jack asked from the hallway.

Her heart leapt in her chest. There was no fighting it—she was grinning from ear to ear and she had absolutely no doubt that she was beaming—yes, beaming. She didn't care. It felt good—it felt so damned incredibly fantastic to be beaming!

"I'd love some. Come in," she told him.

She heard the door open and then gently close. Anticipation wrapped around her heart as she listened to the sound of his footsteps move across the sitting room, and then he peered into her bedroom.

"I didn't wake you, did I?" he asked.

"No … I just got in bed. I hadn't even turned out the light," she assured him.

"Good." He sat at the edge of her bed.

She was most surprised at how she felt. She was comfortable and confident, so she lifted the blanket and said, "It's chilly, c'mon, join me."

She watched his reaction, and he didn't disappoint. His lips curled. He scooted under the blankets next to her, while she fluffed a pillow against the headboard behind his back, and then set one up for herself—it was contentment beyond belief, and it felt as natural as if she'd been doing it for years.

He handed her a plate with a slice of pie and a fork on it. Without hesitation, she scooped up a piece and put it into her mouth. She closed her eyes, savoring the rich apple flavor, except it wasn't just the pie she tasted. It was the tang of her perfectly picturesque September afternoon spent with this wonderful man, who was now sitting next to her in bed, eating pie.

Yum, yum, yummy!

"I'm not the type of man who beats around the bushes, Rayne."

She stopped mid-chew. *Oh no. Oh God no. This wasn't the part where he apologizes for what happened this afternoon, is it? Please dear God, don't let him say something like: I'm really sorry. I was out of line. It's not you—it's me. I'm not really ready for a relationship right now.* Suddenly the pie felt like a large lump of cement in her stomach.

Slowly, Rayne gathered herself together. Wincing inside, she set the plate on the nightstand, and dragged her gaze to meet his. "I hope not. I always want you to be straight with me, Jack."

"Good … because I have strong feelings for you, and I'm hoping that maybe you might feel the same way. I don't make love by accident, Dr. Lee, and I don't think that you do either."

She could barely control herself. She wanted to shove him into the mattress and make mad crazy love to him. Instead, she smiled, and replied, "Oh that was no accident, Mr. Haliday. And besides, a man who makes this good of a pie has my undying affection always."

He looked thrilled and relieved at the same time. Pointing to himself and then to her, he said, "Sooo, this can happen?"

"Try to make it stop, Haliday," she stated, wrapping her arms around him, she pulled him to her lips. He tasted of cinnamon and apples and lust and a brand new beginning.

* * * * *

Amazonian Valley

"Please, dear God, let Patrizia's English satisfy Luis," Bibiana prayed into the dark, while her exhausted daughter lay sleeping across her lap. The moon's light rippled into the cruddy hut where they'd spent two long hot frustrating days. They were tired and hungry and dirty. The stench of body odor clung in the humidity that consumed the room.

In the suffocating heat, she drilled her daughter mercilessly. She had no choice—she had to be firm with Patrizia or death was in the offing. Her trembling hand cupped over her mouth. She tried to stifle her crying. She begged for deliverance from a god that she wasn't sure could hear her or felt her worthy of his aide. Surely Patrizia was worthy. Surely he wouldn't let this child who had already suffered so much in her short life fall victim to the likes of Luis Chaves.

The helplessness and hopelessness made her feel hollow inside. Tears streamed from the corners of her eyes down the side of her cheeks. Her strength was waning; her fight was cowering in the dark corners of the hut. There was nothing left but prayer. There was nothing left but the hope that Patrizia would speak clearly—if she chose to speak at all.

Yesterday when Luis demanded a sampling of their progress, Patrizia froze. She could not utter a single word. Enraged, Luis repeated his promise to kill them both if she didn't come through the next day, and now there were only mere hours until he would burst through the door and order Patrizia to say the words that he wanted to hear in clear concise English.

Patrizia's English and understanding of the language had greatly improved in the past two days, but Bibiana had no idea if it were to the standards that Luis required. If not, how could she convince him to give them more time? She was well aware that she had a better chance to beg for time than for mercy. Luis Chaves was known to kill his own men if they looked at him the wrong way.

The darkness was fading, giving way to the morning. Her stomach coiled. She could see the sun rising through the thatching and she knew that the moment of reckoning was drawing near. She pulled her daughter closer to her chest, fearing that these could be the last hours that they would be together. Unable to hold it in for another moment, Bibiana broke down. Her shoulders pumped from weeping. The tears flowed from her eyes down her hot flushed face.

And then she felt Patrizia's small hands on her cheeks, brushing her hair away. She spoke to Bibiana in Spanish, "Don't cry, Mama. I will do good. You will see. Luis will not kill us. We will be fine and return to our village and live in our hut, and maybe I can help you teach the children English."

Bibiana took Patrizia's hands into hers, kissing each finger. She spoke to her daughter in their native tongue, "I believe in you, Patrizia. You will do your very best today, and Luis will be pleased." She took a moment to gather herself, and then asked, "Will you be able to do as he asks when it is time to do whatever dirty work he is planning?"

Patrizia lowered her gaze to her lap. "I must."

Angst spilled into Bibiana's heart. What would Luis expect from this child, and how many would be hurt by her actions?

As the morning approached midday, Bibiana became tenser. She did not drill Patrizia. She left her daughter to sleep. Fatigue would only exacerbate the dire situation so she let her rest, hoping that it would help her to perform.

Soon it was late afternoon and Luis had not shown his ugly face. The guard came in with food and a pitcher of fresh water toward evening, and still he had not come to test Patrizia. Bibiana had kept Patrizia busy all day with word games. She kept her speaking the English language, but did not apply any more pressure than need be.

Darkness fell over the hut and the long stress filled day withered away into night. While Bibiana was relieved not to have to deal with Luis, she knew that he would soon surface and Patrizia would have to speak the way he demanded.

The sound of a nearby waterfall gave her a small sense of solace. The water beating against the rocks as it fell was quieting, although throughout the night she only managed to doze. Every noise, every slight movement brought her to alertness, fearing that Luis would burst into the hut with his knife drawn and wicked intentions in his heart. Early in the morning, the guard brought in a meager breakfast.

"Luis will be here soon," he told her before he stepped out of the hut.

Bibiana's chest tightened. Patrizia ate very little. It was only an hour later that the door opened again, and Luis stepped through.

"Are you ready to speak, Patrizia?" he asked. He was surprisingly calm.

The girl rose from her chair at the table. She dragged her gaze to meet his. She said, "I am Sierra Lee."

Luis' jaw clenched. His eyes narrowed. "I can still hear the accent, Bibiana! We have no more time! Guards!"

Two men rushed into the hut. One grabbed Bibiana by the arm, and the other grabbed Patrizia.

"Take them outside! I can't stand the stench in this hut!" Luis bellowed.

The guards dragged them through the door. Patrizia screamed and kicked, while Bibiana begged, "No, Luis! Do not do this! Please spare Patrizia! Please!" The guards drug them down the short steps into the open and tossed them into the dirt. Luis' men gathered round to witness the brutality of the killing. Pumping their weapons over their heads, they hooted and hollered their approval.

Bibiana had to act fast, she had to find a way to make them useful to Luis or he would kill them. She screamed at the top of her voice, "The slight accent is more believable! Do you not see?"

Luis raised his arm. Silence fell over the camp. "What do you mean?" he asked her.

Trembling and breathless, Bibiana rose to her knees, she explained, "This girl, Sierra, was only four when she was separated from her mother. If she were living here for four years, she would have picked up an accent. Don't you understand? If Patrizia spoke perfect English, it would not be believable. Whoever you are trying to fool would be suspicious. Speaking with a slight accent would be more … convincing."

The men in the camp looked to Luis. Bibiana grabbed her daughter and held her close to her chest, waiting for his reaction. Luis stood on the last step of the hut contemplating what he had just heard.

Stepping away from the hut, he pulled a cell phone from his pocket. He thumbed the numbers into the phone. "You will have one chance to prove this to me. My connection provided me what I needed as I knew that he would. When the woman answers the phone this is what I want you to say, Patrizia …"

* * * * *

Rayne tugged the ribbon holding Lil's hair atop her head into a bow, and then kissed her on the cheek. "You're ready. Today is a big day, and I know when you step off that bus later this afternoon, you'll be full of stories about the kinder-garten and new friends for your daddy and me at dinner."

Lil brushed her finger across the saltwater pearls. "I hope so, Dr. Rayne. I'm hoping that nasty boy from my preschool, Landon Rawlings, isn't in my class. He's a real brat."

Rayne was hoping the same. Lil was right, Landon was very hard to deal with and his mother wasn't much better, but she smiled brightly, and said, "Don't worry about Landon. I'm sure Mrs. Bower knows how to handle troublemakers. C'mon, your dad is waiting to take you to the bus."

Lil's eyes widened. "Aren't you coming, too?" her voice was laced with concern.

"Of course I am. I wouldn't miss it." She helped Lil slip into her bright pink backpack that sported a large sparkling capital L on the flap, and then taking her by the hand, they walked down the corridor toward the grand foyer where Jack was waiting.

When they rounded the bend Jack called out, "Wow! Don't you look all grown up!" Giggling, Lil ran into her father's arms. She hugged him with all her might and all her love. "You're gonna have a great time in kindergarten and I'll be at the bus waiting for you when you get home." He kissed her on the cheek. Setting Lil's feet to the floor, he looked up at Rayne, tossing her a wink and a smile.

Smirking, she looked away. She was reminded of last night's lovemaking, and the way Jack quietly gathered his clothes from the floor, kissed her lips, and then snuck back to his bedroom around six a.m. so Lil wouldn't know that he'd been in her room. It was almost as if they were teenagers trying not to get caught by their parents, while making love in the backseat of the car. It was difficult, but she managed to stifle the giggle that was fighting to bubble to the surface. She was certain that her cheeks were flushed, hence the very reason she needed to look away.

"C'mon you two lovebirds, let's get to the bus before I change my mind about going to kindergarten," Lil said, as she yanked and pulled on the heavy door that she could never quite get open. Jack's eyes snapped to Rayne's. Both of their jaws were dropped wide open, until Rayne had the presence of mind to cup her hand over her mouth.

Pulling the door open for the child, Jack asked, "What are you talking about?"

Lil rolled her eyes. "*Pleeeze* ... I might only be five, but I know that look," she pointed to Jack, "You look at Dr. Rayne like Prince Eric looks at Aerial ..." she fluttered her eyelashes, "... all *lovey-dovey*," she teased, as she trotted out of the door and down the steps to the waiting SUV in the driveway.

"Well, I'll be damned," Jack muttered.

"*Lovey-dovey*?" Rayne put in.

"Apparently," Jack replied with a chuckle in his voice. "Now what?"

Rayne shrugged. "We take her to the bus and send her off to kindergarten, as planned."

"I suppose so," Jack agreed.

They waited for the bus outside the wrought iron gates at the end of the driveway, and when it appeared at the end of the road, Lil turned to Jack and Rayne with her jaw clenched and her lips spread wide across her face, posing an exaggerated apprehensive expression.

"Everything's gonna be fine," Jack assured her. "It's gonna be great."

Lil fingered the pearls, hugged her father, and then Rayne. The bus screeched to a stop with the red lights blinking back and forth above the windshield. The door squealed as it folded open with a flashing stop sign extending outward. Peering into the bus, they saw a tubby woman sitting in the driver's seat wearing a green sweatshirt with the words Harverton Elementary School scrolled across the chest in white. She had bright red curly hair and a wide welcoming grin.

"Hi there," she said, "I'm Caroline Johnston, what's your name, sweetie?"

Lil studied the woman for a moment. "Lil Haliday," she informed her, and then she turned back to Jack and Rayne. "Goodbye," she said as if she were being bravely led to the lion's den. The bus doors folded closed. All the lights stopped flashing and blinking, and the bus slowly rolled away.

Rayne glanced at Jack who seemed dumbfounded by Lil's theatrical departure. "Whatta drama queen!" she declared, unable to contain her laughter.

Jack turned pulling her into his arms and kissing her playfully on the neck. "She knows how to get to me, and somehow I think you do too. I'm gonna to have to work on that or instead of being the king of the castle, I'll be a hostage."

"Oh, I think it's way too late for that, Haliday."

"You might be right. Do you want a ride back to the house?"

"I think I can make it on foot," Rayne said.

He pulled her closer. "I could drive you back, and walk you inside, and stick around for a while."

"Then you'd be late for training, and I don't think Uncle Walt would be too happy about that," she pointed out, while zipping his hooded sweatshirt up a little higher.

"Probably not. I'll be back early afternoon," Jack said.

She kissed him on the nose. "See you then."

When she turned to walk away, he pulled her back into his arms, kissing her with heated possessive passion, and then he pulled away. "Now that's a proper good-bye." He slid into his vehicle and pulled onto the road.

The leaves twirled and swirled over the gravel like a wispy cyclone behind his SUV as it rolled down the road. Rayne pulled her sweater closer around her body while stepping through the gate and pushing the buttons to make it swing closed. As she made her way down the long winding driveway, she breathed in the morning. It was crisp and fresh.

She felt like skipping.

She felt like singing.

Hell, she felt like doing cartwheels all the way back to the house!

She was just stepping passed the first fat round pillar on the porch when her cell phone rang. A smile stretched across her lips. It was most likely Jack calling with some snappy remark that would make her laugh, but when she pulled the phone from the pocket of her sweater, the screen announced, *Unavailable.*

Disappointed and disgusted that a telemarketer had probably gotten a hold of her number, she pressed the green button with every intention of telling them never to call her again, but rather than a salesman on the other end, she heard a tiny trembling voice. "Mama ... this is Sierra ..." the next thing she heard was a shuffling, a gasp, followed by the growl of a man's voice, and then the line went dead.

Rayne stood stunned. She couldn't breathe. Had she heard what she thought she just heard?

Did the little girl call her mama?

Did the voice say that she was Sierra?

Her *daughter* ... Sierra?

No! How could that be?

Sierra was murdered four years ago!

She fell against the pillar, staring at the dark screen on her cell phone. Her chest felt tight like a steely fist had grabbed her heart and squeezed with all its might.

* * * * *

"That is all!" Luis growled, grabbing the phone from Patrizia's hand, pressing the red stop button. Patrizia ran into the mother's arms. Luis turned to Bibiana. "You have earned another day of life. We will see how Dr. Lee reacts in the coming days, and then we will see if you live or die."

CHAPTER SIX

It was a wrong number. It was a bad connection. Perhaps the child did call her "mama" because that's who the child thought she had dialed, but obviously she hadn't. Most likely she only *thought* that the little girl called herself Sierra. It was very possible that the girl said *Sarah*. It didn't matter. There are plenty of little girls named Sierra. It was a cruel coincidence.

Raking a harried hand through her hair, she rolled her eyes at her ridiculous musings. It simply was not possible that Sierra was calling her—because Sierra was dead. The end. That's the way it was. That was a fact of life that she'd spend several years in therapy to accept, and she wasn't about to allow a simple misdial to distort all the progress that she'd made.

A breeze lifted her hair from her shoulders, reminding her that it was a chilly morning. Pushing away from the pillar, Rayne stuffed the cell phone back into the pocket of her sweater, and decided to go inside and make a nice hot cup of tea to still her absurd thoughts. Fingering the phone deep in her pocket, she knew that hitting the redial button would be futile. Unavailable numbers were just that, unavailable.

Pushing through the door, she exhaled the bad feelings that had consumed her, and inhaled good ones—that's right, good ones, because she had the ability to have good feelings—not better, as Dr. Lockhart used to encourage, but good, because incredibly good things were coming her way—she just had to let them in.

Her hands were shaking ever so slightly when she dipped the tea bag into the cup and set it in the microwave.

"Mama … this is Sierra …"

She shook her head. No! She wasn't going to allow the girl's words to play over and over in her mind. She looked up at the clock—Jack had only left twenty minutes ago—it would be at least three hours before he returned. The buzzer on the microwave went off, making her jump.

Enough!

Hokay, after she steeped her tea, she was going to march downstairs into the medical unit and take inventory of supplies—even though she'd just done an inventory two weeks ago. Regardless, she was going to drive into Harverton to get anything that the unit required—even if it was one lousy box of gauze. She was not going to sit around the house, allowing wild thoughts to molest her.

Yanking the cell phone from her pocket, she tossed it onto the breakfast bar, and then gathering her cup. She made her way downstairs, turning on the lights in the hallways that led passed the gym, the three hospital rooms that they kept ready at all times, the small operating room, and then into the supply room.

She snatched the clipboard that hung on the wall just inside the door and began counting the boxes of bandages on the shelves. No matter how she tried to concentrate on how many of this or that was on hand, she couldn't help but think, *please Jack, come home soon.*

* * * * *

Rayne was right. The medical unit was well equipped. There was very little that was needed, and what she may have been running a tiny bit short on wasn't of much concern. Never the less, she made the fifteen mile trip into Harverton to the pharmacy to purchase a box of 4X4 gauze pads, antibacterial hand scrub—the dispenser in room two was looking a bit low, and a large box of band aides—it was always a good idea to have plenty of those on hand with Lil around.

With the radio up louder than usual, she was on her way home. She'd managed to chase away the sound of the little girl's voice in her head for most of the day, yet something about the voice haunted her. It wasn't just that the girl called herself Sierra, it was the way the call ended—the man's harsh voice, the shuffling sound that the phone made, like it was being ripped from her hand, and the abrupt disconnect. The child sounded like she was in distress—she wanted her mother. No matter if she said her name was Sierra, or Sarah—something was terribly wrong.

Allowing her mind to drift back to the phone call from early this morning, she was not paying much attention to the pickup truck approaching from the opposite direction. She began to wonder if the child had been abducted. Somehow she'd gotten a hold of her kidnapper's cell phone and dialed.

The pickup crossed the center line.

Rayne's cell number must have been similar to her mother's—perhaps only a digit off. Her thoughts were quickly stifled when she realized that a pickup was heading straight at her Explorer—close enough that she could see the young man at the wheel, texting!

She slammed her hand on to her horn, and swerved hard to the right, out of his path. Fishtailing, the truck kept on going, but she was unable to steer her vehicle away from the deep ditch in the side of the road. The Explorer came to a crashing stop, stuck in the gully to its axle. Even though she was wearing her seatbelt, she hit her forehead on the steering wheel. Blood dripped down her nose. She was disgusted with her own loss of focus and the kid texting while driving, however, she was thankful that the airbags hadn't deployed.

Unbuckling her seatbelt and reaching across the cab to the glove box for some napkins, blood dripped from her face onto her jeans.

"Damn it!" she cursed. That's when she heard the rapid tapping on her window. Flinching, she turned to see Jack rapping his knuckles against the glass. Relieved, she let down the window.

"Are you okay?" His voice was laced with concern—he looked anxious.

"I think so."

"Open the door, Rayne. You've got blood all over your face!"

Quickly, she began wiping the wound with a fistful of napkins. "It's okay. Stay calm—it probably looks worse than it really is. The face always bleeds quickly and a lot because the blood vessels are so close to the surface," she explained.

"Stop with the doctor babble, and unlock the door! I want to make sure you're okay," Jack insisted.

Whoa, Jack's face was turning red. *Doctor babble?* At first she was offended, until she looked into his eyes. This was a man who was truly concerned, and when he was concerned, there was no candy coating an issue. She unlocked the door. He yanked it open, immediately pushing the clump of bloody napkins aside to examine her forehead.

With his eyes narrowed and that strong square jaw clenched, he tenderly dabbed at the abrasion just below her hairline. He was so intense, so possessive, so empathetic, and she felt so cared for, and … loved.

"I don't think you need any stitches, but you're gonna have a nice goose egg. We need to get you back to the house so we can clean it and get a bandage on it," Jack said. "What the hell happened?"

"Oh … some stupid kid was texting and driving. He crossed the centerline and I had to swerve. I guess I swerved a little too far," she told him, and then she smiled at her protector—her handsome knight in shining armor.

"What are you smiling about? I'm driving down the road and suddenly there's your vehicle in a ditch." He ran his fingers through her hair, brushing it away from her face. He softened his tone, "You scared me half to death."

She pulled him close to sweep her lips over his, and then she whispered, "Well, since you're here, and I'm okay, could you pull my car out of the ditch, *lovey-dovey*?"

* * * * *

Her head was beginning to throb during the drive home. Jack didn't want her to drive. He wanted to call one of the guys from the team to take him back to the car so he could drive it home, but she convinced him that she was all right and could manage the last seven miles just fine.

She considered telling Jack about the phone call, but what would she tell him? Oh, by the way, a little girl called today. She said her name was Sierra, but she could have said Sarah, and I'm totally freaking out. Yeah ... that's way off the charts. He would think she was a complete lunatic, and she wouldn't blame him. No, it was best to keep this to herself—at least for the time being.

Today was Lil's special day, and she didn't want to do or say anything that would dissuade the attention from that. It was bad enough that she'd drove her vehicle into a ditch and bumped her head. She'd planned a special dinner for tonight—spaghetti and meatballs—Lil's favorite. Tonight would be about celebrating the first day of kindergarten—not a bizarre phone call or her bruised head.

When she drove the Explorer into the garage, Jack pulled his SUV in and jumped out. He hurried over to the driver's door to help her out. "Take it easy now," he said, taking her by the arm.

"Jack ... I'm all right, and we are not going to mention this to Lil, okay?"

He tossed her a cocky smirk. "We're not? How are you gonna hide that big ol goose egg in the middle of your forehead?"

"You leave that to me." She checked her watch. "You'd better get to the bus stop. She'll be home in about ten minutes or so," she urged.

"You're okay?"

She rolled her eyes. "I'm the *big* girl. Please go take care of the *little* girl."

"It's not gonna take me ten minutes to drive up the driveway, Rayne."

"Good … now go!" she insisted, shooing him with her hands toward his vehicle.

After Jack backed out of the garage, Rayne hurried into the house and into the medical unit where she could clean the wound, put a tiny round band aide on it, and then part her hair to the side, brush it over the wound, and finally place a headband over her hair to hold it in place. It didn't take long to clean up—the cut was as she thought, tiny and bloody and yes, the goose egg was starting to pop out, while the skin around it was beginning to discolor. As long as she didn't get a black eye out of the deal, she'd be happy.

Once her wound and her hair were to her pleasing, she hurried upstairs to change clothes. Some of the blood had splashed onto her shirt and jeans, so she tossed them into her bathtub, filled it with cold water to let them soak. She yanked a fresh pair of jeans from the drawer, and a comfy sweatshirt.

She took a moment to listen at her sitting room door. Jack and Lil hadn't come in yet, so she plunked down on the loveseat, and turned on her laptop that was sitting on the coffee table. Her fingers raced over the keys to bring up the national AMBER alert site. She was eager to see if there were any missing children in the area, or in the surrounding areas. The site announced that there were no AMBER alerts anywhere in the United States at the present time.

Falling back against the cushions, Rayne let out a relieved breath. Good. Okay, now maybe she could relax and enjoy the evening and the dinner that she'd planned for Lil. Enough was enough. She'd tortured herself to the point of distraction, and what did it get her? A bump on the noggin, that's what. It was time to dismiss the entire incident for good. Just then she heard the front door close and Lil's laughter echoing from the grand foyer.

Lil called out, "Where are you, Dr. Rayne?"

Slapping the lid of the computer down, Rayne jumped up from her seat. "Here I come." She quickened down the corridor, touching her hair to make sure it was still covering her bump. When she rounded the corner, she saw exactly what she wanted to see, Lil's smiling face. She was filled with joy and excitement. Jack looked relieved for his daughter, but wary for Rayne.

121

Lil ran into her arms, hugging her tightly. "It was wonderful! I had the best day! Mrs. Bower is so nice and she's pretty, too! And guess what?"

"What?" Rayne inquired with great enthusiasm.

"Landon Rawlings isn't in my class. He's in the other kindergarten class across the hall, and he already got yelled at. On the first day of kindergarten, can you believe it? He wouldn't stand in line when they went to the bathroom. His teacher got mad. We could hear him yelling at Landon from our room. I think he got a pink slip—on the first day!"

"Oh, that Landon Rawlings," Rayne laughed. Lil's joy was simply infectious.

"He'll probably end up becoming a SEAL or something like that," Jack put in.

"I wouldn't be surprised," Rayne added, smirking. She took Lil by the hand. "C'mon, let's get a snack to hold you over 'til dinner. I've got some strawberry Greek yogurt."

"C'mon, Daddy," she grabbed his hand, merrily skipping toward the kitchen between them. "I can't wait to tell you about lunchtime," she laughed. "Maggie spilled her milk!"

* * * * *

Lil's fervor didn't dwindle as the evening wore on. She had so many stories to tell and she couldn't wait for the next day to come so she get on the bus and go back to kindergarten. After she'd had her dinner, practiced drawing her capital A's across a dotted work sheet with a red crayon, and took a hot bubble bath, it was time to climb into bed and read the first chapter of one of her new books, *Ramona the Brave*.

"Good night, Lil," Rayne said, as Jack took his daughter by the hand to lead her to her bedroom.

"Won't you come with us, Dr. Rayne? I'd like it if you came to read with us," Lil said.

It was no use to decline. Rayne simply couldn't say no to that face. She couldn't refuse that adorable child that, yes, she had grown to love, and she wasn't afraid to feel that way anymore. "How can I say no? I love Ramona, too," Rayne confessed.

"Good," Jack began, "You can read. I suck at little girl voices."

"I'll bet your teammates would just love to hear you do little girl voices," Rayne teased.

"I'll bet they would too, but it's never gonna happen."

"That's okay, Daddy, Little Big Man isn't very good at little girl voices either," Lil told him.

Rayne and Jack exchanged wide-eyed, eyebrow raised glances at the mere thought of Stewart Little— the man who ate bullets for breakfast doing voices while reading a book to Lil. For that matter, they were still trying to wrap their heads around the fact he would even agree to read to her at all.

Rayne did most of the reading, while Jack sat at the end of the bed with Tickles on his lap leaning into his fingers while he stroked her ears. When the first chapter was done, Lil's eyes were very droopy. It had been a big day and it was finally taking its toll. Jack pulled the blankets up to her chin and kissed her on the forehead.

"Good night, baby," he whispered, and then he followed Rayne to the bedroom door.

"Dr Rayne …" Lil said.

Rayne turned back. "Yes?"

Lil spread her arms wide for Rayne to come to her, and when she did, Lil hugged her tightly, whispering in her ear, "Thank you so much for the bravery necklace. It helped me to go into my class, but there wasn't anything to be afraid of, kindergarten is great—just like you and Daddy said it would be."

Rayne kissed her on the cheek. "I'm glad the necklace helped you, and I'm glad you like kindergarten." Joining Jack at the bedroom door, she said, "Sweet dreams, sweetie." With that she closed the door.

Jack pulled her into his arms. "You are so good for us." He pressed his lips to hers.

"I know you're kissing!" Lil called from her bed.

Jack smiled against Rayne's lips. Pulling away from the kiss, he called back, "Are not!"

"Are to!" Lil retorted.

"Good night, Lil," Rayne said.

"Good night," she called with a giggle in her voice.

* * * * *

Rayne wanted so much to sleep with Jack tonight. She didn't want to sleep alone in her bed. *"Mama ... this is Sierra ... "* began playing over and over in her head the moment she was alone in her suite. Usually she found her sitting room cozy. The pale blue walls and white lace curtains lent for a comforting Victorian charm. But tonight it seemed like those pretty blue walls were folding in on her.

She found herself stopping at her bedroom door, staring at the bed. She was almost afraid to lie down for fear that the disturbing phone call would trigger a nightmare. Standing at the threshold to her bedroom, she checked the clock on her nightstand, two a.m. She was exhausted. She'd been reading, pacing, and switching channels on her TV all night. Her head was thumping. She needed to sleep, yet she was frightened to close her eyes. She was terrified of what sleep might bring.

CHAPTER SEVEN

"Rayne ..." a soft voice whispered in her ear. His warm breath feathered her neck. His strong arms embraced her, and then lifted her from the loveseat. "Why aren't you in bed?" Jack murmured into her hair.

She stirred with the movement and the sound of his voice. Her arms wrapped around his neck and she felt safe. Snuffling deeper into his chest, she muttered, "I couldn't sleep."

Jack laid her in her bed and pulled the blankets over her. "Sleep now," he said.

She was exhausted, mentally and physically. He didn't have to insist. He didn't have to talk her into anything. Rayne continued to sleep as he crept from the room, closing the sitting room door behind him. Click ...

Sipping a cup of Chamomile tea, she sat at the breakfast bar reading the newspaper. A golden sunbeam glimmered through the arched window over the sink, warming her face. The mansion was quiet.

Lil must be at school, she thought to herself.

She looked around the kitchen. Through the window, she could see that the skies had suddenly turned ashen. The wind had kicked up. Leaves of gold, red, and orange whipped passed the window in a fury. A moment ago she felt at peace. The tea was so warm and tasty, except now there was a sense of unease washing over her. Darkness blanketed the kitchen like a thick menacing fog.

Frantic pounding on the kitchen door had her turning to see who was there. The trembling tiny voice that had recently become so familiar called from the other side, "Mama … this is Sierra …" The pounding turned into beating. She repeated her plea filled words, "Mama … this is Sierra …"

She pushed from the stool, trying to find her way to the door.

She had to get to Sierra!

Sierra was at the door!

Sierra was calling to her!

Her daughter needed her!

Her heart beat madly in her chest. She couldn't find the door—the fog was so thick and the wind growled so fiercely, yet the child's voice still resonated through the room. She continued to cry out, "Mama … this is Sierra …"

Finally, she made it to the door. She grabbed the knob. She twisted, turned, and yanked until her fingers burned with ache, and still the door would not open.

"I'm coming, Sierra!" she cried. "I'm coming!"

At last the door sprung open, and there on the back porch stood Esteban Rojas with her daughter in his steely grip. He was laughing. She remembered the laugh oh too well. She suddenly felt naked and vulnerable and ashamed—all the feelings that tortured her for the seven months that she was his captive and for years afterward.

Around a wicked chortle, he announced in Spanish, "You cannot have her! She is mine! You will never see your daughter again!"

And then they were gone …

Wailing, she reached her arms into the wind and haze, but they were gone! Falling to her knees, she felt helpless and empty once again …

Gulping for air, Rayne pressed up from the mattress to her elbows. Her sweaty hair clung to her face. Her chest rose and fell in a quick panicked rhythm. Realizing that once again she'd fallen victim to a dream, she fell back against the pillow, praying that she hadn't been screaming, and that Jack wouldn't come bursting in to the room to find her in this miserable state.

She wanted out of the bed as quickly as possible. So she tossed the blankets aside and jumped to her feet. The sun was shining outside. There was no wind or fog. Glancing at the clock on her nightstand, it was almost one o'clock. She looked back at the twisted bedding. She vaguely remembered Jack carrying her to the bed earlier in the day—she had no idea what time that had occurred. It didn't matter. All she wanted was a hot shower to wash away the dream, the image of Esteban Rojas, and the sound of the girl's voice that had held her prisoner since yesterday morning.

Prior to the call, she'd experienced two nightmares without a trigger that she could come up with. Who knows why dreams come when they do. Perhaps it was karma, warning her that something was amiss.

Now, she completely understood what was causing the dream—her brain was in high gear with censored memories that were surfacing in convoluted visions that were terrifying, hurtful, and confusing.

Stripping out of her nightgown, she reached into the shower, turning the knob to hot.

* * * * *

"Hey, there's sleeping beauty," Jack said when Rayne walked into the kitchen. He was busy making himself a sandwich at the counter near the window. "Want something to eat? I can whip you up some oatmeal or eggs."

"No, thanks, I think I'll just have some tea. I can't believe I slept so late," Rayne said.

"Well, you said that you couldn't sleep last night. Is everything okay?"

Again, Rayne had the urge to tell Jack about the phone call, except again she felt ashamed of the way she'd blown the entire incident out of proportion. She'd literally allowed a wrong number to cause her night terrors. It was ridiculous, and she couldn't bring herself to show Jack what a complete Looney-tune she'd turned into. Instead, she lifted a shoulder, and said, "Sometimes I have trouble sleeping, that's all. I'll have to buy some melatonin." Stretching up on her toes, she wrapped her arms around his waist to whisper in his ear, "Thanks for putting me to bed. Too bad you didn't join me."

Slathering mayonnaise over the bread, his lips curled. "Now, now, I wouldn't want to spoil you. Besides, Lil's on to us—she asked me if we were getting married when I took her to the bus this morning."

Burying her head into his spine, Rayne chuckled. "Oh no, what did you tell her?"

He turned and kissed her on the forehead. "I said, yeah, someday." With that, he carried his plate to the bar, sat on a stool, and took a bite of his sandwich. Rayne was stunned. She remained frozen at the counter, trying to play back in her head what the man had just said.

"*Seriously*? That's what you told her?"

"Uh, huh," Jack said around a mouthful of BLT on rye.

"I'm … I'm … I'm not sure that was the best … um, approach," Rayne stammered.

"I told you that I'm not one to beat around the bushes—"

"Well, yes, but—"

"I've never lied to Lil. She asked me a straight question, and I gave her a straight answer. What's wrong with that approach?"

How could she argue with that? In reality, if Jack Haliday asked her to marry him, wouldn't she say yes? In a freaking New York minute! Wait, was he asking her to marry him, or was he saying that he would eventually be asking her to marry him? She was confused—but in a good way. She could feel a heat climbing up her spine to her cheeks. It was happening so fast, but hey, maybe this would give her something else to dream about.

Releasing a sigh of surrender, she said, "Nothing … nothing's wrong with that approach at all."

* * * * *

When Lil stepped off the school bus she spread her arms out wide, opened her mouth even wider, and in a high-pitched vibrato, she sang out, "I'm ho-o-o-o-me!"

Blinking back, Jack and Rayne exchanged baffled looks. The bus driver chuckled as she pulled the door closed, and the bus bumped and rocked down the road.

After she'd let go of the boisterous note, Lil explained, "Today was opera day at kindergarten. Our music teacher, Miss Morelli, asked Mrs. Bower if we could have opera day every Thursday, and she said yes!"

"Ho, boy," Jack sighed.

Seeing the sheer delight in Lil's face, Rayne asked, "What exactly is opera day?"

"It's so much fun! You're not allowed to talk. You gotta sing everything. Can we do it at home, too? Can we have opera day every Thursday?" Lil cajoled.

The child was serious. Rayne glanced at Jack, who was leaning against the SUV, holding his forehead in his hand. She admitted, "I'm not exactly J-Lo, but I'm willing to give it a try."

"Oooh gooood!" Lil sang out. Lowering her voice, she turned to Jack, "Your turn, Daddy."

Jack's face jerked from his hand. He looked at Rayne, who was tossing him an expecting expression. He inquired, "Do you seriously want your ears to bleed?"

"Oh, I can't wait to hear you sing," Rayne sang, and then she mouthed, "Lovey-dovey."

Jack rolled his eyes, and then after taking in a deep breath, he let out a loud horrible sound—something like a moose dying. "You two are cra-a-a-a-zy!"

Wincing and turning away, Rayne hiked her shoulders to her ears. Lil crinkled up her face while slapping her hands over her ears. Rayne suggested, "Maybe your dad can be exempt from opera day."

Lil laughed, and then pointing at him, she sang, "You stink!"

Jack chased her around the SUV several times until she jumped in the back passenger door, giggling.

"C'mon you two, Lil needs a snack before she goes to dancing lessons," Rayne sang as she slipped into her seat.

"Will you take me to dance tonight, Dr. Rayne?"

"Sure."

* * * * *

Grant Ketchum's wife, Silja, had been a principal dancer for a ballet company in Russia. When she returned to the United States and married Grant, she opened a ballet academy. Lil was one of her first sign-ups. Her ballet school fit right in with the charming shops and restaurants along the main street of Harverton. A lovely blue awning trimmed in white that came to a peek in the middle with the silhouette of a ballerina in arabesque hovered over the door.

The Harverton Ballet Academy was an overnight success. The classes were overflowing with little girls in black leotards, white tights, and pink ballet slippers. Their hair was drawn up in buns, as was Lil's.

The waiting area was rather small. Folding chairs lined the perimeter. Rayne was amazed at how many women were crammed into the tiny space. Some of the women were gathered around the large window that looked into the ballet studio, several sat in the chairs, tapping at their cell phones, tablets, or laptops, while others were busy trying to keep young children under control.

Not wanting to miss a single moment, Rayne stood at the window. She wanted to watch Lil learning to plie and relieve. She was also interested in watching Silja teach the class of kindergarten girls. She was so patient, and the girls adored her. Rayne couldn't blame them. Silja was beautiful. She had long lean legs, and the body of a dancer—slender, muscled, and elegant. Her golden brunette hair was twisted on top of her head into a bun. She wore a black leotard and skirt, pale pink tights, and a darling pink wrap-around ballet sweater. Her students called her Miss Silja. Rayne had to chuckle—the moms called her that as well.

The girls chased after Silja like little ducklings in a line, following every move she made, bourrees, chasses, and even a few skips. The moms at the window were in awe of their children's progress. Yep, all was right with the world—at least this tiny little corner of it.

As Lil passed the window, she looked up to find Rayne. With a huge grin stretched across her face, she waved. Rayne waved back, and then her cell phone vibrated in the hip pocket of her jeans. Not able to tear her eyes away from the tiny ballerinas making one last sweep passed the window, she answered the cell, "Hello ..."

"Mama ... it's really me ... Sierra. I need your help ..."

Rayne's chest clenched. She couldn't exhale. Her mouth was instantly dry and her hand began to shake. She was barely able to keep hold of the phone. Stumbling away from the window, and ear shot of the women, she managed, "Sierra ... where are you? Who are you with?"

She had a million questions, except those were the only two that tumbled from her lips. Pressing the phone harder to her ear, she listened for Sierra's response. It was a poor connection. She could hear other voices, but she couldn't make out what they were saying. It sounded like they were speaking in another language—Spanish. Rayne was fluent in

Spanish, yet she couldn't make it out. There was a woman's voice and a man's.

Sierra said, "I must go …" And with that the connection was broken. The line went dead. Rayne stood in the middle of the room while little girls spilled out of the ballet class, running into their mother's arms. It seemed that the world was crashing down around her, and then she felt a hand cup her shoulder.

"Are you all right, Rayne?" Silja asked. "You're completely pale. You have no lip line. I have another class, but I could call Jack to come drive you and Lil home."

Rayne blinked back into the moment. "No … no … I'm fine. I've just got a headache." Thoughtlessly, she rubbed her fingers through her hairline exposing her black and purple goose egg.

Lil pointed toward Rayne's head. "You've got a bump on your head, Dr. Rayne. What happened?"

Involuntarily, Rayne's hand jerked away from her wound. Faking a laugh, she lied, "Oh … I … um … bumped my head on a door. I went to walk out of my bedroom last night and walked right into the corner of the door. I'm such a klutz. I'm not nearly as coordinated or graceful as Miss Silja."

Unconvinced, Silja asked again, "You're sure you're all right?"

"I'll be fine. I loved watching the class. You do a terrific job, and all of the girls do great. You're a lovely dancer, Lil," Rayne said, trying to shake off the trembling that was churning her gut.

Before putting the Explorer into drive, Rayne checked the last call on her cell phone—it came up as unavailable. Rayne took in a deep calming breath. If it were Sierra calling—and that was a huge if—she was either calling from out of the country, or from a burner phone, or both. Regardless, with everything she'd witnessed through First Force, she knew that it was most likely untraceable, too. Frustration climbed up the back of her neck. While Lil put her dance bag aside and fastened her seatbelt, Rayne laid her head against the headrest.

Hokay ...

It was time to stop panicking.

It was time to start thinking and acting rationally.

No, it wasn't time to tell Jack anything.

She needed more information, otherwise she'd look foolish. Everyone, including herself, believed Sierra to be dead, and if she started voicing doubts it would appear that she was having some kind of breakdown—especially with all the nightmares of late.

"I'm ready!" Lil sang from the backseat.

"Okie-dokie!" Rayne replied in a sing-song voice.

Pulling out of the parking space, Rayne decided that she would wait for the next phone call.

She had no doubts that there would be another call. The girl said that she needed help.

Sierra needed help.

The thought made her stomach coil.

On the other hand, if Sierra needed help that meant that her daughter was alive.

It was time to stop being crazy emotional.

It was time to kick into survival mode.

Her daughter might be out there somewhere in need of her help—not an emotional head case. When the next phone call came, she'd be ready.

* * * * *

Snatching the phone from Patrizia's hand, Luis pressed the end button. His mouth curved into a toxic grin. "This is working better than I could have ever imagined," he crooned. "Dr. Lee believes that there is a chance that her daughter is alive. We will soon make our demands." He made his way toward the door.

"Dr. Lee? There was a Dr. Lee that came to our village years ago. He cared for Patrizia when she was very small. He gave her medicine for an ear infection—but this doctor was a man," Bibiana said.

Luis turned. "*Si*, Patrizia is talking to his wife, Dr. Rayne Lee."

Bibiana was taken aback. "What do you want from this woman, Luis? What is so precious that you would lead her to believe something so hurtful?"

"This is none of your concern. Your concern is making sure that your daughter says the things that I want to her to say. Your concern is living from one day to the next," Luis reminded her. He looked down at Patrizia. "You have done very well so far. You will continue to do well, if you want to return to your village in one piece."

Just then Renzo came into the hut with a cell phone extended out. "The phone call you were expecting," he said.

With one last abrasive glance at Bibiana, Luis took the cell phone from his fighter, and then stepped through the door, closing it behind him.

"What will he do to Dr. Lee, Mama?" Patrizia asked.

"I don't know, but I'm sure it won't be pleasant. He is right, Patrizia. Our concern is to do what we must so that he will not kill us," Bibiana explained to her daughter whose beautiful brown eyes were filled with angst.

A tear flowed over the rim of her eye. Quickly Patrizia wiped it away, she said, "I don't want to help him hurt this woman, Mama."

Bibiana's lips curled. She brushed the back of her fingers over the child's cheek, and then tucked her hair behind her ear. She said, "I know you don't. I don't want to either, but we must take things as they are, and pray for a just outcome—whatever that may be. Come … they brought us some bread to eat. You must keep up your strength, and so must I."

"I hope Dr. Lee is strong," Patrizia put in.

"I hope so too," Bibiana whispered. Closing her eyes, she repeated, "I hope so too."

* * * * *

Deciding that she would avoid her bed tonight, Rayne waited until she was certain that Jack had tucked Lil into bed, she slipped into a silky night-gown, and then made her way down the corridor to the west wing of the house. She needed Jack's strength. She needed to feel his warm, safe embrace, and she wanted to make love to the man she was or possibly had already fallen in love with a long time ago.

The moon gleamed through the tall arched windows that lined the corridor, backwashing the trees moving like phantom dancers in the gentle breeze. The light and the sinewy shadows through each of the four windows ushered her through the dark hallway into the large open grand foyer where tall vintage China palace vases stood like proud soldiers at attention. She passed the staircase to enter the corridor that led to Jack and Lil's quarters.

She hesitated at Lil's door, making sure that all was still. Satisfied, she continued on to Jack's room which was set up much like hers. There was a spa-cious sitting room that led into his bedroom. Jack's sitting room wasn't pale blue like hers. It was a rich mocha color. A cool beige leather sofa that reclined sat along the wall that faced a big flat screen TV on a handsome oak bookcase. It was a manly room— not quite a man cave, there was no bar or pool table, or colorful lights that exclaimed, Budweiser, or Rolling Rock Beer. Nonetheless, the room reeked of masculinity. She tapped on the door, but no one answered. She pushed the door open just a little to peek inside.

"Jack …" she whispered.

She could smell his musky scent the moment she stepped foot over the threshold. He wasn't sitting on the sofa. The TV was off, so she crossed the room. His bedroom door was ajar.

"Jack …" Rayne whispered into the bedroom. The light on his nightstand was on. His clothes lay on the floor in a pile. She could see the light glimmering underneath the bathroom door, and she could hear the water crashing against the wall in the shower.

Jack was in the shower.

She eased through the bedroom door.

Yep … Jack was taking a shower.

With measured steps, she made her way passed the bed, stepping over the pile of clothes.

Mmmm, Jack was naked in that shower.

Her fingers wrapped around the knob of the bathroom door.

She could imagine the water pelting his flawlessly defined, supple, vibrant muscles ... hot, steaming water rushing over every part of him—a reverent river washing over his skin.

She eased the door open and stepped into the bathroom. Steam billowed over the top of the glass shower stall, slithering throughout the small area. The mirror was fogged and so was the lower half of the glass that encased Jack, but it only added to the sultry allure of his body.

The water was washing over his face as he dipped it into the spray, allowing it to soak his hair. The muscles on his beautiful wide back flexed and moved as he scrubbed his fingers through his dark locks. His ribcage eased into his lean hips, moving lower was his rounded tight buttocks. Rayne took in a gulp of steam.

Hot dayum.

Turning, Jack's eyes met hers. She suddenly felt ashamed of her brashness to walk into his bathroom uninvited and watch him bathe. He smiled. She smiled back.

"Well, don't just stand there, Dr. Lee, join me," he said. His erection began to grow, stretching away from the apex of his thighs toward his naval.

Her tummy tightened, as did everything else. Slowly she slipped the strap of her nightgown from her right shoulder, allowing it to slide down to the elbow, baring her breast. Peeking at him through her lashes, she slipped the left strap away, letting the gown fall to her waist.

Jack's hands were pressed against the glass. She knew that he was enjoying her demure display. She reached her arms over her head to stretch, arching her back. Slowly she lowered them, pinching the gown between her fingertips to push it over her hips, letting it fall and pool at her feet.

One slow foot at a time, she stepped away from the fabric, making her way to the shower. He pushed the door open to give her entry, and then he pulled her into his possessive embrace, kissing her. She could sense his primal need. She was surrendering to her own. Wrapping her arms around his neck, she climbed onto his hips, slowly lowering her sex over his. The feel of his penis sliding inside her filled her with the urge to pump and squeeze, while the heat and the steam consumed them.

Jack leaned against the wet wall, holding her derriere in place, while kneading with his fingers. The feel of his fingers, the heat of the water, and the sensation of him inside her climbed and climbed. Tossing her head back, giving him full access to her breasts, she found that place where elation and passion collide, igniting sensations so powerful that every cell in her body celebrated. She dug her fingers into his shoulders, feeling Jack reaching the same pinnacle of pleasure.

She stayed in place, kissing him, until his erection had diminished, slipping out of her body. Jack reached behind to turn off the water.

"That was an amazing shower," he murmured.

"Best I've ever had," Rayne agreed.

Opening the door, he grabbed a towel. "I'd better dry you off. Wouldn't want you to catch cold." Pressing his lips to hers, he wrapped the towel around her shoulders, gently caressing her body, and then he ran the towel over her hips and down her legs. On his way back up, he dragged his tongue over her clit hungry and promising of more to come. She shivered. Her nipples instantly stood up at the thought.

Grabbing another towel from the rack, he handed it to her. "You're turn."

She was breathless. She wanted him to use that tongue to bring her to climax. She managed to take the towel from his hand. She dragged it over his body, spending most of the time making sure his rising erection was enjoying the drying more than anywhere else.

Jack took the towel from her hands and guided her out of the shower. Grabbing her nightgown from the floor, he tossed it through the door into the bedroom. "Won't be needing that anytime soon," he remarked, and then he turned, picked her up by the waist and sat her on the counter. He kissed her mouth, her throat, making his way to her breasts, sucking each pebbled nipple until she thought she would burst.

"Lean back," he said in a husky voice.

She complied.

He spread her legs, knelt between them, and laid them on his shoulders. She could barely contain her excitement. She could feel the wetness between her legs, anticipating the feel of his tongue, and when it caressed the delicate folds of her intimate spot, she arched savoring every swipe, every flutter, and every probe. She moaned, immersed in the glorious sensation.

Jack stood, lifting her from the countertop to carry her the short distance to the bedroom. He laid her upper body face down across the bed. He trailed kisses down her spine, while his hands smoothed up and down her hips and ribs. His hands were big and strong and the skin was coarse. He didn't have the soft hands of a man who made his living in an office, sitting in a cubical, drinking coffee, tapping at a computer. Jack's hands were used and abused, and even though they were rough, they felt good against her body. Using his legs, he spread her legs apart and then he took her from behind, sliding into her wet warm sex. She grabbed a fistful of the bedspread in each hand, relishing every moment of his love making.

His whisper was raspy with heat, "Come for me, Rayne. Come for me now, darlin'."

He didn't have to ask her twice. She obeyed his appeal without hesitation. The sting of her climax filled her with complete gratification, turning her bones to liquid. Jack collapsed on the bed next to her. He took in a deep long sated breath.

"Stay with me tonight," he whispered.

"Mmmm," was all she managed, "my turn to sneak back to the bedroom at six a.m."

"Better set an alarm," Jack suggested.

After he set the alarm for six, he gathered her into his arms. Lying with her head on his chest, she watched the trees outside the window swaying to and fro. She could hear a distant *ting-aling-aling* of a wind chime that hung in a tree in the yard. She'd forgotten all about the chime. Now it was a beautiful sublime sound. Adding to the gentle cadence, rain began to patter against the glass. It felt so right in his arms. She wasn't sure where the mysterious phone calls would lead her. But she was certain of one thing, nothing or no one could harm her when she was in Jack's arms—wrapped in his love. Reaching up, she brushed an errant strand of hair from his forehead.

"Good night, lovey-dovey," she whispered. The shadows fell across his face. She could see his lips curl.

He kissed her on the forehead, only it wasn't a comforting kiss, it was the kiss of a lover—a warm sincere lover. Jack said, "G'night."

* * * * *

Washington D.C.

"Good night, Mrs. Pérez," Smitty said to Justice Alejandro Pérez's wife, Paullina, as she made her way passed him toward the staircase. Nodding, she favored him with a half-smile. Smitty sensed that she considered the three men in her home a necessary intrusion. Smitty and Grant perused the downstairs area while another man from Orlando, Florida was assigned to the upstairs. Paullina was polite to the men in a curt sort of way. As she began her climb up the stairs, Smitty muttered into his tiny microphone attached to his lapel, "Mrs. Pérez is coming upstairs for the night."

"Roger that," the upstairs bodyguard said into his earpiece. Once the judge's wife had disappeared at the top of the stairwell, Smitty returned to his post outside Justice Pérez' office. He was amazed at how late the judge worked and how little contact he seemed to have with his wife. They barely spoke at dinner, and what infrequent conversation took place was spoken in hushed tones of Spanish. They didn't realize that Smitty was fluent in the language, but not wanting to intrude on their private moments, he excused himself to stand outside the dining room.

Smitty noted that Paullina didn't seem offended or upset by the judge's disregard for her. Rather, she seemed accustomed to the cold shoulder that wafted across the dinner table. He knew that they had been married for twenty plus years through the briefings he'd sat through the day before.

Smitty tipped his chair against the wall, wishing he were anywhere but on this lame assignment. Grant meandered from the living room toward him.

"All quiet on the front lines," Grant said.

"This is gonna be two of the most boring weeks of our lives, dude," Smitty complained. A nano-second later Judge Pérez' voice boomed from the other side of his office door. He was yelling at some-one in Spanish. He was angry and his tone was threatening. His bellowing brought Smitty to his feet. Grant's head jerked toward the door. Smitty slowly shifted to lean in close to the door to listen.

"What the hell's going on in there?" Grant questioned over Smitty's shoulder. "Is he talking on a phone or did someone break in there?"

Smitty shushed him. His eyes narrowed. He pressed his ear closer to the door. Judge Pérez was speaking so quickly that Smitty couldn't make out what he was saying through the thick oak door.

"No one's in there with him. He's definitely on the phone. He's mad as hell and he's threatening someone, but I can't make out what he's saying," Smitty whispered. With that the judge suddenly became silent. Smitty cocked his head, listening to the sound of the man's footsteps pacing over the floor beyond the door. He gestured for Grant to get lost, while he quickly returned to his seat.

The door opened with a fierce whoosh and then Justice Alejandro Pérez stomped through. Smitty jumped to his feet. The judge's face was flushed. His eyes burned with an angry fire.

"I will be retiring for the night," he said to Smitty with a voice that could have spit nails into a steel wall.

"Yes, sir, good night, Justice Pérez," Smitty said, and then he informed the guard upstairs, "Justice Pérez is on his way up for the night."

"Roger that," the guard returned.

Smitty stood at the foot of the stairs while the judge made his way upward. He blew out a breath when the judge rounded the banister into the upstairs hallway. Loosening his tie, Grant came up from behind. He muttered, "Something's up his ass. He was mad as a rattlesnake."

"Yeah, and I'll bet he's twice as deadly," Smitty noted.

CHAPTER EIGHT

He had spent the past five days keeping a close eye on Chaves' men, and the men he once served with under Esteban Rojas. Juan trusted no man. Since Luis Chaves and his guerillas attacked their camp killing most of his colleagues and Rojas, those who had survived were anxious to prove their loyalty to their new commander. Tongues were loose and betrayal was looming.

Juan scanned the camp before he dipped his hand into the bucket of water to splash his dusty face. The sun had raised with much the same fury as the day before. The tepid water felt good on his face. After mopping away the excess with a rag, he opened his eyes to find Luis Chaves and two of his henchmen surrounding him. As always, Luis had a resolute look in his eyes. Instantly Juan was filled with unease. It appeared that betrayal was no longer a looming threat—it was now in his face.

"You have pledged your loyalty to my militia," Luis said.

Hesitantly, Juan responded, "*Si* …"

Luis circled him like a vulture circles his supper as he spoke, "I find it very hard to trust a man who quickly changes his allegiance when threatened with death. You were loyal to Esteban Rojas for several years, and yet now you are willing to serve under my command. Why is this, Juan?"

"As you said, a man must find a way to survive when faced with his own mortality. I have looted, killed, and burned for Esteban. I will do the same for you," Juan explained.

Luis studied him. His eyes were like torches burning into another man's soul. Luis was no man's fool. A man can only lead as long as he remains stronger than the rest. The moment he shows any weakness at all another man will rise up to strip him of his reign. He said, "I have been told by another who has joined my militia that you knew Esteban well—he confided in you and that you took part in helping him to put the chip in Dr. Lee. Is this so?"

Juan couldn't read what was in Luis' eyes. He didn't know if his answer would lift him up or be his ruin. Considering his few options, he took in a breath, and then he said, "*Si.*"

"So, you placed the chip in the doctor?"

"No."

"Then who did?"

"A doctor from a nearby village."

"You will go and get this doctor. I want him here as soon as possible," Luis instructed.

"But this took place four years ago. The doctor was a very old man. What if he is dead?" Juan asked.

Luis poked him in the chest, hard. "For your sake I hope he is not. Go now and return quickly."

Juan could feel the sweat forming on his brow. Only the sweat was not from the blazing sun, it was from the tightening in his chest. He muttered, "Of course."

As Juan hurried away, Luis nodded to Renzo, standing to his right. "Go with him, and if the doctor is not there—kill him," he instructed.

* * * * *

Bibiana did not look up when Luis entered the hut. She continued to eat her breakfast as if no one had entered their space.

Luis slapped the paper down on the table in front of her. "I have written what I want Patrizia to say to Dr. Lee the next time we call."

Bibiana's eyes flicked to the paper, reading what she would have to practice with her daughter. She clenched her teeth at the words, and then in a stiff voice she asked, "When will we call her?"

"When I decide. Work with Patrizia until the words are perfect."

Still Bibiana did not look at him. The sight of this man made her want to wretch. She simply stated, "Patrizia will be ready."

"*Very good*," Luis said.

When Luis had left the hut Patrizia asked her mother, "What does he want me to say, Mama?"

Bibiana took in a long breath and then let it out. She slid the paper across the table to her daughter. Patrizia gathered the paper in her hand to read the script that Luis had prepared for her. A moment later, she tossed the paper down and slid it back to her mother.

* * * * *

It had been a long eventful week. Rayne was happy that Lil had settled into kindergarten so well. She loved her teacher, Mrs. Bower. She was making friends and blending in very well with her classmates. She already had a birthday party invitation for the next weekend. Every day she came home filled with stories to tell and pictures that she'd drawn, and even though Landon Rawlings wasn't in her class, she seemed to be up to date with his misadventures.

Rayne's relationship with Jack was moving at warp speed and that was okay. She wasn't interested in slowing things down. She was interested in full speed ahead, and it appeared that Jack was feeling the same. Yep, everything was coming up roses, except for the phone calls.

Rayne was determined not to let them send her into a tailspin. She was determined to get to the bottom of whatever was going on. She kept her cell phone within reach at all times—even when she was in the shower. She hoped that the girl—Sierra—would call back soon so she would have the information that she needed, and then she could share it with Jack without looking like a whack-job.

Sierra had called two days in a row, Wednesday—Lil's first day of kindergarten, and last evening during dance classes. Rayne was hoping that she would call today, and the day dragged on and on.

Deep down she feared that Jack and the team would be called out on a mission before she could gather the intel that she needed to justify an investigation. She was well aware at how quickly a desperate phone call could come in, and after careful preparation, the team would roll out. Everything had been unusually quiet over the past two weeks. She could feel a storm brewing.

Jack had joined team members Dan Garrison, Stewart Little, and Clark Rhodes at the shooting range for some target practice. The house was quiet. She was on edge, waiting for the phone to ring. Trying to ease the tension, she decided to put together the lasagna that she'd planned for dinner when the buzzer that announced a vehicle was coming through the gate sounded. She jumped. Her eyes snapped to the security screen mounted on the wall. Letting out a breath, her lips curled at the sight of Casey Rhodes' silver Viper rolling along the driveway toward the mansion.

Casey was the team's sniper. Her twin brother, Clark, was the team coordinator. The two shared a womb, but little else. They had been separated at birth and reunited only three years ago. Casey was raised in a rural setting, learning to hunt and fish and shoot and she was damned handy with a bow, too.

Her brother was raised in Philadelphia. Both of his parents were professors at a university. While Casey was rough and tumble there was a softer side to the woman. She was very attractive with long dark hair that she usually kept pulled in a severe braid that cascaded down her spine. She was tall and lean with an athletic yet feminine body.

Over the years Rayne had grown to love Casey. She so enjoyed when Casey would drop by to drink some wine and talk. Rayne felt a flutter of excitement in her tummy. She was anxious to share the news of her relationship with Jack, although she didn't think that Casey would be terribly surprised. She suspected that Casey could sense the electricity between her and Jack. She would toss a smug smile at Rayne every once in a while after a quirky exchange between her and the overtly handsome

Navy SEAL in front of the team. Yeah, Casey knew. Hell, the entire team probably knew. The butterfly in her tummy stirred again. She couldn't help herself—she was darn right giddy to tell her BFF the news: she and Jack were now an item— a couple—they were having hot sex for crying out loud!

The blue light over the kitchen threshold blinked letting her know that a door had opened, and then the security screen flashed a picture of the front door, as Casey stepped through. All of the team members had the access code to First Force Headquarters.

"Rayne! Are you here?" Casey called from the foyer, pushing her sunglasses from the bridge of her nose onto her head.

Rayne was already plucking two glasses from the cupboard and hunting through the fridge for the bottle of Riesling that she'd been chilling, and a block of Gouda cheese. Her eyes flicked to the clock—one o'clock—perfect, not too early for a nice glass of wine with a friend. The Riesling and the cheese would make for a great afternoon treat.

"In the kitchen," Rayne called back. Setting the wine and cheese on the counter, she grabbed a box of crackers from the cabinet.

Stepping into the kitchen, Casey asked, "Hey girlfriend, what's up?"

She was looking so smart in a pair of tightly fitted Levis, a rhinestone zebra print belt with a huge rhinestone belt buckle, cowboy boots, while sporting an electric blue silk blouse that draped flawlessly over her shoulders.

Casey was an unlikely sniper suspect. Dressed so casually chic, one would never imagine her hiding in the brush or a tree or on a hilltop with an eagle eye and a steady finger on the trigger, taking out bad guys. No, one would think she was a super model arriving home after a shoot on a balmy beach somewhere in paradise.

Wearing a sly smirk, Rayne poured the wine into the glasses and handed one to her friend. Casey's eyes got a little wider. Her eyebrows rose a little higher. Before taking a sip, she said, "I know that look. You're either up to something, or something's already up. Spill it."

"You're awfully impatient," Rayne pointed out, while slicing the block of cheese into little squares and placing them onto the crackers.

"When it comes to something juicy … yes. Now tell me … what's going on?"

"How do you know that anything's going on?"

Casey tossed her a baleful look. "You're glowing."

"Goodness, I'm not pregnant," Rayne quickly put in.

"Okay, okay, you're … *beaming*. Now tell me before I go get my gun."

"Well … Jack and I are—"

"Having hot sweaty sex!"

Rayne blinked back, "How did you know?"

Lifting a shoulder, Casey snitched a piece of cheese and tossed it into her mouth. "You look like someone whose having hot sweaty sex."

"I—I do?"

"I told you—you're beaming. Good?" Casey inquired with a lifted brow.

"Mmmm … *very* good."

They shared a chuckle.

"I'm happy … for both of you, but I have to admit—I knew that it was just a matter of time," Casey informed, just as her cell phone whistled at her. Rayne's stomach clenched. Was it Uncle Walt calling the team to headquarters for a mission? Unable to breathe, she watched Casey pull the phone from the hip pocket of her jeans. As she read the message, her lips drew upward into a sultry curl.

Nope. Not this time.

Thankful, Rayne took a sip of her wine. With a fresh taste of the Riesling in her mouth and faux innocence filling her tone, she asked, "A mission?"

Casey dragged her gaze to meet Rayne's. "Not exactly, Peyton Mattock."

"Hot sweaty sex?"

"No. I'm afraid we haven't, but he's in D.C., which is much closer than Russia, sooo … ya never know, maybe," she said, pumping her eyebrows up and down once again.

Rayne laughed. Casey was such a good friend— a confidante. She felt the urge to tell her about the calls. What would Casey say? Would she think that she was losing it? Would she think that she should run as fast as she could to Dr. Lockhart's office? No. Casey was a friend, and friends supported one another. Casey would believe her. Casey would know what to do.

"Rayne … woo hoo … Rayne …" Casey called, waving a hand.

Snapping back into the moment, she realized that Casey had been trying to grab her attention for a while. "I'm sorry … you were saying …"

"Wow, you were deep, and it didn't look like you were thinking about hot Navy SEAL sex." Her eyes narrowed. "Something else is going on. What is it?"

Yep, Casey was a good ally. She could sense when something was amiss. It was time to tell someone about the calls—someone she trusted. It wasn't that she didn't trust Jack—that wasn't it. They were just forging a relationship. He knew that she had struggled with emotional issues for years, and she didn't want him to view her as weak or … or … unstable.

"Rayne …" Casey coaxed.

"Yes … there is something else," Rayne finally divulged.

"Tell me."

Casey listened intently while Rayne told her about the first phone call that came Wednesday morning. She explained how she tried to dismiss it as a wrong number or perhaps the little girl said Sarah, and not Sierra.

When she paused Casey said nothing. Rayne could tell that she was processing what she'd been told and was patiently waiting to hear the rest. She appreciated Casey's fortitude. After another sip of wine, she told her about the second call that came Thursday evening during Lil's dance class. This time Rayne was certain that the little girl had indeed called herself Sierra.

"She said, 'Mama … it's really me … Sierra.' And then she said, 'I need your help.'" Rayne took in a cleansing breath. She touched her cell phone lying on the counter. "And that's it—that's the last phone call I've received. I'm keeping the phone close at hand. I know she's going to call back. I just don't know when."

Rayne studied Casey's face. She was contemplating all the information. Rayne could see that Casey didn't think she was crazy or over emotional.

Pouring another glass of wine, Casey sat back against the seat. She swirled the wine around the bottom of the glass, watching the golden liquid sparkle in the afternoon sunshine glimmering through the kitchen window. After she took a long sip, she asked, "Were there any voices or noises in the background?"

"Yes, there was a man's voice. And right before she hung up, I heard a woman's voice, too. Sierra hung up very abruptly, like someone caught her on the phone and they took it away," Rayne explained. She added, "The man spoke in Spanish, I believe."

"But they didn't make any demands?"

"No."

"You need to tell Walt. Have you told Jack?" Casey asked.

"No. Frankly, I'm surprised that I'm telling you. I really didn't want to tell anyone until I knew what kind of trouble Sierra's in, and who's causing the trouble," Rayne told her.

"And where the calls are coming from," Casey put in.

"I have a plan. I just have to wait for the next call to come, and then I promise that I'll let everyone in on what's been going on," Rayne said.

Casey leaned forward. Her eyes scanned the counter top like she was searching for the right words before she spoke, and then she said, "Rayne … I hope you're not getting your hopes up that Sierra is still alive. I mean … I suppose it's possible, but not probable. I don't want to see you lose all the progress that you've made." She placed her hand over Rayne's, and squeezed.

Squeezing her hand back, Rayne replied, "I can't help but have hope that somehow my daughter is out there and she needs me. That said ... I assure you that I'm trying to keep it all in perspective, but I've got to find out, Casey. I've just got to know."

Casey wrapped her arms around Rayne, hugging her tightly. "I'm with ya all the way—no matter what, girlfriend. Now, tell me your plan."

"I've downloaded an app to my phone. I want to record the next call," Rayne said.

"I think I know where you're going with this. The app you're talking about can be a bit tricky to use, so let's practice a little so you're completely prepared when she calls. Sooner or later the calls are going to accompany some sort of demand or deal— I'm sure of it. You'd better be ready. All of that said, don't think that just because you've recorded the call that Clark will be able to trace it. They are most likely using a burn phone—they're untraceable," Casey explained.

"Yes, I know. But at least I'll have all of the information. I won't accidentally leave out any details, and they may hear something in the conversation or in the background noises that I'm missing. Okay, you're the expert on running missions—teach me what I need to know."

Casey smiled. Bowing her head, she said, "Let us begin, grasshopper."

* * * * *

Rayne was thankful that Casey had dropped by. She was also relieved that she'd finally unburdened herself, and she'd picked the perfect person because Casey spent the rest of the afternoon helping her stabilize her strategy, while they put together the lasagna. She was well aware why Casey was helping her put dinner together—it was a calming device, a way to keep her mind on something else while working on her plan. Casey wasn't just a good friend—she was the best. Rayne only hoped that she would have the presence of mind not to panic when the phone call came. She had no choice—she had to keep it together.

Casey stuck around until Lil came home. Jack pulled up just in time to greet his daughter as she stepped off the bus. Lil was thrilled to see Casey at the bus stop, and Casey took the time to look at Lil's papers and listen to some of the day's events.

"Are you sure you won't stay for some of that yummy lasagna we made this afternoon?" Rayne asked.

"No, thanks, I'm going to go home. I've got some things to catch up on—like laundry, or I won't have anything to wear by Sunday," Casey said, as she slid into her Viper. With a wink and a wave, she drove out of the drive.

Slipping his arm around Rayne and taking Lil by the hand, Jack suggested, "How about we celebrate a successful week—Lil's first week at kindergarten, and …" he was suddenly tongue tied. He wanted to say, and a new beginning for him and Rayne, but he needed to talk with Lil first. He couldn't just blurt that out.

Lil stopped. Looking up at him, she cocked her head. "And what, Daddy?"

He glanced at Rayne who was waiting for his answer as well. His jaw was working, but nothing was coming out. Finally, he managed, "Well … the Steelers made a lot of touchdowns Monday night …"

"And we made a fabulously scrumptious pie on Tuesday," Rayne put in accompanied with a smirk.

"And Landon Rawlings isn't in my kindergarten class!" Lil exclaimed.

"Well, that right there is reason enough for celebration," Jack said with relief. "Let's go to dinner and a movie."

"But I've made lasagna for dinner," Rayne said.

"We'll have that tomorrow night. It's in the fridge, right?" Jack asked.

Rayne was suddenly hesitant. The moment she stepped into the movie theater, she would have to silence her phone. She might miss Sierra's call. She could feel panic welling inside her. She stammered, "Well, yes … I suppose—"

"It's settled then. We'll look up what's playing on the computer, pick a place to eat and see a movie. It'll be a great night out," Jack said.

"Woo Hoo!" Lil declared, jumping up and down.

It was decided. They were going out for the evening, and somehow Rayne would have to keep a line of communication open for Sierra.

* * * * *

They went to Rayne's favorite Italian restaurant in Harverton, Lombardo's. It was a quaint little place with red and white checked tablecloths and a waxy candle stuck in a fat olive oil bottle in the middle of the table. The restaurant wasn't very busy as they arrived before the rush, but as their dinner was served, the crowd began to filter in and the restaurant buzzed with conversation and laughter.

Afraid that she wouldn't hear her phone ring over the noise, Rayne took it from her purse and set it next to her plate. She was aware that Jack noticed, but he didn't say anything.

The evening was a little crisp but pleasant so they decided to walk to the small movie theater down the block—it was playing the latest Disney flick. Lil was most excited.

After they purchased their tickets, popcorn, and soda, and they had slathered the popcorn properly with butter, they made their way into the theater to find seats and watch previews of the upcoming movies. During the previews they were asked to silence their cell phones. Rayne glanced at Jack. He pulled his cell from his pocket and pressed a button and then put it back.

Lil was sitting between them, so Rayne leaned over her head and whispered, "Did you power-down your cell?"

"I can't do that, Rayne. I put it on vibrate in case Walt needs me," Jack whispered back.

"Oh, of course," she muttered, and then she pushed the buttons on her phone to the vibrate mode, too, making sure the phone was against her leg so she would feel the vibration should there be a call.

It was almost nine-thirty when they left the theater and strolled along the main street of Harverton toward Jack's vehicle. Sierra had not called. Rayne's heart sank. She was anxious to hear from her again. She was feeling desperate to know what she could do to help—if anything.

When they arrived home, Jack put Lil to bed. Rayne went to her bedroom to slip into a soft lilac nightgown, and then she wandered into her sitting room and plopped down on the sofa. She went through her phone to make sure there weren't any missed calls—and there it was—a missed call from, unavailable, Sierra! Panic crowded

Rayne's chest. How could she have missed the call? She didn't feel a vibration against her leg in the theater. So when did Sierra call?

Okay, she'd missed the call.

There was absolutely nothing she could do about it; after all she couldn't redial an unavailable number. She would simply have to wait for her to call again. Lifting her feet onto the coffee table, she decided to try to relax—there was absolutely nothing she could do but wait. Wait … wait … wait …

"Hey, want some company?" Jack asked, leaning through the doorway.

"Sure, come in," she said. Happy with the distraction, she laid the phone on the end table. Jack sat next to her and she snuggled against his chest. Rayne asked, "What chapter are we on with Henry Huggins?"

Caressing her bare shoulder with his fingertips, Jack said, "We were on chapter four, but tonight we read chapter five because, get this, Little read chapter four to her before dance class yesterday. I didn't even know Little was here."

"Yes, he was down in the garage for a while. After she got dressed in her leotards, she grabbed her bag of books to show him what she'd bought. He must've read some to her then. I think it's adorable," Rayne said, thankful for every tiny tingle against her skin from his touch.

Jack snorted. "Little is a lot of things, but adorable isn't one of them. Lil loves him, and I guess that's all that matters." He adjusted his caress to running his fingers through her hair. "Am I assuming too much to think that it's okay to sleep with you again tonight? And when I say sleep, I don't mean we have to have sex, I just want to be with you."

She laid her head back against him. With a smile in her voice, she said, "You may assume anything you like, Mr. Haliday. But I do think that we should have a conversation with Lil—and I mean *we*. If we're going to be together then we should talk to her together."

His embrace tightened. He kissed her on the top of her head. "I agree."

Rayne pushed up from the sofa and extended her hand out to him. "C'mon, let's go to bed. I'm pooped."

"Is that a medical term or did you just come up with that off the top of your head?"

"It's a medical term. I know a lot of medical terms. Any time you want to play doctor—I'm your girl."

He took her hand and she led him into the bedroom. Jack shed his clothes down to his boxers, and then climbed into the bed. Realizing that she'd left the phone in the sitting room, Rayne hesitated. "I'll be right back," she said. She hurried into the sitting room to retrieve the phone from the coffee table, and then returned to the bedroom to place it on the nightstand.

Jack's brows fell into a "V". "You've been nursing that phone all evening. Are you expecting a call?"

Her eyes flicked to his. "No ... no not at all. I usually keep the phone on the nightstand."

"I haven't noticed it there the past several nights."

Rayne glanced at the nightstand on his side of the bed. His phone was there, but that was different. Jack had to keep his phone with him at all times in case Walt called the team out. "Well ... I usually do. I guess you've had me a bit off balance the past several nights." She smiled.

Jack reached for her. "I like keeping you off balance."

* * * * *

Patrizia's grip grew tighter and tighter as the Dr. Lee's phone rang and rang. She wasn't answering. Luis' mouth went from a stiff hard line into a stiff glower.

"She is not answering," Patrizia told him.

Grabbing the phone from the girl, he barked, "I can see that! I hope the doctor has not caught on to our little scam." He turned to Bibiana. "I hope for both your sakes she answers the phone the next time we call, or I will have no more use for you or your daughter." With that Luis marched toward the door.

Bibiana hated the phone calls that Patrizia was forced to make, but at this point, the phone call were their lifeline. She called out to Luis, "When? When will we call again? Perhaps the doctor is in a place where the reception is bad or perhaps she simply does not hear the phone ringing. I'm sure that she will answer the next call ..."

Hesitating at the door, Luis merely glared at the desperate woman making excuses for the unanswered call. With a loud harrumph, he walked out the door.

Bibiana brought her hand to her mouth. Had the doctor caught on? Would she answer the phone the next time Patrizia called, and if so, would she want to hear what Patrizia had to say or would she tell them to never call again?

CHAPTER NINE

With the old doctor sitting in the back seat of the Jeep, Juan and Renzo arrived at the camp early in the morning. The old man's face was weathered and gaunt. His thick hair was white as the snow that drapes the peaks of the Andes Mountains. His fingers were long and boney and his toes that peeked out from his sandals were twisted with arthritis. He groaned as Juan helped him stiffly step out of the vehicle to shuffle bent and slow through the camp toward Luis, who was sitting among a large group of his men.

Luis' lip curled in derision. Juan was formerly of Esteban's group. The man had not done anything since pledging his loyalty to Luis to appear that he was not sincere. Yet again, one can never be too careful.

Luis asked his new recruit, "This is the man who put the chip in the woman?"

"*Si*," Juan replied.

"You are certain?"

"*Si*, this is the man."

Turning to the old man, he asked, "Did you put a sub dermal chip into an American woman for Esteban Rojas about four years ago?"

The old man did not appear to be frightened. Luis figured that it was because he was so old that death was always imminent. The old man replied, "*Si*, I am a doctor for the village just beyond the second hill."

"How difficult is it to take the chip out?"

"You must be very careful. The chip may have moved over time, and if you slice too deeply or too quickly, you could damage the chip, and never retrieve the information from it," the old doctor explained.

"Did Esteban show you what was on the chip?"

"I did not wish to know, and I don't want to know now."

Luis turned to Juan. "Take the doctor to the hut just passed where we are keeping the two women. He will stay until the chip is removed."

"I cannot stay. I have patients to care for. The village depends on me," the old man bit out.

"The village will have to manage on their own. I need you, and you will be here when the American woman arrives." He looked at Juan askance and then back to the old man. "I assure you, it will not be long."

Taking the old doctor by the arm, Juan started for the hut that he was instructed to take him to when Luis called out to him. "Juan ... the latrines, they are in need of cleaning. You will do this before you eat."

Fury ripped through Juan's gut. Esteban never treated him with such impertinence. Luis' men eyed him, while fingering their weapons. Renzo's mouth lifted into a greasy grin. Feeling the burn that started at the base of his throat slowly crawl to his face, Juan replied, "*Si.*"

* * * * *

Washington D.C.

Smitty and Grant bumped fists with their replacements at five a.m. They pulled their ties from the collars of their shirts while making their way down the sidewalk of the Pérez estate toward their SUV parked at the curb. They felt a tinge of pity for the poor guy who stood vigilance in the upstairs of the home. His replacement did not come until later in the morning. Poor schmuck. The Secret Service preferred that Justice Pérez and his wife were up and about before the switch of the upstairs guard took place so they would not be disturbed.

Both First Force operatives were thankful that neither had been assigned to that area of the house. They were looking forward to getting out of their suits and getting some much needed sleep.

Smitty climbed into the driver's seat, while running a weary hand over his short hair. "Walt said this assignment would last about two weeks. I should grow most of my hair back in that time, and no, I am not getting a trim before this is over."

"Screw that, Peyton Mattock's got a full head of dreads. Wish we would'a got the house and yard assignment. Too late now, I'm just glad they gave us separate rooms at the hotel. At least I don't have to listen to your freakin' snoring," Grant groused.

"I don't snore," Smitty stated.

Grant rolled his eyes. "Let's put it this way, dude, the guys on the team have seriously considered smothering you with a pillow."

"Speaking of grumpy old men, Justice Pérez sure has been a bear since his telephone conversation the other night. He was bitchin' Mrs. Pérez out pretty good at the dinner table last night," Smitty supplied.

"What about?"

"He doesn't seem too fond of her brother. But that's the most I could make out of it. He's got a nasty tone, and he keeps it nice and low. I was a little too far away to really catch the whole conversation. But I'm keeping my ears perked." He turned into the parking lot of their hotel. "I think something's up with our good friend, Alejandro."

"Maybe Mrs. Pérez used to be a stripper, and he's afraid that her past will compromise his appointment to the Supreme Court," Grant suggested, pushing a shoulder against the door to get out of the vehicle.

"Ya never know," Smitty agreed around a snort. "Let's keep close eyes and ears on the Pérezes. It seems to me like he's worried something's out there that could ruin his big opportunity."

* * * * *

"Didja like the movie last night?" Jack asked Lil as he slid a plate of macaroni and cheese down in front of her.

"Yep," she said, picking up her fork to dig in to the gooey cheesy pasta. "When are you and Dr. Rayne gonna get married?"

Jack leaned a hip against the counter, crossing his arms over his chest. "What makes you think we're getting married?"

Lil lifted a shoulder. Around a mouthful of cheesy goodness, she said, "You're kissing, right?"

Jack was amazed at how absolutely nothing got by this child. Denying the kissing was an exercise in futility, so he decided to just roll with it. He replied, "We've kissed a few times, yes."

Lil flipped her right palm upward. "Then you should get married."

Children view things in such simplistic terms. They are blessed with not being aware of any complexities of situations. It is all part of the innocence that they get to experience for a very short time, until it is ripped away by the realities of a cruel world.

Jack wondered, so he just came right out and asked her, "What do you think Mommy would think about that?"

Lil smiled. "I think she would love it. You wouldn't be sad anymore, and I would have a mommy again. I think she would be happy, don't you?"

Relief washed over Jack. She was so wise for her age. His heart swelled with love for his daughter. Hugging her, he kissed her on the top of her head, and whispered, "Yes, I know she would want us to be happy, because she loves us, and I love you, baby girl."

"I love you too, Daddy," Lil said. Just then the blue light above the kitchen door blinked and Stewart Little stepped through. "Hi, Little Big Man," Lil called out.

He grunted, and then he went to the sink to wash his hands. Jack was mystified by the relationship between his daughter and the huge operative who never spoke unless he absolutely had to. Pleasantries in general were never an option for the big man.

"Hey, Little, what's up?" he asked.

"I'm gonna wash and wax the helicopter today. Might as well, been pretty dead as far as missions go," he replied, while he opened the refrigerator door and grabbed a beer.

"That's for sure." Jack scrubbed a hand across his chin. "So … have you read any good books lately?"

Little stopped mid-opening the beer. His eyes narrowed. "When the hell do I have time to read a freakin' book, Haliday?"

Jack instantly regretted his question. Little never engaged in conversation with anyone, but there wasn't a more reliable man on the team. If his life was on the line, he knew that he could count on Little to pull him or any of the team members through—he just wouldn't talk about it—ever.

"I—I don't know, I was just trying to make conversation."

"Whatever," the grump bit out, and then he started for the door, hesitating long enough to bump fists with Lil, and then slamming the door behind him, rattling the glass on the windows.

"I thought you said he reads to you," Jack said.

"He does. He likes Ramona better than Henry," Lil put in.

"That a fact?"

* * * * *

Saturday had dragged. Lying in Jack's arms, Rayne listened to the thrum of his heart and the steady rhythm of his breathing. When would Sierra call? Was she upset that she didn't answer the last time? Would she call directly after the team was called away? Should she tell Uncle Walt and Jack what was going on? Her mind was on constant speed dial.

Casey said that sooner or later they would call to make a demand or a deal, but when? What would they want? Several times each day she would review how to use the recording app that she'd downloaded to her phone, making sure that she pushed the buttons just as Casey had shown her.

There was no room for panic.

There was no room for error.

There was no room for impatience, and yet, impatience was welling inside her like a geyser ready to explode.

"Rayne … I hope you're not getting your hopes up that Sierra is still alive. I mean … I suppose it's possible, but not probable. I don't want to see you lose all the progress that you've made." Casey's words ran through her mind. She was right, of course. But how could she not hope that her daughter was alive?

She had to find out. Sierra had to call … soon.

* * * * *

Sunday morning

The sun was shining. An easy breeze stirred the trees. The leaves lightly fell to the ground like twirling ballerinas free falling from Heaven. The lawn was covered in a layer of leaves, so Rayne decided to grab a rake and occupy her mind with a little physical labor. She was in desperate need of a distraction—any distraction would do at this point.

One couldn't ask for a more perfect Sunday afternoon, so her chore was more a delight than it was work. Tickles had followed her outside and seemed to be enjoying the task as much as she was. The kitten batted and tackled the leaves as they fell from the trees. Soon Lil spotted her from a window and came running out the front door to join in the fun.

Rayne swept the leaves into a meager pile—there really wasn't enough to form a large mound, but Lil made good use of what was there. She would take a running start from across the yard, and then plunge into the leaves, sending them flying in all directions. Rayne was amazed at how many times Lil could repeat the routine. She was getting tired just watching her run and jump and run and jump.

Her cell phone rang.

Rayne stiffened.

Pulling it from her pocket, she checked the screen, *unavailable*.

It was Sierra.

The phone rang a second time.

"Excuse me, Lil, I'll be right back," she said. She needed some space to concentrate on what Casey had instructed her to do. Swallowing back her panic, she carefully pushed the buttons to activate the app, as Casey had shown her, and then with as much calm as she could muster, she lifted the phone to her ear.

"Hello …"

"Mama, it's me, Sierra. I need you to help me. They are willing to let me go, if you will do as they say," the voice told her. Rayne noticed that the girl didn't seem as uncertain as she had during the past calls. Her voice wasn't as anxious as it had been. She seemed steadier—more confident.

"Where are you, Sierra? Who are you with?" Rayne blurted out before she could stop herself.

"I am in Peru, but I can come home …"

There was a shuffling of the phone, and then a man's harsh voice spoke to her in Spanish. "If you do as you are told, we will reunite you with your daughter, but if you do not, you will never hear from her again. Do you understand what I am saying to you, Dr. Lee?"

She was breathless. She thought that she would never forget Esteban's voice, but she wasn't sure. Was it Esteban on the other end of the call? The voice was as harsh and demanding as she remembered, but she couldn't be certain. She stammered out in Spanish, "Esteban ... what do you want?"

"*Muy bien*," he said. "You will come to Peru. If you cooperate, you will be united with your daughter."

"When? Where do you want me to go?"

"I will tell you soon. You will wait for my instructions, and you will follow them exactly, but most importantly, you will tell no one, or we will kill your daughter for real this time."

The line went dead.

The world spun out of control around her.

Trying to suppress the panic that was churning inside her, she examined the phone to make sure that the call had been successfully recorded. Pressing her eyes closed, she drew the phone to her chest. Yes, she had pressed the correct buttons, and yes, the phone call had been recorded.

It was time to act. It was time to tell Jack, Uncle Walt, and the team about the calls. Casey was right. Esteban Rojas wanted to make a deal of some sort. Only First Force would be there to thwart his plans, and if this girl was her Sierra, she would be reunited with her daughter.

She was afraid to hope. She was terrified to let it into her heart, except hope spilled into her heart as naturally as it was beating.

With trembling fingers, she texted her uncle. *I need you to come to HQ ASAP. Very important!!*

She hit the send button, and then she hurried toward the house. She needed to talk to Jack immediately.

She pressed through the front door to rush through the foyer and into the living room, where she found Jack with his feet propped up on the coffee table, watching a football game.

"Jack!" Rayne exclaimed.

Jumping to his feet, Jack's hand went to the gun that he always kept stuffed down the back of his jeans. "What? What's wrong?" he asked, looking passed her for someone who may be chasing her or some other urgent situation.

Extending her cell phone out toward him, Rayne hurried around the couch. "Listen!" she insisted. She pressed the play button, and then handed the phone to him. His eyebrows furrowed and his face hardened as he listed to the conversation between Rayne and a girl claiming to be her deceased daughter, and then the conversation switched to a man speaking Spanish, with Rayne answering him back in the same.

Jack shook his head, giving the phone back to her. "I speak a little Spanish, but not enough for this. What's this about? What's going on?"

"I need to sit," Rayne said, sinking down onto the couch. Returning his gun to its hiding place, Jack sat next to her. She explained, "The girl you heard on the phone contacted me on Wednesday and then again on Thursday. She said she was Sierra ... my daughter, Sierra, and that she needed help."

"What? Why didn't you tell me?"

"Because it sounded insane. I didn't believe it myself, at first. So I downloaded an app onto my phone so I could record the conversation the next time she called. Casey said—"

"Whoa! Casey? You told Casey, but you couldn't tell me?"

Rayne could see the irritation and the hurt crowding Jack's eyes. Her heart sunk. She could understand his frustration, but this was no time for a lover's spat. She didn't know what to say. She didn't know how to explain without making the situation worse. She muddled through as best she could. "Please, Jack, try to understand. Our relationship is new. I was afraid that if I told you ... you would think I was losing it. I didn't want you to think that I was unstable."

Jack dropped back against the couch. "You don't trust me?"

"That's not it. I trust you. Please believe that I do. I just wanted to have all the information before I came to you. Please ... please don't be angry with me. Not now," Rayne pleaded.

"Please, Daddy, don't be mad at Dr. Rayne," Lil's voice came out watery.

Jack and Rayne turned to find the curly haired girl standing behind them with her kitten in her arms. Leaves were tangled in her hair. Her face was flushed from playing outside, and her eyes were wet with tears about to fall down her cheeks.

Jack dropped his chin to his chest for a moment, and then he quietly said, "I'm not mad at Dr. Rayne." He dragged his gaze to meet Rayne's. "I love Dr. Rayne, and I just want her to be honest with me at all times and not hide anything from me. Dr. Rayne needs to understand that trust and honesty is the most important thing to me in a relationship."

Tears bursting from her eyes, Rayne threw her arms around him. She whispered in his ear, "I love you too, Jack, and I will never hide anything from you again—no matter how crazy it sounds."

Lil ran around the couch to join in the hug, and they welcomed her into their embrace.

Tickles purred.

Rayne's cell phone whistled.

Wiping her eyes, Rayne peeked at her screen. It was a text from Walt: *I'm on my way. Do I need the team?*

Rayne showed Jack the text.

"Tell him to call for Clark. We need to gather some intel, and then we'll need the team."

* * * * *

Disconnecting the call, Luis smiled. "You have done well, Patrizia. I think Dr. Lee believes that her daughter is still alive, and she believes that she will be meeting with Esteban. Many surprises wait for her when she arrives."

"*Bien*," Bibiana snapped. "It seems that you have what you want. Now perhaps one of your men can take us home."

"I will let you know when our business is done, Bibiana," he said, as he shoved the burner phone into his pocket, fetching a different phone from another. "Don't worry, you will know when I am finished," he repeated through a wicked chuckle. Thumbing numbers on the phone, Luis made his way out of the hut.

Patrizia said, "I wish there was a way to stop him, Mama."

Around a drained sigh, Bibiana asked, "I do too, but how?"

Folding her arms one over the other atop the table, Patrizia laid her head down. She didn't know the answer, but somehow there must be a way to help Dr. Lee.

* * * * *

Washington D.C.

"The house has been completely quiet all day," the day security guard told Smitty and Grant when they showed up for their shift. "Mrs. Pérez is upstairs in her room, and the judge is in his office. Upstairs security has already arrived. He's in position," he added, whipping his tie from his collar.

Making his way from the kitchen area while munching on a blueberry muffin, the second security guard bumped fists with Grant on his way toward the front door. "See ya tomorrow, dude, they're all yours."

"Have a good sleep," Grant told them, while closing the door, turning the dead bold, and activating the alarm system.

"The Pérezes seem like a happy-go-lucky couple, don't they?" Grant said quietly.

"Head-over-heals in love," Smitty wryly added. "I'll take my usual position outside the judge's office. You can roam the living room and dining areas."

On his way into the living room, Grant groused, "I'd give my right arm for a beer and a football game."

"What? No heated night with Sil?"

"That's a give, dude," Grant said.

"I would hope so. She's one gorgeous woman," Smitty told him.

"Hey, that's my wife you're talking about."

"Lucky bastard," Smitty stated.

Pitching him a proud smirk, Grant rounded the bend into the living room.

Letting out a sigh at the sight of the chair poised next to the judge's office door, Smitty took his seat, unbuttoned his suit jacket, and leaned back, crossing his arms over his wide chest. It would be a long-ass afternoon, evening, and an even longer night. Yeah, it was Sunday, and he had to agree with Grant—a beer and a football game on the tube would be a welcome relief from this torturous boredom.

He had just laid his head against the wall when he heard the soft ringing of a phone from inside the office. Immediately, he jerked his head upward, rose from the chair, and placed his head as close to the door as he possibly could.

"What do you want now?" the judge demanded in Spanish. "I gave you the information that you requested. I told you not to contact me again."

The judge kept his voice low, except Smitty could hear the sheer malevolence in the tone. Whoever was on the other end of that call was a threat. Smitty had serious doubts that it had anything to do with his wife being a former stripper as Grant had jokingly suggested. No, it was direr than that.

"I told you before I want nothing to do with these things anymore!" The judge was quiet, like he was listening to the caller's response, and then he bellowed, "I can't help you! Don't you understand this? It would destroy everything that I have worked so hard to build!" Again the judge was silent. This time his retort was hushed and concise, "I will consider what you have said, now leave me alone to think. Do not contact me for several days, and don't do anything that I will regret!"

Smitty heard him toss the cell phone down hard. Hearing the judge's footsteps stomping across the floor, Smitty quickly returned to his seat. When the door yanked open, he jumped to his feet.

"Summon my wife, I want to speak with her immediately," Judge Pérez commanded.

"Of course, Justice Pérez," Smitty said. With that the judge retreated into the office, slamming the door behind him. Moving away from the door, Smitty spoke softly into the mike on his lapel. "Please send Mrs. Pérez down to the judge's office. He wishes to speak with her."

"Rodger that," the upstairs security guard confirmed.

Moments later, Paullina slowly made her way down the staircase. Her fingers gripped the banister so tightly that her knuckles were white. Smitty noticed the disquiet in her expression as she stepped away from the stairs to walk across the foyer toward her husband's office.

"Good evening, Mrs. Pérez," Smitty said, while he opened the door to the office for her.

"Is it?" she quietly replied, considering him through her long dark lashes. Even though her skin was dark, Smitty could see the flush in her cheeks and the tiny beads of sweat forming along her hairline. It was most obvious that Paullina Pérez was nervous about the conversation that she was about to have with her husband.

The judge was pacing his office. When he heard the door open and his wife step through, he turned. His face was filled with agitation, his shoulders squared in righteous indignation. In English he said to Smitty, "Please go to the kitchen for your dinner. I want complete privacy with my wife."

Bowing his head, Smitty said, "Certainly."

He closed the door feeling a surge of sympathy for Paullina—he wouldn't want to be on the receiving end of the judge's frustration. He couldn't help but wonder what Paullina had to do with the phone calls. On his way into the kitchen, he recalled a small portion of a conversation he'd overheard during dinner Thursday night ...

"I cannot control what my brother does," Paullina said.

"He is your brother. Surely you can reason with him. He has been nothing but trouble for me. I cannot afford to deal with his demands. You must talk with him, Paullina," the judge said in a seething voice. "He could destroy our lives." She said nothing in return. The room fell silent.

Smitty sat at the kitchen table, scrubbing his fingers across his chin.

"What are you doing in here?" Grant's voice broke through his deliberation. "I thought you were supposed to be sitting next to the office door."

"The judge got another phone call, and now he's having a conversation with his wife about it. He didn't want me around. Something's up, and he's worried that something is gonna ruin his invitation to the big dance. I think it's time to tell Walt about this and see if Clark can do some digging around into the Pérezes' past—specifically Paullina Pérez."

Grant sank into the chair next to Smitty. "Looks like this assignment isn't going to be the cakewalk that we thought it would be."

"They never are, my friend. They never are."

CHAPTER TEN

Rayne could barely sit still while waiting for Walt and Clark to arrive. She was happy that she'd been able to record the phone call from Sierra and her conversation with Esteban Rojas, but would it add up to anything?

Jack had been upset that she hadn't told him about the phone calls when they first started, and she worried that her uncle would be unhappy with her, too.

Clark Rhodes was the First Force mission director. He gathered intel and helped her uncle organize the missions. Clark was ex-FBI and a whiz with a computer—he could hack just about any system to get whatever information he needed. If Sierra was out there, Clark would find her.

When Clark first came to the team he had very short dark hair. As an FBI agent he lived in black suits. The moment he joined First Force he traded that look in for a more casual wardrobe. Being September, she expected the tall lean director to sport a pair of flip-flops, tan cargo pants, and a loose fitting T-shirt. His dark hair would sweep across the collar of his shirt, and brush across the top of his black squared-off glasses. Clark wasn't quite as big or chiseled or muscled as the operatives, but make no mistake in taking him to task—the man was an expert in martial arts. Oh yeah, Clark Rhodes was one kick-ass behind the scenes operative.

The blue light over her sitting room door blinked, alerting her that a door had opened somewhere in the mansion. Her eyes flicked to the close circuit screen stationed near the ceiling in the corner of the room—it flashed a picture of Walt walking through the front door with Clark directly behind him. Walt had his trusty briefcase in hand, while Clark toted a laptop case. Yep, she'd hit the nail directly on the head—flip-flops, cargo pants, and a chocolate brown V-neck T-shirt.

Continuing to study the screen, she saw Jack and Lil approach the two men. Lil hugged them both, and then she saw Jack direct his daughter to take her kitten and go into the living room. Lil scooped up Tickles and, with a wave, did as she was told. Jack and Clark followed Walt into his office.

On a braced breath, Rayne pick up her cell phone from the coffee table and stepped out of her suite to join them. It was time to find out who was making the ambiguous phone calls. It was time to find out if Sierra was really out there in need of help to return home.

When she entered her uncle's office, she found the three men discussing the state of affairs. Walt leaned a hip against his desk with his arms crossed over his chest, while Jack and Clark sat in the leather winged back chairs that faced him.

Looking up, Jack said, "I was just about to come get you."

"I saw them come in," Rayne put in. Quickly crossing the room, she handed Clark the phone, as if she'd been protecting a top security item and was glad to be rid of it. Pointing she said, "Press this button to hear the recording."

Clark was fluent in as many as six languages, so Rayne knew that he would have no problem understanding the conversation between her and Esteban Rojas. Leaning forward in his chair so that everyone could hear, Clark pressed the button. Rayne's heart sank when she heard the girl's voice on the recording ...

"Hello ... "

"Mama, it's me, Sierra. I need you to help me. They are willing to let me go, if you will do as they say,"

"Where are you, Sierra? Who are you with?"

"I am in Peru, but I can come home ... "

Rayne found it most interesting that the shuf-fling of the phone from Sierra's hand to Esteban's sounded harsher in the recording than it had during the actual call, and then the conversation turned to the Spanish language …

"If you do as you are told, we will reunite you with your daughter, but if you do not, you will never hear from her again. Do you understand what I am saying to you, Dr. Lee?"

"Esteban … what do you want?"

"Muy bien," he said. "You will come to Peru. If you cooperate, you will be united with your daughter."

"When? Where do you want me to go?"

"I will tell you soon. You will wait for my instruc-tions, and you will follow them exactly, but most impor-tantly, you will tell no one, or we will kill your daughter for real this time."

The recording ended. Walt, Clark, and Jack looked up at her, questions filling their faces.

Clark went first, "How many calls have you received from this girl?"

"This was the third," Rayne told him.

"Was this the first time you spoke to Esteban Rojas?" he inquired.

"Yes, although in the other calls I heard a man's voice in the background. It must've been Esteban."

"When did you receive the first call?" Walt asked.

"Wednesday morning. The second came Thursday evening. What now?" Rayne was anxious to put together a strategy, except she knew that there wasn't enough information to move forward promptly.

Walt and Clark exchanged befuddled glances. Rubbing the back of his neck, Clark said, "Well, there's not much to go on. We have to wait for his instructions. We don't even know where he is sending you. That said, he hasn't told you what he wants in exchange for a reunion with the girl." Clark was careful not to dub the girl on the phone as "Sierra," because he believed that Rayne's daughter was dead. He didn't want to initiate any false hope. He continued, "We will have to have a course of action in place ASAP. Let me see what's been going on with Esteban since our last run-in with him."

"The moment you hear from Rojas, contact me," Walt stated. He pulled his cell phone from the briefcase. Thumbing a message, he said, "I'm going to put the team on alert. They will be ready to report here and to move out at a moment's notice. In the meantime, make sure you record the next call—we don't want to miss any details. I'm going to stay here so that I'm available when the call comes through."

"I think I'll stick around, too," Clark said, while he slid the laptop from the case onto the desk.

Just as Walt pressed the button to send out his text message to the team, his cell phone rang. He looked at the screen. "Looks like Smitty's checking in." He placed the call on speaker. "Wabash …"

"Yo, Walt, I think we've got a situation with Justice Pérez and his wife. I've overheard several heated cell phone conversations. It appears that someone's blackmailing him, and I've got a feeling that its Mrs. Pérez's brother," Smitty explained.

"Whose Mrs. Pérez's brother?" Walt asked.

"Hell if I know, but I'll bet Clark can find out right quick."

"No doubt," Walt said. "Keep me in the loop. I'll get back to you soon." With that he ended the call and turned to Clark. "Looks like you've got some double duty on the horizon."

A blue hue illuminated Clark's face. He had already slid into the seat at Walt's desk and was tapping at the keys on his laptop.

Jack commented, "I'll bet the feds just love you hacking into their system."

"Then they shouldn't make it so freakin' easy," Clark remarked.

"Easy for you," Rayne pointed out.

"I am amazing," Clark supplied wearing a sly curl on his lips. "Here it is … Paullina Pérez was born and raised in Peru. Her full name is, Paullina Chaves-Pérez—which has a very nice ring to it. She left Peru to attend Georgetown University through a scholarship program. That's where she must've met the judge. He attended Georgetown as well. They were married thirty-five years ago. Mrs. Pérez has three siblings: Anita Chaves who is deceased, Francesco Chaves is a dentist in Callao. Paullina is third in line, and the youngest brother's name just happens to be, *Luis Chaves.*"

"Ouch," Walt said.

"Ouch indeed," Clark agreed, lacing his fingers behind his head, while leaning back against the chair.

"Who is Luis Chaves?" Jack asked.

"He was Esteban Rojas' partner in extra-curricular activities like drugs and weapons trafficking. He was also his cohort in the killing of Senator Billings. So one would have to ask, what does the Honorable Justice Pérez have to do with the death of Senator Billings?" Clark mused.

"Senator Billings, Matt, and possibly my daughter, Sierra," Rayne adamantly put in.

"It looks like this mission is turning into more than an alleged mother and daughter reunion," Walt noted.

* * * * *

Amazonian Valley

A cock crowed somewhere in the camp, waking Bibiana. It was early in the morning yet the heat filled their hut like the fires of Hades. Patrizia was curled up against her on the inadequate cot that had been provided for them. She watched her daughter sleep, hoping that today was the day that Luis would force her to make her last phone call, and then announce that their imposed obligation was satisfied and they could return home.

It was a sad situation. No one from their village came looking for them. No one would dare. They had vanished into thin air, and although people from their village would wonder where they were or what had become of them, not a soul would venture out to find them. Not even Bibiana's elderly father. He was fretting over them, no doubt, yet there was little that he could or would do.

Carefully as to not disturb Patrizia's slumber, she slipped off the cot to pad across the dirt floor. She poured some water from the pitcher into a bowl and washed her face. She wished for a hot bath and clean clothes, but for now just being alive was a blessing.

As she sat in the chair using her fingers like a comb, the door opened. The man who stood guard came in with a plate of bread and some fruit. He told her, "Wake the girl. Luis will be in soon, he wants to call the woman this morning." He sat the food on the table, and then retreated from the hut.

Yes, today would be the day, and while she felt a deep sorrow for what would happen to Dr. Lee, she felt a relief that this nightmare would soon end for her and Patrizia.

* * * * *

It wasn't long before Luis stomped through the door. "We will call the doctor now, and I will give her instructions," he announced. He dialed the phone and handed it to Patrizia. "This is what you will say, Patrizia, Mama, please do as they say. I want to come home."

"And then you will let us go home?" Bibiana asked.

"I told you that I will let you know when you can go," Luis barked.

"If the woman agrees to come, why would we remain here?"

"Because I want you to, and you will do as you are told!"

Patrizia stared at the number that Luis had dialed on the phone. Closing her eyes, she committed it to memory. She wasn't sure what good it would do, but she memorized the numbers all the same.

"Patrizia!" Luis bellowed.

She flinched, realizing that he'd been trying to get her attention for a few seconds.

"You will say what I have told you to say now!" He pressed the send button on the phone in her hands, it began to ring.

* * * * *

"Why is Uncle Walt and Mr. Clark staying at the house?" Lil asked over her bowl of Cheerios. The happy-go-lucky sound that usually filled her tone was absent replaced with hesitance and wariness. Lil knew the score. She'd been living among the operatives long enough to know that when Walt and Clark were in the house, a mission was fermenting.

Sipping her tea, Rayne leaned a hip against the breakfast bar. "Something has come up that needs their attention, so they're staying here until it's all figured out."

"So Daddy's going away?"

"Possibly."

"But I'll stay here with you, right?"

"We'll see," Rayne said.

Jack came into the kitchen with Lil's backpack in hand. Taking her lunch bag from the counter, he asked, "Ready to go to the bus?"

Slipping off the stool, Lil inquired, "Are you going on a mission?"

"Maybe," Jack said, slipping her backpack over her shoulders, and then handing her the bag.

"Will I stay here with Dr. Rayne?"

"Yes," Jack firmly replied.

"*Jack* ..." Rayne scolded over her mug.

Quickly glancing at her over his shoulder, while he tugged the door open, he said, "C'mon, we'll be late." With that he shooed Lil out the door, abruptly ending any conversation on the subject.

Rayne straightened. Did he actually think that she wouldn't be involved in the mission? After the meeting with Walt and Clark last night Jack had turned stiff. He was quiet, preoccupied. While Clark worked in Walt's office gathering intel, they sat in the living room watching TV with Lil, except Jack would jump up from the sofa every half-hour to check on Clark's progress, and when he returned he seemed on edge, and cranky.

Running a hand through her hair, she recalled how he hugged her tightly before he retired to his suite for the night. His body felt rigid. Every muscle was tense, unyielding—even to her touch. He wasn't the cool, fun-loving Jack Haliday that she'd spent a year with and had fallen head-over-heels in love with. Rather he was a bundle of apprehension. He seemed to be filled with words that he wanted to say but couldn't find a way to allow them to tumble from his lips.

He would work through it.

They would work through it.

Everything was going to be all right—at least that's what she had to keep telling herself. Last night she could see in Clark's eyes that he was concerned for her mental and emotional state. She could see that he was worried that she truly believed that it was Sierra on the other end of those phone calls. She took in a ragged breath. Did she believe that it was Sierra calling?

No.

Yes.

Maybe … maybe … may—

Cupping her hand over her mouth, she sucked back a sob before it could completely escape her throat. Was it too much to hope that her daughter was still alive? Was it too much to ask?

Her cell phone rang.

Her eyes flicked to the device vibrating on the countertop.

The screen read, *unavailable*.

She needed to calm down.

She needed to press the correct buttons to record the call.

Inching her way toward the phone, she carefully picked it up, and even more carefully she pressed the button to activate the app to record, and then she lifted it to her ear.

"Yes …"

"Mama, please do as they say. I want to come home," Patrizia pleaded.

Luis snatched the phone from her hand. "Are you ready to make your journey?" he asked in Spanish.

Rayne demanded, "What do you want from me, Esteban?"

"You will find out soon enough. You will come to Nanay, Iquitos. There is a hotel there, Hotel Dos Rios. You will check in and wait. I will be in contact."

"I don't understand. How much money do you want?"

"You will give me more than money. Remember, you will tell no one. You will come alone, or I will kill the girl," Luis reminded her.

"Let me talk to her," Rayne insisted.

"Very well," Luis gave the phone to Patrizia. Before he permitted her to speak, he waved a warning finger in her face. She nodded her understanding.

"Hello …" Patrizia said.

Rayne wanted to ask her a question—something that would prove that she was or was not her daughter. Her mind was racing. She needed to come up with something quickly, while she silently scolded herself for not thinking of this earlier. Esteban wasn't going to let her talk for long. What could she ask? What would Sierra remember? She was only four when she was snatched from her arms—never to be seen again. How much trauma had the girl been through in the past four years?

Quickly she spit out, "Do you remember your favorite cookie? I … I could bring some with me."

Patrizia froze. She didn't know what to say. She certainly didn't know the answer to the question. What if she got the answer wrong? It could ruin Luis' plans, and that would surely mean death for her and her mother! Her eyes snapped to the scowl on Luis Chaves' face, and then to the angst on her mother's.

After swallowing hard, Patrizia replied, "I am sorry, Mama. I do not remember."

Rayne's heart broke. Giving it one last shot she asked, "Do you remember the flavor?"

"Flavor?" Patrizia repeated. This was a word that they hadn't gone over. She wasn't sure what the woman meant.

In Spanish, Rayne said, "El chocolate … vanilla … fresa?"

The woman wanted an answer. Patrizia knew why. Dr. Lee was trying to figure out if this voice really belonged to her long lost daughter. How was she going to pass this test? How could she convince this woman that she was her daughter when in fact she was not?

Still Luis glowered at her. Anxiously, her mother shifted from one foot to the other, while Dr. Lee waited for a response. She felt trapped. Finally Patrizia managed, "It was long ago, Mama. But … I remember … chocolate."

Luis had had enough of this game! The woman was trying to trick Patrizia, and he wasn't having it. He seized the phone from her hand. "You have talked enough! You will come or she will die! I will expect you no later than Thursday! Do you understand?"

Tears running down Rayne's face, she answered, "I understand."

The line went dead.

Tossing the phone aside, Rayne leaned on the counter, bowing her head to weep. Warm hands cupped each shoulder, squeezing. Clark soothed, "It's okay, Rayne. You did good. You did very good."

She wished Jack were there to hold her. She needed to be held, so she turned around to hug Clark with all her might, clutching his shirt with her fingers, burying her face into his shoulder to let her tears flow freely. The girl didn't know the answer to her question, but that didn't prove that it wasn't Sierra. Rayne was more uncertain now than before.

"What happened?" She heard Jack's voice from the doorway.

"Get Walt," Clark said, "Tell him to call up the team."

* * * * *

Within an hour, vehicles filled the driveway in front of the Georgian mansion. Jack, Stewart Little, Casey Rhodes, and Dan Garrison were all gathered in Walt's office for a briefing and to hear the tactic that Clark had composed. Smitty and Grant were doing their part in Washington D.C.—keeping a close eye on Judge Pérez and his wife.

This was the first time that Rayne would sit in on a meeting. Her palms were sweaty. She was nervous. Casey tossed her a reassuring wink when she entered the office. She sat next to Jack on the sofa. Rayne wanted to take a seat between her friend and Jack, but instead she retreated to a far corner of the room to listen and observe. She couldn't help but notice that Jack was on edge. His jaw was so tight that the skin rippled over the bone. He fidgeted in his seat. He seemed to be filled with trepidation. He'd been on so many missions as a SEAL, and now with team First Force. She couldn't figure exactly why he was so bent over this mission.

Once all of the operatives had taken seats in the office, Walt explained that Rayne had been receiving phone calls from a young girl claiming to be her deceased daughter, Sierra. There was no reaction from any of the operatives. They sat very stiffly listening to all the information without so much as a raised eyebrow. Rayne noted Stewart Little grinding his right fist into his left palm. The big man hated bad guys, but even more, he hated bad guys who messed with those he cared for.

When Walt was finished briefing the team, Clark stepped forward to play the two recordings on

Rayne's cell phone. Again, no one had a reaction. They listened, processed.

"With all due respect," Dan Garrison, an ex US Marshall, spoke up when the recording ended. "We don't believe that this girl is Doc Rayne's daughter, correct?"

Hokay, it was out there.

Dan had verbalized what everyone was thinking. Rayne wasn't quite sure if Clark was relieved or pissed. Everyone in the room seemed to be waiting for the answer, and yet a little wary of what would be said in Rayne's presence. She knew what they were thinking. Each one of them respected her as a doctor, a colleague, and yes, a friend. They knew how difficult this situation had to be for her, and leaving the obvious question unanswered was a comfortable preference, but not a realistic one.

This was the first reaction she saw in the team members. Each one looked at the floor, not really seeing it, waiting for Clark's response.

"We're not ruling that possibility out, just yet. Please draw your attention to the screen," Clark said, nodding at Walt who turned out the lights. Clark pressed the button on the remote to flash a photograph of Esteban Rojas on a large screen behind Walt's desk. "Most of you may remember Esteban Rojas from four years ago—drug and weapons trafficking. We went into his camp to extract Doc Rayne. We took out quite a few of his guerrillas, but

207

Rojas escaped. Now as you heard in the recordings, Rojas hasn't made any clear demands of Rayne—only that she arrive in Peru at the Hotel Dos Rios by Thursday and wait for him to contact her. So at this point we don't know what his objectives are." Clark noticed the intense glare in Jack's eyes. He was leaning forward in his chair with his elbows resting on his knees, and his hands clasped in fists so tightly that his fingernails and knuckles were white. |He tapped his right toe.

Clearing his throat, Clark continued, "Our objective is to make sure that Esteban Rojas does not escape this time. We want to take him and his operation down. Rayne and Dan will travel to Nanay, Iquitos on a commercial flight. I made sure that Dan's seat is toward the back of the plane to observe anyone who might be tailing Rayne, and so that no one suspects that they are traveling together. The team, including Walt, will follow several hours later on a flight through the military base." Instantly, Jack straightened. His eyes narrowed.

From the corner of his eye, Clark saw Walt watching Jack. It was just as he and Walt had suspected. Jack and Rayne had become very close—most likely intimate.

Remaining on course, he said, "Rayne will check into the hotel—Dan will get a room next door." Clark changed the screen to a map of Nanay Iquitos. "The team will arrive several hours before Rayne and Dan because they have connections to catch and a bus transfer, while your flight will be direct and an SUV will be waiting for you at the base. While Rayne and Dan wait for Esteban to contact her, the team will have taken positions on the hills above these roads that lead in and out of Nanay Iquitos." He used a pencil to indicate the locations of the stakeouts.

"Of course we will stick like glue to Rayne after she has been contacted, and she travels to Esteban's camp—"

"Find another way," Jack firmly interrupted.

Having an idea of what Jack was indicating, Clark asked anyway, "What do you mean?" All the operatives turned their attention toward Jack.

"I mean, find a different way. Rayne is not going in as a decoy. There is no reason to put her in this position and I won't have it," he told them in a concise, no uncertain terms tone.

Rayne pushed out of the corner that she had been occupying. "Jack ... I've got to go. Esteban—"

"No you don't," Jack bit out. He turned toward Casey. "Casey is a trained operative. She's about the same height as Rayne, and just about the same build. They both have long dark hair. Esteban hasn't seen Rayne in four years. There is *no reason* that we can't send Casey in as the decoy, and leave Rayne right here out of harm's way."

"I understand your concern, Jack," Walt said. "But Esteban isn't stupid. He used Rayne as a slave for seven months. I don't think he's going to forget what she looks like."

Jack jerked from his seat. "I knew this was what the plan was going to be. Well I'm telling you to find another way, because I'm not going to let you put Rayne's life at risk! She's not prepared for what could go wrong out there! Casey's trained. At least if things go FUBAR, Casey knows how to handle herself."

"I don't think Jack is wrong, Walt," Casey put in. "We don't really look alike, per sai, but there are enough likenesses that we could pull it off long enough to get the team inside the camp."

"Whoa!" Rayne called out. "You're all talking as if I'm not even in the room. Well I *am* in the room, and this is *my* daughter we're talking about!"

"Rayne—"

Rayne threw her hands up in a halting manner, "No, Jack! I know what you're going to say, and don't think I don't know that Esteban could be bluffing, but what if he's not? I won't risk it!"

"And what if he is bluffing, Rayne? What then? I'll tell you what, you'll be in a bad situation that you won't know how to handle," Jack argued.

"He wants something from me. Casey doesn't have whatever it is that he wants, and the moment that he realizes that he doesn't have the right woman, your mission is going to go FUBAR in a big hurry, and then Casey will be in a very bad situation. No! I'm in, and that's that!"

"You don't get it, Rayne!"

Walt bellowed, "Stand down, Haliday!"

Jack stopped. He glared at Walt. He could feel the stares of his comrades burning into his back. He couldn't bear the thought of letting Rayne go into a hot zone that she or the team couldn't control—no matter how well prepared they might be.

Frustration exploded inside him. He spun on his heels and marched out of the office, slamming the door behind him. The room was silent. Rayne ran a harried hand through her long tresses.

Walt said, "Haliday needs time to cool off." He turned to Clark. "For the moment, let's move on to the other issue at hand."

"Excuse me," Rayne said in a hushed voice.

"Of course," Walt said.

Quietly, Rayne crossed the room to slip out of the office.

Clark pressed the button again to bring up a photo of a dark-haired Peruvian man with evil eyes. "This man is Luis Chaves. He is a notorious drugs and weapons dealer in the same region of the Amazonian Valley that we will be traveling to. He and Esteban work together and have a powerful network. I have recently uncovered the fact that Luis Chaves is Paullina Pérez's younger brother."

Clark noted the baffled look on the team member's faces. He wasn't sure if they were baffled by the parallel between Paullina and Chaves or the display that Jack and Rayne had just put on, but he decided to go with the parallel. He clarified, "Paullina Pérez is the wife of the Honorable Justice Alejandro Pérez—the judge that Smitty and Grant went to Washington to protect until his senate nomination to the Supreme Court."

"Whoa," Dan let out. "How did all the president's men miss that little tidbit?"

"Good question," Clark said. "According to Smitty, Justice Pérez has been receiving phone calls of a blackmailing nature. Now we can only speculate that these calls are coming from Luis' camp. We're not sure if this is connected to our mission, but my gut is telling me that it is."

* * * * *

Rayne made her way across the foyer and down the corridor to the west wing of the mansion. The door to Jack's suite was open, but the lights were out. She peered into the dark sitting room to find him on the couch with his legs propped up on the coffee table—his left ankle crossed over his right. Resting his head against the cushions, his eyes were closed.

"If we were trying to hide the fact that we're lovers, we just blew it," Rayne whispered into the dark.

Without opening his eyes, he whispered back, "I can't lose you, Rayne. I can't lose another woman that I love. I don't want you to go."

Her heart swelled. He was trying to protect her. She got that. Jack protected those he loved and he couldn't bear the prospect of being in a position—like he was a year ago—where he couldn't shield his loved ones. Being rendered helpless was terrifying to him. This mission was hitting home like a wrecking ball smacking a mighty fortress.

She made her way to the couch to curl up on his lap. He took her into his arms, pressing his lips to her forehead, holding them there.

"You know that I have to go. Maybe, just maybe, we could get away with sending Casey in my place, and God bless her, she'd do it, but we both know that I have to go—I *need* to go."

"Missions go wrong all the time. Mistakes happen. Situations change in the blink of an eye and we have to readjust our strategy just as fast, but we're trained to do it. I'm terrified that something will go very wrong and I won't be there to protect you. But most of all, I'm terrified that Esteban is playing with you. I don't want you to have unrealistic hopes that—"

"I'm not a fool, Jack. Oh, I want Sierra to be there so badly, but I also know that there's a very good possibility that this is some kind of game. Why would he contact me after all this time? There's got to be something to it, and we have to find out what it is." She pulled his face to hers and kissed him. "I love you, Jack, and I love Lil, but how can we be a family until we put this behind us?"

Pushing up from his lap, she held her hand out to him. "Now, c'mon, there's much to do and only a few hours before Lil gets home from school." She cajoled. "If you're a good boy at the meeting, maybe we can make some pie later."

"Are you trying to *handle* me, Dr. Lee?"

"I think I just did."

CHAPTER ELEVEN

It was set. Rayne would travel back to the place where she lost everything that mattered in her life and was forced into sexual slavery to a tyrant for seven months. It had been the darkest time of her life. What could Esteban possibly want from her now? He wasn't demanding money. She had no drug connections in the U.S. or Peru.

Rolling over in her bed, she checked the clock: 3:00 a.m. She couldn't sleep and it had nothing to do with nightmares. Her mind was a live wire, snapping and jumping through dreadful memories, and the contemplation of returning to the Amazonian Valley.

What did he want?

What did he want?

What could Esteban Rojas want from her four years after the fact?

Suddenly a thought crossed her mind. What if she was not his real target? What if it was some kind of a trap to bring First Force into his territory and destroy them? Surely, Esteban knew by now who her rescuers had been. He also had to know that she would not come alone—there was no way that her uncle's security team would allow such a thing.

First Force took out most of his militia, and those who were left were badly injured or were turned over to the authorities. She considered that an exercise in futility. The authorities in the Amazonian Valley were almost as evil as the drug militias that pillaged it.

Was Uncle Walt the target?

She shuddered at the notion.

The plan was that she would leave twenty minutes ahead of Dan Garrison for the airport early Wednesday evening. By the time she made all the connections and hopped a bus, she would arrive in Nanay, Iquitos late in the day on Thursday. She was terrified, but she knew that Dan would be right on her heels the entire trip. He wouldn't let her out of his sight—until they went to their perspective hotel rooms to wait for Esteban's directives.

She took in a braced breath. Oh how she remembered his directives. She remembered how he loved her hair. He would run his sausage-like fingers through it when he returned to the hut for the evening, and then he would grab her by the hair and toss her onto his bed and rape her.

Night after night, she would cry into the dark for God to take her. She prayed that Esteban would grow bored with her body and kill her. After the rapes, he would make her lie close to him while he smoked his rancid cigarettes. If she had not pleased him as he thought he deserved, he would put them out on her shoulders. She still bore those scars—and so many others that were not visible—deep cutting scars that therapy could not expunge.

The memories drove her to sit up in her bed. Her silky hair fell over her shoulders. Caressing the long strands with her fingertips, she considered cutting it shorter before her trip. If the mission went south, she didn't want to provide Esteban with anything that gave him pleasure. Covering her face with her hands, she could almost feel his toxic touch on her skin. She shivered again.

Okay, the tossing, turning, and fretting was doing her no good. Dr. Lockhart would reprimand her good if she knew that she was harping on the past. She whipped the blankets to the side to swing her legs over the edge of the bed, and then she pushed from the mattress. She was going to go into the kitchen and make some tea.

After pulling on a robe, Rayne arrived in the kitchen to find Clark brewing a fresh pot of coffee. His jaw was filling with dark whiskers, his feet were bare. He had changed into a pair of fleece lounging pants that hung low on his hips, and an old faded T-shirt that read: *Someday you'll pay to sleep with us—Penn State Hotel and Travel Management.*

Rayne's lips curled. Clark had just rinsed out a mug when he turned to find her standing in the threshold. His eyes flicked to the clock above the stove.

He asked, "It's almost three-thirty in the morning, what are you doing up?"

"I could ask you the same question," she replied, on her way to the cabinet for a cup.

"I seldom sleep while planning a mission. What's your excuse?"

"I seldom sleep when I know that I'll be coming face-to-face with Esteban Rojas."

"I'm sorry. I know this has to be hard for you," Clark said, stirring creamer into his coffee. "So … how long have you and Jack been … um … a thing?"

Dropping a tea bag into the cup, Rayne could feel a slight blush warming her cheeks. "Probably longer than either of us was aware of. But we made it official about a week ago."

"Mmmm, I figured. He was pretty hostile this afternoon."

She winced. "Sorry about that. He was just protecting me. It's only been a year since he lost Laura. I'm sure all that is rushing back to him with this mission."

"I get it, but he's too close to the situation, Rayne. We'll have to keep him at a distance on this one—emotions will be running too high, and that can blow a mission right out of the water," Clark explained.

"I understand."

"Let's hope that Jack does, too," Clark said.

* * * * *

Washington D.C.

The daytime security team briefed Smitty and Grant. They said that the judge had cancelled all appointments and court appearances for the day. He'd spent his time behind the closed doors of his office, having meals delivered by the maid. Thusly, Paullina had remained in her room all day, only coming downstairs for her meals, eating alone in the dining room, and then retreating back upstairs.

Yeah, something was up. The judge had spent a lot of time on his phone in the past two days, but there was no yelling as there had been earlier in the week, only muffled conversation that Smitty couldn't make out.

Smitty had just taken his post outside Judge Pérez's office when the doorbell rang. The maid rushed from the kitchen to answer it. Smitty waved his hand to stop her. She shrunk away from the door. With his handgun at the ready, he peeked through the peephole to find Peyton Mattock on the other side. He couldn't see beyond the Hawke International operative, but that didn't mean there wasn't someone off to the side holding him at gunpoint. When guarding an important political figure, caution was imperative.

Just then Grant rounded the corner, with his gun in hand to back Smitty up, if necessary. Smitty nodded at Grant to keep on alert while he opened the door. With a nod, Grant complied, while gesturing the maid to leave the foyer. She scurried into the dining room.

Smitty nodded at Grant again, and then opened the door. Peyton stood on the front stoop dressed in a pair of work overalls with his arms crossed over his chest. Judge Pérez's voice made Smitty and Grant turn, "Thank you for your prudence, Smith and Ketchum, but I've called for Mr. Mattock. Please invite him in."

"Do come in, Mr. Mattock. Justice Pérez is expecting you," Smitty said, his tone laced with just enough sarcasm for Peyton to detect.

Peyton smirked. "Thank you, Smith."

The judge motioned for Peyton to join him inside his office. Smitty and Grant stepped aside. The judge called out to the maid, "Viviana, please bring some fresh coffee to my office."

"Yes, Judge," Viviana said, peeking out from behind the threshold of the dining room. With that the judge closed the door.

"What's that all about?" Grant asked, while stuffing his gun into his shoulder holster.

"I dunno, but I'm sure as hell gonna find out," Smitty stated.

Peyton and the judge spent several hours behind closed doors. Once again, the conversation was too muted for Smitty to make out. Finally, Peyton emerged from the office, leaving the judge seated at his desk. Grant slipped into Smitty's chair, as he unplugged his mike from his suite to place it on a decorative table in the foyer, and then followed Peyton out the front door.

Easing the door closed, Smitty asked, "What was that all about?"

Peyton stopped on the top step. "I'm not at liberty to say, my friend."

"Did the judge discuss who's blackmailing him?"

Peyton hitched his chin toward a beat-up pick-up truck parked alongside the Pérez's townhouse. After they were inside the pickup with the windows up, Peyton inquired, "What've you got?"

"He's been getting threatening phone calls. We think they may be coming from his wife's brother, Luis Chaves. What've you got?" Smitty insisted.

Peyton scrubbed his fingers over his chin. "These judges are pretty untouchable no matter what level they've risen to, but when they get to this echelon," he whistled. "You'd better have some solid shit to accuse them of anything, and it gets really hard to gather that shit when they decide to go straight for several years, like Justice Pérez did. He's kept his nose clean since the Billings killing, but Hawke's kept waiting and watching. We knew that sooner or later his old comrades would raise their ugly heads. As predicted, here they are to grab their opportunity now that the judge has been invited onto the big boy bench."

"Isn't that the senator that was killed in Peru during a humanitarian mission?"

Peyton snorted. "Yeah … that's what ole Frank Billings was into, humanitarian aid—the kind where you deliver weapons to guerillas in the Amazon in exchange that certain businesses are not attacked, while certain businesses are. Only they got greedy, and when they demanded more than the good senator could provide to keep the operation on the down low, he ended up dead—at least that's what we believe went down. Judge Pérez was able to clear himself of any connection, or even suspicion of a connection, and since that time, he has steered clear of *humanitarian aid*."

"They were delivering weapons?"

"In amongst the medical supplies, yes," Peyton said.

"And Luis Chaves?" Smitty inquired.

"Yeah, he was mentioned. The judge is looking for Hawke to extract his brother-in-law from the Amazonian Valley, although he doesn't seem willing to say exactly why, but I've got my theories. I'm hoping that he hires us, and then we can do what we wanted to do years ago—bust him," Peyton explained.

"Our team is heading to the Amazon tomorrow. I think your assignment and ours just might be tightly connected," Smitty said.

"How's that?"

Smitty went on to explain the set of circumstance surrounding Esteban Rojas and First Force medic, Dr. Rayne Lee.

"I remember the doctor," Peyton began. "She was at the mansion when I visited after our mission in Russia. I remember Rojas, too—bastard. Was she married to Dr. Matthew Lee?"

Smitty nodded.

Peyton continued, "I know that Chaves and Rojas were buddies. Rojas took part in the goodies that Billings provided. I didn't make the connection when I was at First Force Headquarters between your Dr. Lee and Dr. Matthew Lee. Then again, I was a little distracted."

"Yeah … I know."

"I'll tell our director, Seamus Hawke, what you've conveyed to me. I've got a feeling that we'll be working closely together on this one, too," Peyton said.

"You know where to find me," Smitty told him, while sliding out of the truck.

* * * * *

Amazonian Valley

"Juan!" Luis bellowed from his cot, where he was chewing on fresh figs.

Juan dragged himself into the hut. He had been instructed to sit outside Luis' hut in the sun until he was called upon. He had been sitting there for hours watching the cool clear water dive over the rocks into the pool below the waterfall. How he wanted to refresh himself with a shower in the waterfall at the far end of the camp that provided Chaves' militia with clean water. Instead, he was tired, sweaty, dirty, and filled with malevolence for his new superior. Now he stood inside the door waiting for whatever directives this insolent man dished out.

Luis hitched his chin toward the pitcher of fresh water on the table. "Have some water, Juan. You look parched."

Juan went to the table and poured a glass of water, and then gulped it down. He poured another glass, drank down half, and splashed the remaining over his face.

Luis said, "You will go with Renzo to the Hotel Dos Rios and bring back Dr. Lee. Renzo has never seen the doctor, nor have I, so we will depend upon your identification that we have the correct woman."

"Do you believe that she will come alone? The militia that rescued her was very organized. I don't think they are stupid enough to let her come to Peru without help," Juan said.

"She believes that we have her daughter. I don't think she will risk her child's life, but if you see any Americanos, find a way to take her without detection." He dismissed Juan with a wave of his hand. Before Juan walked out the door, he added, "Juan ... she also believes that she will be meeting with Esteban. Do not tell her otherwise."

* * * * *

"When you get off the bus tomorrow, we'll be taking you to Grandma Dale's house for a couple days," Jack explained to Lil at the dinner table.

"Why?" she asked. "Why can't I stay here with Dr. Rayne?"

"Because Dr. Rayne is going on the mission, too," Jack said.

Lil's gaze rotated from her father to Rayne. "Why are you going, Dr. Rayne? You never go on missions with Daddy."

Rayne had prepared for this question. Lil was quite familiar with the team's protocol. Smitty provided medical care for anyone injured in the field, while Rayne tended to the more serious wounds if it were possible for the patient to be delivered to headquarters, as Jack and Lil were a year ago.

Jack had a firm "no lying—no matter what" policy for his daughter, so she had decided to tell her the truth in as vague a manner as possible.

A kernel of unease swept through her as she began. "Well, you know that my daughter, Sierra, was killed some time ago, right?" Lil nodded. Rayne swallowed, and then continued, "The team is going to Peru to see if she might be alive."

Lil's eyebrows fell into a "V". She cocked her head. "Why do you think she might be alive?"

Pretty insightful question for a five-year-old, Rayne thought. She had hoped that her short explanation would satisfy the child, but she was Jack's daughter—how could Rayne expect it to be that simple? It was okay. She had another explanation on deck just in case this very circumstance arose.

"I've been receiving some phone calls from someone who says that she might be alive, so we're just going to check it out." She glanced across the table at Jack. Wearing a svelte smile, he nodded his approval of her explanation.

Whew.

"Sounds like a good idea," Lil said, picking up her fork to dig into a juicy beef tip.

Rayne let out the breath that she'd been holding. She put in, "We thought so."

And then Lil looked up at her with questioning concern in her brown eyes. "Are you nervous?"

"Nervous?"

"Yeah … nervous that maybe she won't be there. I'd be really nervous if someone told me that Mommy might be coming home, and then she didn't."

Rayne's eyes flicked to Jack, who was now shuffling the food around on his plate with a fork. The slight smile on his lips had drawn into a thin line. Nervous wasn't quite the right word—devastated would be more like it. Nevertheless, Rayne said, "Yes … I suppose I'm a little nervous. But I have to believe that it will all work out the way it should—however that may be."

* * * * *

The night had been long. Rayne tossed and turned in her bed—her hair falling across her face. Although she'd been spared a night of bad dreams, her memories made up for it. She could feel Esteban's rough hands in her hair, over her body, and his hot breath on her face. When the sun finally peeked through the blinds, she was relieved that it was time to get up and prepare for the journey she was about to take—a journey into the past, where she would come face-to-face with the harsh realities of her angst, and that was worse than any nightmare the night had to offer.

After she and Jack had put Lil on the bus, they returned to the house to pack. Jack went into his section of the house to pack a go-bag, and a small suitcase for Lil, while Rayne packed a go-bag of her own. She didn't need much. She had to travel light, so as she stuffed the small backpack with absolute needs: bug spray, antiperspirant, panties, a brush, and just in case, a box of tampons.

Her mind wandered to unwelcome thoughts of Esteban Rojas. She didn't invite him into her thoughts; rather he pushed in with all the brutality that he possessed. Finally, she zipped the bag closed, tossed it aside, grabbed her car keys, and hurried for the door. She was going to rid herself of at least the one thing that Esteban loved—if for no other reason than to ease her own mind.

* * * * *

When Rayne returned to the mansion just a few short hours later, she was greeted by Jack's wide-eyed expression.

"You cut your hair," he said, eyeing her chin length hair with a wedged cut in the back.

"I did." She studied his expression. Feeling a sudden shade of regret for her abrupt decision, she fingered the short tresses, hesitantly asking, "You … you don't like it?"

Jack blinked back. He stammered, "Um … yeah … yeah. You look …" Pulling her into his arms, his said, "You'd look beautiful with no hair at all."

"I'm sorry," she said into his chest, trying to hold in the ache. "Esteban loved my hair. He used to run his fingers through it and pull it. I … I just didn't want it to be there for him when—"

"Shhh … you don't have to explain anything to me." He tipped her face upward with his fingertips. "You are one brave woman, Dr. Rayne Lee. Not too many would have the guts to return to the place where so many hurtful things took place, and you're worried about a haircut? Are you kidding me?" He kissed her, and then he said, "Look at it this way, it's almost worth going to Peru."

"How do you figure?" Rayne asked.

"Tomorrow is opera day."

He was back. The Jack Haliday that made all the bad feelings run and hide in the dark hole where they belonged—the Jack Haliday who could make her smile in the face of any bad situation. This was the Jack Haliday that she needed. Because the uptight, tense Jack Haliday from yesterday only made tonight a scarier place to be, and Peru a scarier place than was already waiting for her.

Rayne tossed her head back, laughing. Burying her face into his chest, she murmured, "Oh, Jack …" She held on tightly. She wanted to cherish this moment, because in a matter of hours she would need to cling to it for strength.

* * * * *

Lil was thrilled with Rayne's new haircut. She told Rayne that she looked like a movie star. Jack and Rayne laughed. Lil chattered and giggled from her seat in the back of the SUV on the drive to her grandmother's house. Both Rayne and Jack made a fuss over the papers that she'd done in school that day. Rayne wished the conversation and the papers could keep her mind diverted from what lay ahead in just two hours: her drive to the airport, and then the flight to Peru.

It was a forty-five minute drive to Dale's house, but it seemed that not less than a nanosecond later they were pulling into her driveway. Jack carried Lil's suitcase, and hand in hand, the three of them walked up the sidewalk to the red brick ranch house.

Dale greeted them with a smile that was unsuccessfully hiding her trepidation. Lil hugged her grandmother tightly, as she announced, "Dr. Rayne is going to Peru to see if Sierra is there."

"So I've heard," Dale said, reaching out to take Rayne into a warm embrace, whispering into her ear, "You will be in my thoughts and prayers. Be safe."

Rayne had to fight to keep the tears back. She said, "Thank you."

"I'm pretty sure that I've packed everything that Lil needs," Jack said.

Taking him into a hug, Dale told him, "Don't worry about a thing. If you've missed something, I'll take care of it. You just be careful and come home safe and sound."

"We will," Jack assured, and then he opened his arms to his daughter. "C'mon, give me a big hug and a kiss." Lil jumped into his arms, hugging him with all her might. She kissed him. He said, "Okay then, you be a good girl for Grandma. We'll see you in a few days."

Lil hugged Rayne, kissing her cheek. She said, "I hope you find Sierra, Dr. Rayne."

It was too much. The tears that Rayne was trying to withhold trickled down her cheek. She murmured, "Thank you, Lil."

Jack took Rayne by the hand to lead her out the door and to the SUV. He opened the door and she slid into the passenger's seat. Jogging around the front of the vehicle, Jack got into the driver's seat, and turned the ignition. Suddenly they heard Lil's voice calling after them. They looked up to see her running down the sidewalk toward the SUV.

Rayne let her window down. "Is something wrong?"

A little out of breath, Lil shook her head no. Quickly, she unclipped the string of saltwater pearls from her neck, and held them out to Rayne. She said, "I don't want you to be scared, Dr. Rayne. I want you to have my bravery necklace. It helped me on the first day of kindergarten, and now maybe it'll help you not to be nervous when you go to Peru."

Rayne's lips quivered. She drew her hand to her chest. This dear little innocent was worried for her. The tears flowed from her eyes. What a beautiful gesture from one so young, and yet perhaps not so naive. At the age of five, Lil knew what it was to be frightened. She knew what it was to have someone you love ripped from your life. She knew.

Unable to utter a word, Rayne took the pearls from Lil's hand. With shaking hands, she clasped them around her neck. Finally she managed, "Thank you so much, Lil."

Lil smiled. "I love you, Dr. Rayne." With that, she turned and hurried back to the house, where Dale was waiting for her on the porch.

Rayne turned to catch Jack wipe a tear from his eye. Swiftly, he pushed the gearshift into reverse, muttering, "That's my kid."

* * * * *

There was so much to do and very little time left. After she'd changed into a pair of jeans, hiking boots, and a black T-shirt, she found herself running around the mansion taking care of last minute details, including some instruction for Clark—which she was not used to doing. She was usually at the mansion while the team was away, so she would take care of meals for Clark and Walt, while they took care of all the intel and communication with the team from Walt's office. This mission was completely different. Not only was she going on the mission, but Walt was as well.

"There's some apple glazed pork chops, beef tips, oh and there's a little lasagna left over in the fridge," Rayne told Clark.

"Nice ... some great Doc Rayne leftovers, and I've got the mansion to myself for several days," Clark said, smiling.

"Well, not exactly," Rayne began. She scooped up the kitten at her feet to plop her into Clark's arms. "Tickles will be here ... and then there's the matter of her litter box," she said, as she whipped out the pooper-scooper from behind her back. Clark winced.

"Rayne, the team is gathered in the foyer. It's almost time," Jack said, leaning into the office.

Rayne's breath caught. It was time. It was for real. On a braced breath, she said, "Give me just a minute. I have to run down to the medical unit for my medical bag."

"Okay, but hurry," Jack told her.

She rushed from the office and down the stairs into the medical unit and into the supply room where she kept her bag. Grabbing the black duffle bag filled with medical emergency supplies for the trip, her eyes fell upon a drawer. She opened it to stare at the one piece of equipment that she rarely used—a pair of clippers. Her breathing quickened. She tangled her fingers in her already shortened hair. She reached in and snatched it, tossing it into her bag. It would be a big decision, but she may just use it.

When she arrived in the foyer, the team was waiting. Go bags were lying over the floor as were weapons in cases.

Taking her into a hug, Casey assured her, "We've got your six, girlfriend."

"I know," Rayne said.

Walt stepped forward. "Are you ready?"

"As I'll ever be," Rayne said around a sigh.

"You'll do good, I'm sure of it. Dan will be right behind you." He handed her an earpiece. "As soon as you get to your hotel room put this on. You'll be in constant contact with Dan. Only take it off to shower, but let him know that that's what you're doing, got it?"

"I do." She glanced at Dan, who was standing closest to the door. Opening the go-bag, she found the box of tampons on top, thinking that the tampons would cradle the earpiece and keep it secure; she slipped the earpiece into the box and closed the lid. Looking up at Dan, she asked, "Are you ready?"

"You betcha," he replied.

Walt turned to Dan. "I'll have the rest of your gear."

Slinging the go-bag over her shoulder and her medical bag tightly in her fist, Rayne glanced around at the team who would support her through the mission. She smiled. "Okay, let's do this."

"Hoo-yah!" Little called out.

"Hoo-yah!" the team retorted.

Jack opened the door and followed her to her vehicle. He opened the driver's door for her to slip in, and then closed the door behind her. She let the window down.

"I'm still not in favor of this," he told her.

"I know. But I've got a great team who cares very much for me, and I know that they won't let anything happen to me."

"*I'm* not going to let anything happen to you," Jack vehemently stated. He leaned through the window to kiss her. "I love you, Rayne."

His kiss was primal, possessive, and oh so loving. She whispered, "I love you, too … lovey dovey." The right side of Jack's mouth kicked up.

"Hey, Haliday! Garrison's supposed to leave twenty minutes after she does. You're holding up the boat!" Walt called from the porch.

Pressing his forehead against hers, Jack whispered, "Be careful."

Rayne bit her bottom lip in an attempt to hold on to what little composure she had left. Quickly she started the Explorer and pulled away from the man who made her feel safe and secure toward the place she never thought she would ever go to again.

* * * * *

Walt was waiting for Jack when he came back into the house. He said, "When Rayne's mother died, I promised her that I would take care of her as if she were my own. I put her through college and then medical school. She's like my daughter— do you actually think I'd let anything happen to her?"

Jack glared at Walt. His nostrils flared. "She's not properly prepared for what could, what most likely will happen out there. I know you'll want me to keep a distance from this mission, Walt, but I can't, I just can't. Once she gets on that plane she's in real danger, and I'm gonna stick like glue."

CHAPTER TWELVE

Walt ticked off twenty minutes, and then gave Dan the nod to leave for the airport. Dan gathered his go-bag and his weapons. He would have to check his guns with security, and it would slow him down when he arrived in Peru, but at least he would be far enough behind Rayne to make it look like they had no connection.

As Dan pulled open the door, Jack stopped him. "Dan …"

Dan looked into Jack's desperate eyes. He knew what his teammate was feeling. "I know, man," he said. "I'll look after her." With that he offered his hand, Jack shook it. He nodded to the team, and then jogged to his vehicle to follow Rayne to the airport. It was go time.

* * * * *

Rayne could feel her stomach coil into a bundle of knots as her flight approached the Jorge Chavez International Airport in Peru. She hadn't laid eyes on Dan since the connection at La Guardia last night. She was trying to read a book when she caught a glimpse of him taking a seat two rows over in the gate area to wait for their connection to Peru. After that, he'd kept his distance.

It was almost time to catch a bus to Iquitos. As the landing gear hit the runway, her stomach flipped and flopped at the thought of checking in to the Hotel Dos Rios and waiting for Esteban to contact her. She checked her watch. It was almost noon—Thursday. She would probably arrive at the hotel by three or four o'clock—if everything went smoothly.

"Welcome to the Jorge Chavez International Airport. If you are a visitor to Peru, we hope you enjoy your stay. If you are a native, welcome home. Please stay in your seats until the plane has come to a complete stop and the unfasten seat belts signs go off," the flight attendant announced in English, and then she repeated the instructions in Spanish.

Beads of sweat formed on her forehead. She asked herself the same question that had been rolling over and over in her mind since he instructed her to come to Peru. *What could Esteban possibly want?* Her fingers caressed the pearls around her neck. Her lips curled. She had so much to look forward to when she returned home. A new life waited for her in Harverton—a life with Jack and Lil. She had so much to live for. Yes, she would survive this trip.

Suddenly, she realized that the passengers were pulling bags from the overhead compartments—they were getting ready to deplane. Dan was standing next to her seat. He helped a woman who was very short retrieve her red duffle bag, and then he held Rayne's go-bag out to her.

"Does this belong to you, ma'am?" he asked.

Hesitantly, she took it from him. "Yes ... thank you."

With a wink and a nod, he said, "You very welcome."

It was Dan's way of letting her know that he had her back, and she appreciated it. Holding her go-bag to her chest, she sat in the seat until most of the passengers had got off the plane, and then she made her way down the aisle and up the ramp into the airport. She saw Dan leaning against a far wall pretending to text, but she knew that he was watching to make sure she'd gotten off the plane safely. He fell into the crowd behind her. She was now facing the last leg of the trip. Her heart clenched in her chest.

How would she react when she finally came face-to-face with Esteban?

How would she react if Sierra really was alive?

How would she react if Sierra wasn't?

As she made her way through the throng of hurried passengers, her mind was in a tailspin. All the cards were in Esteban's favor. Even with the team close at hand, they didn't know what his demands were, or where he would take her. She still worried that this might be a trap. Along with the din of the crowd and the constant feed of announcements repeated in many languages, her quickened heartbeat boomed inside her head. What if she'd led the team into a trap?

* * * * *

Running a harried hand through his thick nest of curls, Jack paced back and forth. They were supposed to have taken off over an hour ago. When they arrived at the base, they were informed that the plane was experiencing some technical difficulties and would take off as soon as their mechanics had the problem fixed.

Casey sat with her leg draped over the arm of a chair reading on her ebook, while Little sat very erect near the large window, watching the mechanics scramble around the plane trying to make it air worthy. Walt leaned against a far wall with his arms crossed over his chest, tapping his foot, while checking his watch every few minutes. His frustration was evident. If the plane had taken off on schedule they would have arrived at the airbase in Peru two hours before Dan and Rayne's flight. They would have had plenty of time to travel to Iquitos, do some recon, and take their positions. As it was now, Rayne and Dan would arrive well before they did—the mission had already gone sideways, just as Jack had feared.

Walt pushed from the wall when an officer came through the door. They had a short conversation, and then the officer went back outside. Letting out a breath, Walt rubbed the nape of his neck. He looked up to lock eyes with Jack. Immediately, Jack knew that he wasn't going to like what Walt was about to tell them.

"Listen up," Walt began. The team gathered around him. "They have to send to the warehouse for a part. Once it arrives, it should only take an hour or so more to make the repairs." He glanced at Jack. "I know, this puts us way behind schedule, but the good news is that when we get to Peru there will be a copter at our disposal. I'll see to it that Clark alerts Dan to this glitch."

Jack wanted to explode. What the hell? This was a military base and their plane is busted?

He wanted to punch the wall.

He wanted to punch Walt.

Most of all, he wanted to hijack a plane and get to where they needed to be.

None of the options were viable. The only option was to wait for the plane, and hope that Dan Garrison could hold down the fort.

* * * * *

Rubbing his weary eyes, Clark set a fresh cup of coffee on the desk, and then with a few strikes to the computer's keys, he checked in on what was new with the police department in Iquitos. He had hacked their files days ago and was keeping a close tab on their movements. So far it was status quo: a few thefts in the open air marketplace, a current list of missing people that he was certain the police had no intention of looking for, and a fresh addition to the list of four young girls—Clark had a good idea what happened to them, and he had no doubt that the police did too.

He was just about to close the site when his eyes fell upon new information that had just been recorded—the body of drug lord and weapons trafficker, Esteban Rojas had been found in a desolate area. He had been shot in the head and looked to have been dead for a week or more.

"Shiiit," Clark muttered. "This can't be good. Rayne hasn't been talking to Rojas at all." Just then the phone rang. Bringing it to his ear, he said, "Rhodes …"

"I need you to get a hold of Garrison A-sap," Walt said.

"What's up?"

"We're still at the military base—plane problems. Let him know."

"That's not the only thing Dan needs to know. I just got some interesting information, and it's a game changer ..."

* * * * *

Gathering her medical bag from the baggage area, she glanced over her shoulder to see Dan at the security window turning in his ticket for his weapons. She knew that it would take him some time to collect them, and he needed to be on the same bus as she was, so she decided to grab a cup of coffee from the stand nearby. The snack stand was located a bit of a distance from where Dan was, but she could still see him.

Taking her first few sips of coffee, she hadn't realized just how exhausted she was. She was thankful to find an empty seat in the busy airport while she waited. Her eyes were burning with fatigue, the muscles in her neck and shoulders ached. Even though it had been a night flight, she couldn't sleep. Every time she closed her eyes, the face of Esteban Rojas came into clear view. She could use a few hours, except she knew that wasn't going to happen. No, most likely she wouldn't rest at all until she was safe in Jack's arms.

Her thoughts were interrupted by the sound of Dan coughing loudly. She looked up. He was standing about fifteen feet away. He hitched his chin toward the exit. It was time to catch the bus. It was time to go to the Hotel Dos Rios and wait for the dreaded phone call from the man that she hoped she would never have to see again.

* * * * *

"It is time to bring Dr. Lee to the camp," Luis told Juan and Renzo. "She should be at the Hotel Dos Rios within a few hours. Be watchful for anyone who may be escorting her—"

"Luis!" a guard called from the door of the hut. "Come quickly, the old doctor is sick. He is not re-sponding at all."

Luis jerked from his seat to hurry out of the hut with Juan and Renzo close behind. The old white-haired physician lay on a cot. His weathered face was pale. "How long has he been this way?" Luis demanded to know.

"I don't know," the guard said. "He was sitting on the cot this morning when I brought him some food. He said nothing. I left the food on the table," the guard regarded the plate of figs and fruit. "He did not eat anything."

Luis touched his forehead. He was clammy. "Bring Bibiana and the girl to this hut. They will care for him until Dr. Lee gets here. *Rapido!*"

The guard hurried away. A few minutes later, he returned with Bibiana and Patrizia. "What do you need, Luis?" Bibiana asked.

"Take care of this sick man. He will be important to us when Dr. Lee arrives. You will make sure that he does not die," Luis told her.

Bibiana approached the still body lying on the cot. She ran her hand over his forehead. He was feverish. His skin had no elasticity. "Patrizia, bring me the pitcher of water and a cup." Patrizia hurried to the table to retrieve what her mother had requested. Bibiana dipped her fingers into the pitcher to gently wet the old man's parched lips. "I will try to help him," she said.

Luis turned to Juan and Renzo. "Bring the doctor quickly. If the old man dies, I will have to cut the chip out of her myself."

"No, Mama," Patrizia gasped. Bibiana grabbed her daughter's hand and squeezed—a gentle warning to be silent.

* * * * *

"We're on our way," Walt informed Clark. "Have you heard from Dan?"

"I've been trying to call, but he's not answering. Maybe he's in a dead zone. I'll keep trying. What's your ETA?" Clark asked.

"We won't beat them to Iquitos, that's for damned sure. It's a straight flight, but it won't be there for several more hours."

"How's Haliday holding up?"

"Like a cornered badger."

* * * * *

Washington D.C.

Smitty had just finished shaving when there was a knock on his hotel room door. "Smitty, open up, it's Peyton."

Wearing a pair of sweat pants, he grabbed a T-shirt off the bed as he passed, pulling it over his head, shuffling his arms through the holes, and pulling it over his torso, while he grabbed for the door knob.

"What's up, Mattock?" he asked, hitching his chin for Peyton to enter.

"Judge Pérez was considering having Hawke travel to Peru to find his brother-in-law, Luis Chaves. He claims that he needs to talk with him about closing down his operations, and rolling over on those he's done business with so that the police in the area can clean up the crime. He said that if Luis will cooperate, he will serve a very short term sentence in an upscale facility. Isn't that nice?"

"That's real sweet. But I don't think that's what Alejandro has in mind. I think Luis has something on him, and I think he wants Luis to visit the U.S. so he can have an accident," Smitty proposed. "What's Hawke gonna do?"

"Nothing now. I was called to his office early this morning, seems he's had a change of heart. He says that he had a talk with Luis and he has agreed to be a good boy. Yeah, right. I think he's hired another team. I told Seamus that First Force had a team on its way, so he's going to be in contact with Clark. We've got to find out what Chaves has on the judge so we can inform the president before this yahoo gets a spot on the Supreme Court. Seamus is going to inform his contact in the CIA of the situation."

"I got a text from Clark just a little while ago. Esteban Rojas' body has been found—he's been dead for over a week. So we have no real proof who Rayne is really going to meet, but we're pretty damned sure that it's Chaves. The question is: What does Rayne have that Chaves wants, and how is this all connected?"

* * * * *

The old multi-colored bus creaked and rocked over the rutty road. Three chickens in a crate on an old woman's lap squawked, while the goat that she had on a leash *baaad* while chewing on a seat cushion. Deep sun scorched wrinkles molested her face akin to a map of a hard-lived life. Her gray-white hair peeked out from under a tattered straw hat. Like most of the passengers on the bus, her clothes were well worn and the sandals on her feet looked like they'd seen many miles. The old woman patted the goat's head, while she eyed Dan sitting diagonally from her seat amongst a group of old men smoking cigarettes. The passengers swayed back and forth in their seats as they haphazardly gazed out the windows. The sweltering heat filled the close space as no air moved through the open windows. The bus stunk of chickens, goat dung, and cigarette smoke.

The radio blared over the clamor of Spanish chatter throughout the rickety transport. Sweat poured from Rayne's brow. Her head was pounding. She was beginning to worry that she'd become dehydrated. She should have drunk a bottle of water rather than a coffee at the airport, but she really needed the caffeine.

Hugging her go-bag to her chest while keeping a firm hold on her medical bag, she managed a quick glance at Dan. He sat very straight. Arms folded over his chest, while constantly scanning the passengers on the bus. She wondered what he was thinking behind the aviator sunglasses parked on his nose. What was he anticipating when they got to the hotel? Had he heard from Uncle Walt?

Closing her eyes, she laid her head back against the metal window encasement. She was hoping to get a long drink of water, an ibuprofen from her bag, and a shower when she got to the hotel. How long would it be until Esteban contacted her? She shuttered at the thought.

* * * * *

Juan and Renzo drove along the dusty road toward Iquitos. The backseat of the Jeep was filled with weapons just in case the American woman had come with protection. Renzo slowed the Jeep when they came to an intersection to see the approach of a bus.

Renzo suggested, "That is the bus that comes from town to Iquitos. Maybe the woman is on it."

Juan lifted a shoulder. "Does not hurt to find out. I will recognize her."

Casually, they waited for the bus to pass, and then they quickly wrapped black scarves over their faces. Juan checked to make sure that the hood he'd connected to his belt was secure, and then he reached back to retrieve two 9mm micro Uzis.

Spitting dirt into the air, the Jeep fishtailed out onto the road. Renzo pressed down hard on the accelerator, while both men shot their guns skyward, yelling for the bus to pull over. Juan decided not to wait; he shot out the back tires. The emergency door flung open and a man fell backward along with several of the passenger's belongings. The bus continued forward dragging its backend for a few more feet before it came to a halt— thick dust billowed around the vehicle like a fierce storm cloud.

Renzo managed to dodge the luggage and the man sprawled on the road as he pulled the Jeep alongside the crippled bus.

* * * * *

From the back of the bus, Dan watched Rayne's head bob against the dusty window. Exhaustion finally took its toll lulling her to sleep. Her head rolled to the side as she drifted farther and farther away. Good. She needed some rest. Guns exploding and panic amongst the passengers pulled his attention from Rayne to the Jeep driving alongside the bus.

"Get down on the floor!" Dan yelled, trying to get Rayne's attention, while he fumbled with his gun case. Suddenly the rear of the bus slammed against the ground sending everyone backward to the floor. A young Peruvian man fell against the rickety emergency door, its hinges broke. Dan tried to grab for the man and his weapons case, but it was no use, the man, his weapons case, and several other bags slid out the door. Dan found himself clinging to the seats, trying not to fall out of the opening.

The bus bumped and pitched to a hard stop. All the passengers were on the floor in the aisle, coughing and gasping. The old woman had landed on top of the chicken crate, clinging to the goat's leash. She was face-to-face with Dan.

In Spanish she said, "Americano ... Don't be a fool. These men will kill everyone on the bus if we do not all cooperate with them. Give them whatever you have without question. Or they will kill us all."

Dan nodded his understanding to the woman, and then felt for the handgun that he'd stuffed in the back waistband of his jeans before boarding the bus. He scanned the bus for Rayne. There were too many people in the aisle, too much panic, he couldn't find her. His gut twisted.

The bus driver opened the door. Raising his hands, he then called out to the passengers in Spanish, "They want us to get out of the bus."

"*Rapido! Rapido!*" A tall skinny man yelled, while the passengers shuffled toward the front of the bus and down the short steps. He pushed them to the side, while a scrawny man lined them up alongside the bus telling them to keep their hands up. He kept a close eye on the driver who was helping the young man who had fallen out of the emergency door to hobble toward the gathering.

Scrawny smiled when Rayne stepped off the bus. Stealthily he gestured to tall and skinny that they'd found their prize. The parade of passengers continued until the vehicle was empty.

The crowd was three deep along the bus with Dan standing in the front. Rayne stood behind the group with her back against the vehicle. The old woman stood directly behind Dan, clutching her crate and keeping the noisy goat on a shortened leash, close to her legs.

After tall and skinny did a check of the bus to make sure that everyone was out, scrawny pushed through the crowd roughly until he stood in front of Rayne. She looked away from his intense scrutiny. Saying nothing, he grabbed her by the arm to separate her from the group. He snatched her go-bag and began rifling through it until he came up with her cell phone. He tossed the phone to the ground and smashed it with his foot, and then he seized her medical bag. Rayne's fists clenched at her side while he searched the contents of the bag. Satisfied with his find, scrawny shoved her into tall and skinny's grip along with a hood.

Tall and skinny dropped the hood over her head, pulling it tight around her neck, and then snapped a pair of handcuffs on her wrists. With Rayne kicking and screaming, he dragged her toward the Jeep, while scrawny kept his Uzi trained on the passengers.

Dan's blood was boiling. He had to keep a cool head. He waited for the moment when the man holding his gun on the group turned his head to pull his gun from the waistband.

"No!" the old woman screamed. With all her might she swung the crate of flapping squawking chickens to hit Dan in the back, sending him forward. He tripped over another passenger, they both fell face down in the dirt.

Scrawny hurried over to grab the gun from Dan's hand. He slammed the butt of the Uzi against Dan's head. He fought to hold on to consciousness. He couldn't afford to lose sight of Rayne. The ground spun beneath him. He could feel the passenger who had fallen with him push from his body and scrambled away, and then everything started to go dark …

"Let's go!" He heard one of the men yell as they hopped behind the wheel of the Jeep, tossing Rayne's bags into the passenger's seat. The Jeep whirled a wide circle, spinning a curtain of dust around them, and then they sped down the road from the direction they came.

* * * * *

Rayne could barely breathe inside the hood. Fingers of dread crawled over her skin. She didn't know what happened to Dan, but she'd heard the scuffle. He was left behind with no knowledge of where these two men were taking her. She would have to face Esteban Rojas with no back-up.

* * * * *

The world spun. Dan's head thumped like ten trombones were playing inside his brain. Slowly he brought his hand to his head to feel the blood trickling down his temple. Spitting dirt from his mouth, he rolled over on the ground to look up into the relentless sun, and then the realization struck that Rayne had been abducted by Rojas' men. Dan tried to sit up too quickly. Dizziness forced him back to the ground. Nausea washed over him.

"Lay still," a man's voice spoke to him in Spanish. "They are sending another bus soon. You will need to see a doctor when we arrive in Iquitos."

He needed more than a doctor. He needed to contact the team and let them know what had happened. He reached for his cell phone. The bus must've been crippled between two hillsides because the zone was as dead as Esteban Rojas was gonna be within the week.

He managed to open his eyes to take in his surroundings. The old woman was perched atop the chicken's crate smoking a cigarette, scowling at him. *Bitch*. He looked at his cell phone again to find that a text message had just come through. Squinting through the throb, he struggled to read the words that Clark had actually sent several hours ago. *Team has been delayed—won't be there when you arrive. Esteban Rojas is dead. Has been for over a week. We think Luis Chaves is behind the phone calls. Will advise ASAP.*

Shit. The entire mission had gone sideways.

CHAPTER THIRTEEN

It had been a wild ride. The Jeep bounced, bumped, and pitched over rough roads tossing Rayne about in the seat. Her captors were silent—not a word was spoken between them the entire way. Finally the Jeep slowed, rolling to a stop. Voices exploded all around her as brutal hands grabbed her by the arm, yanking her from the vehicle. It was an exercise in futility to resist. Someone had a steely grip on her right arm, while another squeezed her left. Her feet barely touched the ground, while they dragged her over the stony dirt. Panicked breathing boomed inside her head as they rushed her toward who knew where, yet she was certain that Esteban was at the end of the trail.

They towed her up a short pair of steps. She tripped once and was roughly hoisted back to her feet. Now she was inside. They shoved her into a chair, tearing the hood from her head. The air was sweltering, but at least it was fresh. She drew in a breath while trying to adjust her eyes to the sudden burst of daylight. It took a moment for the blur to clear only to find a man that she did not recognize standing over her with a toxic smirk on his mouth.

"Dr. Rayne Lee?" Luis confirmed.

She dragged her gaze to meet his. Her voice came out like sandpaper. She asked in Spanish, "*Si*, who are you?"

"Get the doctor a drink of water. Remove the handcuffs," Luis instructed with a snap of his fingers.

Juan took away the handcuffs, while Renzo went to the table and poured a glass of water and brought it to Rayne. Rubbing her irritated wrists, she tried to control her nerves. She didn't want to show the fear that was coiling through every fiber in her body, except her hands shook as she took the glass from him to gulp down every drop.

Rayne licked her lips to wet them, and then handing the glass back, she said, "More, please."

Renzo looked to Luis for permission. Luis nodded, so he refilled her cup. She drank it down, and then with her voice a bit stronger, she repeated her original inquiry, "Who are you?"

"I am Luis Chaves."

"Nice to meet you, *Senor* Chaves, what do you want from me and where is Esteban?"

His smirk grew intensely venomous. He bragged, "He is dead. I killed him. He is unimportant. You have been brought here to assist me."

Rayne should have been thrilled to hear of Esteban's demise, but it was wasted on the trepidation that spilled like acid into her gut. The unrealistic hope that her daughter was alive and waiting to be reunited with her lay broken on the floor around her. The only thing left was to cooperate with this man and pray that Jack and the team would find her. Shifting in the chair, she asked, "What am I to assist you with, *Senor* Chaves?"

"Take her to the doctor," Luis commanded.

Immediately, Renzo and Juan hauled Rayne from the chair and lugged her roughly from the hut. Clutching her arms until she thought they would break, they marched her swiftly through the camp, filled with guerrilla fighters who ogled her, whistled, and called out vulgar comments as she passed. She kept her head down and her gaze to the ground so she would not have to look at them. The old familiar feelings of subjection and nausea came rushing in to molest her.

She was escorted into a hut where an old man lay on a cot. A dark-haired woman sat on a stool next to him, while a young girl quickly moved to cower behind her. Rayne caught a glimpse of the girl's deformed lip.

Luis asked, "How is he?"

"No better," Bibiana replied.

Turning to Rayne, Luis told her, "You must save this man's life. He is a doctor and if he survives, he will operate on you. If he does not," he yanked his knife from its sheath to hold it at the tip of her nose, "I will cut out what I need myself. It is to your benefit that he lives."

Rayne's eyes widened, her jaw dropped open. "What are you talking about? What are you going to cut out?"

"You have a sub dermal chip in your neck which contains a valuable recording. Esteban had this doctor put it inside you four years ago. We need it, and you need the doctor," he explained.

Her hands immediately went to her neck, frantically feeling for any little bump or bulge that she'd overlooked over the past four years. Finding nothing unusual, Rayne blinked back and blinked back again. She could barely take in what she'd just been told. She couldn't feel anything under her skin. How deep had they planted the chip? What had the chip possibly attached itself to over time? Panic rushed through her like fast white water.

"Dr. Lee …"

Her eyes snapped to Luis'. She realized that he'd been calling her for a few seconds. "Yes ... Of course," she muttered.

Bibiana vacated her seat so Rayne could sit at the old man's bedside for a quick evaluation of his vital signs and general condition. As she examined him, she asked Bibiana in Spanish, "He appears severely dehydrated. Has he had any convulsions?" Keeping her eyes to the floor, Bibiana shook her head no. "Has he been conscious?"

"Sometimes, but only for short periods," Bibiana replied in English.

Rayne favored her with a svelte smile. Looking over her shoulder at Luis, she said, "I had a medical bag with me, which your men took away. If you want me to help this man, I need it, now."

Luis turned to Renzo. "Get the bag."

Renzo rushed from the hut and returned with Rayne's black duffle and her go-bag, but as he attempted to hand them off to Rayne, Luis grabbed his arm. He asked, "These have been searched for weapons?"

"*Sí*," Renzo assured. Luis gave him the nod, and he passed the bags off to Rayne.

Setting the go-bag aside, she sorted through the contents of the medical bag. Forgetting herself, she said in English, "Good, nothing seems to be missing." She pulled an IV pack; a bag filled with saline solution; surgical tape; a bottle of alcohol, and a tunicate from the duffle. She said to Bibiana in English, "By the way, I'm Dr. Rayne Lee."

"Yes, I know," Bibiana replied. Hiding her face, Patrizia peeked at the beautiful doctor from behind her mother's hip. Bibiana added, "I am Bibiana Vasquez. This is my daughter, Patrizia."

Rayne pitched Bibiana a curious glance. How was this woman connected to Chaves? She seemed uncomfortable in his presence—they didn't appear to be lovers.

After attaching the bag to the tube, she said to her, "Please hold this. We need to hydrate him intravenously. I will need you to hold it up so the solution can flow into his arm."

Nodding her understanding, Bibiana took the IV bag from Rayne. The location was quite primitive. There was no sink to scrub up or purified water to scrub his arm. She prepared the old man's arms by swabbing it down with alcohol, and then wrapped a tunicate around his arm to locate a vein that had not collapsed. She thumped at his arm with her middle finger, and then half smiled at finding a usable vein. She inserted the needle, taping it down to hold it tight.

She stood to face Luis. Switching back to Spanish, she said, "Hopefully the fluids will bring him back."

Stuffing the knife back into the sheath, Luis told her, "For your sake, I hope so." He waved for his men to follow him outside. When they were beyond the door Rayne heard him say, "It doesn't matter if the old doctor recovers, they will all be dead within a day or so."

Bibiana held the IV bag, while Rayne continued to examine the old man. She asked, "What's his name?"

"I do not know," Bibiana replied.

Rayne peeked askance at the young girl watching her from behind her mother's skirt. She favored the child with a smile. "May I examine your face, Patrizia?" Rayne asked in Spanish. "I managed to see that you have a cleft lip. May I have a look?"

With her free hand, Bibiana gently tugged Patrizia from behind her. "Let the doctor see," she told her in English.

Tears filling her eyes, Patrizia stepped out from her hiding place. Unable to hold back, she cried, "I was the one who called you, Dr. Lee! Luis forced me to tell you that I was your daughter. I did not want to do it, but I had no choice." She tried to swallow back her tears, but it was useless, they flowed down her face, dripping from her chin. "He said … he said that he would kill Mama and me if I did not do what he wanted." She buried her face in her hands. "I am so sorry for what I have done!"

Rayne's heart broke for this child. She couldn't be more than seven or eight, and yet she held the life of her mother in her hands by pretending to be someone that she'd never met. The weight of a cruel world that forced her to do something so shaming and a deformity to bear stood firmly on her minute shoulders. Rayne understood the pain she was feeling—she felt it like a dagger in her stomach. Unable to instantly find the words to soothe this poor innocent, she tenderly brushed back several errant strands of hair from her flushed wet face.

Tears pooling in her eyes, Rayne whispered, "Shhh … Shhh … it's okay, Patrizia. I think I understand what you and your mother have been through." Taking her by the shoulders, she guided the girl to the chair, and knelt down before her. Holding her hands, Rayne tried to transfer any strength that she could spare. "I don't want you to worry about it anymore. Everything will be okay. We will find a way out of here." She pulled a tissue from her duffle and wiped Patrizia's eyes. "Now, I want you to let me examine your face. I want to see your lip and check to see if your pallet is in tack."

Trying to be calm, Patrizia sat as still as possible, while Rayne examined her face and lip. Pulling a small flashlight from the duffle, she said, "Now lean your head back and open your mouth as wide as you can."

The girl did as Rayne requested, while the girl's mother bit her lip as if to control a sadness that was threatening to bubble to the surface.

Relieved, Rayne turned off the flashlight, patted Patrizia on the cheek, and then stood to face
Bibiana. "Thankfully, Patrizia does not have a cleft
pallet, and her lip is not the worst that I've seen.
While it is very deformed, there is quite a bit of
flesh, therefore it would be an easier surgery than
most. I'm not a cosmetic surgeon, but I don't think
that she would have much of a scar when it was
healed."

Bibiana explained in a watery voice, "We are
poor, Dr. Lee. We do not have the money for such
an operation that you speak of."

Touching Bibiana's shoulder, Rayne said, "I understand. The good news is there are agencies in the
United States that I am familiar with and have connections to that can help your daughter. We can fix
her lip. She doesn't have to go through life with this
deformity."

Tears poured from Bibiana's eyes. "You would
help her? You would do this for the girl who lied to
you? We may very well be responsible for bringing
you to a place that you will not ever leave."

Rayne turned to Patrizia. "You are not responsible for what happened, Patrizia. You must understand that. You were forced to tell me those things
by an evil man. We will get out of here, because you
need surgery, and I have a man to marry. If that's not
huge motivation, I don't know what is. "

* * * * *

It was early evening by the time they had sent a fresh bus to pick up the stranded passengers. Dan felt like shit, and he looked like ten miles of bad road. His head was pounding. Most likely he required a few stitches. Fuck that. He had not fulfilled his objective: to keep Rayne safe and within his watch at all times. He had failed the team. Worse, he had failed Rayne.

As the bus drove toward town filled with relieved travelers, he managed to get a phone call in to Walt. The team would meet him at the hotel to regroup, and figure out how to find Rayne. He dreaded facing the team. Walt sounded as he should: pissed. Most of all, he dreaded facing Jack. He had given his word to Jack that he'd keep Rayne safe. He couldn't bear the thought that he would be solely responsible if anything happened to that dear sweet woman.

The bus rolled to a jerking stop. The passengers wasted no time exiting. Dan stepped from the stifling bus into the stifling street. The long street was lined with colorful buildings of pink, blue, red, and green stucco.

"*Americano estupido*," the old woman muttered as she shuffled passed him, lugging her crate of chickens, towing the obstinate goat behind her.

Dan watched her plod down the street a short distance, hoping that he'd never bump into her again, and then he turned to the bus driver. In

Spanish he asked, "Which way to the Hotel Dos Rios?"

"Turn left at the first street. It will be three buildings down on your right," the bus driver told him.

"*Gracias*," Dan said, tossing his go-bag over his shoulder while carrying the dented up weapons case in his right fist. When he took his first step, nausea rolled through him to remind him of his head wound. The street before him blurred, and then came back into clear view. It didn't matter. There was a mission to fix, and a member of the team who was in dire straits.

When he arrived at the door of the small hotel painted bright yellow, he noticed a black SUV parked at the end of the block—the team had arrived. He shouldered through the door to find them filing out of the small lobby toward the rooms. Rather than say anything, he simply followed along.

"Jack, you're bunking with me—room eight. Little, you'll be with Garrison—room four, and Casey, you have your own room—number six," Walt told them as they made their way down the dimly lit hallway. The hotel was as hot and sticky as it was outside—at least in the hall. Dan had no doubt that each team member was hoping for at the very least a window air conditioner in their room.

"We'll have a short meeting in my room, and then you can go to your rooms until Garrison arrives," Walt put in.

"No need to wait. I'm right behind you," Dan announced.

The team turned. Before Walt could stop him, Jack pushed his way through to come nose-to-nose with Dan. Grabbing him by the front of his shirt, he growled, "I thought you were supposed to take care of Rayne! What the fuck were you doing?" With that he pulled back his fist, but before he could throw the punch, Little grabbed his hand.

"Dial it back, Haliday. This isn't going to solve any of our problems," Little said, forcing Jack against the wall across the hallway from Dan.

"Stand down, Haliday!" Walt insisted, and then he turned to Dan. "I want a full explanation when we get into my room."

"Yes, sir," Dan replied. His heart felt heavy at his miserable failure mixed with the way Jack was glowering at him from under Little's huge hand against his chest, holding him against the wall.

Walt turned to Jack. "Take a deep breath and calm down. We'll get her back. Everyone drop your excess off in your room, and then report to mine in ten with weapons. Garrison ... *now*."

* * * * *

Evening cast a fray of disquiet over the hut. One of Luis' guards had brought two candles with a meager meal. The flames would provide scarce light for Rayne to take care of the old doctor who still had not stirred. His vital signs were strengthening, and his skin was suppler, yet he laid quiet, unconscious. Rayne feared that he was too old and had been dehydrated for too long or other ailments that he suffered from were taking their toll because of the dehydration.

The IV that she had inserted to provide fluids had emptied over an hour ago. She had only brought one. Bibiana insisted on taking turns, sitting by his bed, keeping a wet compress on the old man's head, moistening his lips with her fingertips often. It was all that was left to do under the circumstances.

Studying him, he did not exude the prominence of a surgeon. He appeared very frail. His hands were twisted with arthritis, and probably shook when he held something. Most likely he was a simple town doctor. Rayne was unnerved by the thought of him cutting her open. True, he had inserted the chip in to her neck, except retrieving it may prove to be a more difficult task, especially if it had attached itself to a muscle or nerve or something more vital in her neck. She had to find a way out before the old doctor was strong enough to operate.

Rayne had little opportunity to look over the camp, but she was certain that it was not the same one that she'd been held captive before. Regardless, the similarities between Chaves' camp and Esteban's conjured frightening shadows of the past to haunt her mind. Desperately she tried to shoo them away with thoughts of escape for herself and the others who occupied the hut with her.

She was sorry Patrizia and Bibiana were forced to be a part of a scheme to get her to Peru. Rayne ached so deeply it was as if she were completely hollow inside. Whether she was willing to admit it to others or to herself, she had hoped to find Sierra alive. It was not to be. Her daughter was dead— a cold reality that punched her in the face the moment she was informed of Esteban's death.

Lifting her weary head toward the ceiling, she squeezed her eyes closed. A tear escaped, trickling down her temple into her hair. She couldn't allow herself to mourn—not again—not now. She had to focus on surviving. She had to focus on keeping the nameless old man alive. She had to focus on Jack and Lil, and the new life she would soon have when she got out of this mess. She was bound and determined that she would. Absently, her fingers caressed the delicate necklace around her throat— Lil's bravery necklace. It was such a *Dumbo* stunt, but it had helped the little girl through, and now the saltwater pearl necklace had been given to her by the darling child to help her find strength, and somehow, on some level, it was working.

Brushing her hair back with her fingers, she listened for any sound from outside. It was her first truly mindful moment to do so. The camp was quiet, although there must have been a breeze. She could hear the palms and large vegetation tossing. And what was the other sound she was hearing? Water—falling water. Cocking her head, she listened more closely. There must be a waterfall nearby. Yes … the water was falling furiously—it was a waterfall. She hadn't noticed it when they drug her to this hut. Then again, she was too busy trying to avoid the stares and catcalls from Chaves' men.

She tiptoed to the door to listen for voices or any other sound. Chaves' men were quiet, unlike Esteban's. She remembered hearing Esteban's men bicker and carouse at all hours of the night. Chaves appeared to keep a tighter rein on his men than Esteban did.

She glanced over her shoulder to see Bibiana propped up in the far corner of the hut with Patrizia draped over her lap, asleep. It was quite surprising to find out how they came to be Chaves' prisoners …

"Luis kidnapped Patrizia to try to get Esteban to tell him where he had hidden the sub dermal chip," Bibiana told her.

"Why? Why would he need Patrizia?" Rayne asked her.

The woman dropped her gaze to the floor. It took her a long moment to muster the courage to tell Rayne. "She is his daughter. Esteban and I were lovers many years ago—before he knew Luis. Once he joined Luis' militia, I had nothing to do with him. He knew of Patrizia, but she never met her father until the day Luis killed him."

Rayne took in a ragged breath. Never in her life had she felt so much hate for another human being as she did for Esteban Rojas. How ironic that now she was going to help his daughter and his former lover escape Luis Chaves, and see to it that Patrizia had a fresh lease on life with a new face.

Everything in life happens for a reason, she reminded herself. *I can't hold this child responsible for the actions of a father that she never knew.* She decided to take a quick inventory of her medical bag. She was most certain that she'd brought at least six quick clot bandages, but she wanted to be sure. Reaching into the bag, her fingers touched the clippers that she'd thrown in at the last minute before leaving headquarters. She let out a careworn breath. *Well, at least I was spared that decision.* Rayne actually allowed herself a snort at the thought of her plan to completely shave her head so that Esteban couldn't touch her hair. The quick change in circumstances on the bus had rearranged the entire scope of the situation.

Satisfied with the amount of bandages she'd packed, she reached for her go-bag for her brush and antiperspirant. As she dug through, her hand fell upon the box of tampons that she'd packed.

"Oh my God," she whispered into the dark. "Oh my God, I'd forgotten all about this." Pulling one of the candles closer, she flipped open the box, fingering the earpiece that she'd stuck inside the tampon box for safe keeping. Evidentially, even badass Peruvian guerrillas feared touching or opening a box of tampons. *Thank God for small— no big, really big, blessings*, Rayne mused.

Hoping a miracle was on the table, too, she pressed the power switch. The device powered on. Bringing it close to her face, she whispered into it, "Mayday, Mayday, are you there, Dan? Mayday, come in First Force ..."

* * * * *

"There wasn't a damned thing I could do, Walt," Dan explained. "I'd take a bullet for that woman. Every person on the team would. You've got to know that." He turned to Jack. "I own it. I feel like shit about it. I'm sorry."

Jack clapped his hand over Dan's shoulder. "I know." Sitting back hard against the chair he added, "I'm sorry I lost my head." Turning to Walt, he asked, "What now? Are we gonna just sit around the hotel licking our wounds, or are we gonna do something to get Rayne back and take those bastards down?"

There was a soft knock on the door. Casey called in, "We're here, Walt."

"Come in."

Casey and Little filed into the small room. Walt said, "It's getting late, but we're gonna drive out to the site where they attacked the bus to see what we can find, and look around in the direction that they came from, and then I'm gonna call Clark and have him do a little recon of the area from his end. Little, I noticed a hardware type store two doors down across the street, stop in a purchase a couple machetes. Let's move out."

The team began to shuffle out of the room, but Casey came to a sudden halt.

"What's that sound?" she asked.

They all stopped to listen, but heard nothing. Walt inquired, "What did you hear?"

"I thought I heard a voice," she said.

"Probably from another room. These walls are paper thin—I guarantee that," Walt said, while the team made their way out of the room.

On the chair where Dan had been sitting, Rayne's muffled voice called from inside his go-bag, "May day, Mayday, please come in First Force ... *please* come in ..."

* * * * *

The old man moaned. Quickly, Rayne stuffed the earpiece back into the tampon box, and rushed to his side. With half-lidded eyes, he picked his head up from the pillow. She took his hand. Even though he was weak and a bit disoriented, she could see the apprehension in his eyes at the unfamiliar face looking down at him.

She said to him in Spanish, "I'm Dr. Rayne Lee. How are you feeling?"

Laying his head back onto the pillow, he rasped, "You are the woman they were searching for."

"I am. What is your name, *Senor?*"

"I am Dr. Emilio Tola." His voice was weak. He tried to explain, "They want me to—" He was cut-off by an attack of coughing.

Rayne helped him to sit up. She brought the cup of water to his mouth. "Drink this, Dr. Tola."

He took several sips of the water, and then waved the cup away. "They want me to remove a sub dermal chip that I placed in your neck years ago. I tried to tell them that this is a dangerous thing. The chip may have moved. I do not know if I will be able to do the surgery." He coughed again. After Rayne helped him to take more water, he added, "Even if I was sure of the surgery, I do not think that I am strong enough. I have a poor heart. I have been without my medication for several days, and I do not think Chaves would wait for me to grow stronger."

"I believe you're right. Do you know what is on the chip that is so important?" Rayne asked.

"I am sorry, Dr. Lee. I do not," Dr. Tola replied.

Fear scraped through her. How long would Chaves be willing to wait? Could they convince him to hold off? She didn't think so. Patting him on the shoulder, she said, "You should rest now. My mother always told me that things will look better in the morning."

"Let us hope that your mother is right," the old doctor said. He closed his eyes to drift off to sleep.

It was as she had suspected. Dr. Tola was suffering from more than just dehydration. Without his medication his heart could give out under the stress. Again she removed the earpiece from the box and lifted it to her mouth, hoping that her desperate message was getting through. "Mayday, Mayday … Come in First Force, please come in …"

* * * * *

"You will do as I have requested, Alejandro," Luis bellowed into his cell phone. "It is only a matter of hours before I have exactly what I need to destroy you—decide quickly what you will do!"

"What happened to the woman that I provided you contact information?" Alejandro demanded.

"She is here," Luis supplied.

"But how? How did you get Dr. Lee to agree to come after her family was killed?"

Luis chuckled. "Esteban's daughter posed as Dr. Lee's daughter. We convinced her that her child was alive and well and waiting for her. But don't worry, Alejandro, there will be no evidence of any of it. I will kill Dr. Lee, the girl, and the girl's mother as well. There will be no one alive to tell what they have seen or heard."

"Kill, kill, kill, that is all you know!"

"Do not belittle me! Your campaign profited well from our former arrangements. These people are collateral damage for a greater cause—your advancement to the Supreme Court, and my complete control of the Amazonian Valley. It was a shame that Senator Billings did not have such insight. It is a shame that he got greedy. He may have been president by now. Make up your mind, Alejandro, or all the world will know what you have done!" Luis thumbed the end button. Pushing from his chair, he made his way out of the hut toward where his prisoners were being kept, while caressing the sheath where his knife rested.

* * * * *

Alejandro pitched the cell phone across the room, smacking into a portrait of himself dressed in his black robe, sitting in a red wing-backed chair with gavel in hand. The phone nicked the painting before it fell to the carpet. The Honorable Justice

Alejandro Pérez on the wall in a gilded frame was now missing most of his right eye.

His decision had been made. He had no choices left now. He had to do what was necessary to guard his appointment to the highest court in the land, and no one was going to stop him—he'd come too far.

He stomped across his office to yank the door open. Smith stood near the man that he had summoned. He wore a dark three-piece suit and tie. He was stocky with broad shoulders. His round face was pocked and his eyes had an edge about them. In his hand he grasped a briefcase with the words, National-Life Insurance Company printed in bright green letters across the lid.

Alejandro was pleased. He didn't have the look of a mercenary. Indeed he looked like an insurance agent. He had considered hiring Hawke Security International or First Force to do his bidding, but upon further investigation, both teams were a bit too by the books for his needs. The man standing in his foyer posing as an insurance agent had a team of killers' void of compunction on his payroll. An anonymous group more fitted to his requirements.

Smitty turned when he heard the judge's door whoosh open. "Mr. Carpenter is here to see you, Judge."

The right side of Alejandro's mouth hitched up. Mr. Carpenter—a very simple yet professional choice for an alias, he forced a pleasant tone, "Thank you, Smith. Please, come into my office, Mr. Carpenter. I'm anxious to go over my policy. Smith … please have Viviana serve you dinner in the kitchen."

Smitty took the hint. The judge wanted privacy with this man that security had checked out to make sure he was legit, so he went into the kitchen to find the maid.

The man followed the judge into his office, discarding his briefcase just inside the doorway. Without invitation, he took a seat near the judge's desk. He skipped the pleasantries and went straight to the business at hand. "I have a team who works the area of Peru that you have told me about. Is there anyone that you would like to spare?"

"No," Alejandro replied, easing into his chair. "Clean out the camp. I have fared well during all the questioning and investigation of my character, but this could be my undoing. I not only need complete anonymity, but I need your task accomplished quickly. My appointment is to be formalized within a day or so."

"Understood. You have wired the money to the account that I gave you?"

"Yes, five hundred thousand."

"Then we have an agreement," the man stated, lifting from his seat.

Standing, Alejandro offered his hand. "We do."

The man did not accept Alejandro's hand. Instead he made his way to the door, picked up his briefcase, and then left the house.

* * * * *

Rayne was pleased that Dr. Tola felt strong enough to sit up and drink, and he even managed to eat a small portion of food. He wasn't strong, but he was showing encouraging signs of recovery. The door swung open. Luis, Renzo, and Juan stepped through. Instantly, Luis' eyes brightened at the sight of the old man in an upright position.

"You are feeling better. That is good. We can proceed with the operation immediately," Luis announced. Bibiana and Patrizia woke at the sound of Luis' voice.

"He isn't strong enough to operate," Rayne said. "He's barely strong enough to hold a cup in his hand let alone a scalpel. You must give him some time."

"I am out of time, Dr. Lee." He pulled the knife out. "Either he operates or I will."

"If you try to cut this chip from her neck you may damage it, and it will be useless," Bibiana put in.

Luis whirled to face her. "Be quiet! I have no more use for you or your daughter. It would be to your benefit to shut your mouth."

Juan stepped forward. "I think the woman has a point, Luis. Give the old man a few more hours to gain his strength. What is a few more hours?"

Luis considered Juan's words. He pulled his cell phone from his pocket to check the time. "We will return in two hours. By then it will be dark. We will bring lanterns and the doctor will perform the operation ... or I will under his direction." With that, Luis waved Juan and Renzo from the hut.

Bibiana turned to Rayne. "What are we going to do, Dr. Lee? He will not be strong enough to operate on you within a few hours, and I fear what will happen if Luis takes a knife to your throat."

"That makes two of us, Bibiana. By the way, the man's name is Dr. Emilio Tola. Please see to it that he keeps drinking, while I try to summon some help," Rayne said, and then she retrieved the tampon box from her bag and pulled out the earpiece.

"What is that?" Patrizia asked.

"It's a communication device. I have friends who came with me to Peru. I'm going to try to contact them. Let's hope they hear me." She brought the device to her mouth. "First Force, come in ... This is Dr. Rayne Lee. Please come in ..."

CHAPTER FOURTEEN

Team First Force followed the dirt road along the direction the Jeep had come that afternoon to attack the bus. They tracked the Jeep's tires to a right turn where the two roads intersected only to come to a dead end where the vehicle could have come out of the jungle in any direction. Breaking off in two teams, they fanned out over the terrain cutting their way through the thick foliage with the machetes, while the mosquitoes devoured them.

Swinging the wide blade, Little cleared the way for Casey, while she kept her handgun at the ready. Sweat poured from the big man. He looked into the darkening sky. "It's getting dark. Time to rendezvous at the road," he told her. He maneuvered passed her to take the lead back to where they'd come from. Without the constant swish and hack of the machete, Casey heard water pounding against rocks in the far distance. Hesitating, she listened. *There must be a waterfall nearby*, she thought. Giving closer attention, she figured it was probably one or two miles away. The sound wasn't strong, but it could be heard, which indicated that it must be a massive body of water. *Whoa, it would feel pretty damned good to step under the water right about now.*

"Hey! Rhodes! You comin'?" Little called out, tearing her from her muse.

"Yeah, sure," she said, making her way through the roughly cut foliage, while slapping a mosquito and swiping the sweat from her face.

* * * * *

Walt was pleased that the small team had managed to cover a good ten miles of jungle in a short time, yet no sign of Chaves' camp. He waited at the intersection with Jack and Dan for Little and Casey. He watched Jack shift from one foot to the other while scanning the jungle that hovered over them for any sign of anything. Dan was much the same, and Walt couldn't help but feel a pang of pity for Dan—he was well aware that the man felt like a failure.

"No sign of Chaves' camp?" Walt asked when Casey and Little stepped onto the road.

"Nope," Little replied.

"Let's get back to the hotel. On our way, I'll feed Clark the intel we have and see what he can do from his end. Hopefully, he'll have something quickly and we can act tonight," Walt said.

* * * * *

When they arrived at the hotel, Walt opened his laptop to find that Clark has sent him a detailed map of the area they had been searching. The team gathered round to study the surrounding areas that they weren't able to explore.

Casey pointed at the screen. "There it is—I thought I heard a waterfall about two miles from where Little and I were before we had to turn back, and there it is. Can you zoom in to see what's around it?"

Walt zoomed in, showing a detailed look at the area. "It falls over a very big cliff, and look what's at the bottom … a big open area—a camp, Chaves' I'd bet." He moved the map around to see where the waterfall's flow led. "Look, the water continues on about four more miles and dumps right into the Amazon."

Jack pointed out, "It looks like it dumps over another very steep hillside into the river, and there's a rope bridge that leads to the other side."

Walt's phone rang. He clicked it over to speaker for the team to hear. "Talk to me, Clark …"

"I was contacted by Seamus Hawke. He has reported our activity to the CIA—we are off the grid and can expect no assistance, but they either want Chaves alive or they want whatever information he has about Justice Pérez. The more I dig on my end, it is looking like it's all directly connected to Senator Billings, but I still can't figure just how. With all that said, they are counting on us to get the intel or bring Chaves in to provide it."

Walt looked around at the tense expressions on the team's faces. He said, "Got it."

"There's a big open area at the bottom of a waterfall about twenty kilometers from the intersection. My program is far advanced to yours, so I can see that there are four huts and three Jeeps in the camp. I'm sending you a visual now. I've succeeded in hacking the CIA's cell frequency in that area. The activity in is hot—it's definitely Chaves' camp. Three kilometers north of the camp is the Amazon. Can you see the rope bridge?"

"Yeah," Walt replied.

"Good, there's plenty of open area for drop and pick up. Little should have no problem maneuvering a copter between the two hills over the river. Pick up would be easier the closer that you can get to the bridge," Clark explained.

"I'll take position at the top of the waterfall. It looks like I'll have a clear view of all movement in the camp," Casey said, indicating the area on the screen. Sitting back, she pulled out a GPS. "Setting my GPS coordinates now."

"That works," Walt said. "Haliday, Garrison, and I will give you twenty minutes to get into position and set up, and then we'll go in from the lower end of the camp, here. One of the huts has to be their armory; one has to be where they're holding Rayne. Hopefully Chaves will be in one of the others. Garrison and I will start at this end setting up the explosives. Haliday, you'll start here. Once Rayne is liberated, and we have Chaves in custody, we meet at the bridge and blow the camp sky high. Little, you've got the explosives ready?"

Little nodded.

Walt continued, "Good. Everybody suit up and get your gear ready, we leave for the airbase within the hour."

Team First Force had their game faces on. Everyone stood and started for the door, and then their spines stiffened, and they all came to a complete halt.

"Mayday, Mayday … Come in First Force. Are you there?" the stifled voice pleaded from the corner of the room.

Jack pushed through the team. "That's Rayne! Where's it coming from?" His eyes scanned the room, spotting Dan's go-bag still lying on the chair in the corner.

A muffled voice from inside the bag implored, "First Force, come in … This is Dr. Rayne Lee. Please come in …"

Jack dove for the chair, ripping the bag open, bringing the earpiece to his mouth. "Rayne! It's me, Jack. Where are you?"

The team gathered around him. He could hear her let out relieved breath. She said, "Thank God. I'm in Luis Chaves' camp. Esteban Rojas is dead. Chaves killed him. I have no idea where I'm at, but I can hear a waterfall very close by. I think it's their water source. I'm not sure, but from the little that I've seen, there are about twenty men in the camp with Chaves."

"Are you okay?"

"For now, but not much longer. I have a sub-dermal chip in my neck. I don't know what's on it, but Chaves plans to have it cut out within a few hours. I'm terrified, Jack," she said, her voice cracked.

Apprehension crowded his chest. He could tell that she was trying to hold on to every shred of composure that she had left. He tried to keep his voice as calm as possible. He said, "We have a location on you, and you've just confirmed our directives as correct. We're getting ready to move. Hold on for just a little while more, darlin', we'll be there soon."

"One more thing ... it's not just me, there are three others. An old doctor in poor health, a woman and a young girl," Rayne put in.

Jack glanced over his shoulder at his teammates. They wore resolute expressions. He knew what each of them was thinking. Without doubt, he spoke for all of them, "We're coming for you all. Hold tight."

"Jack ..."

His heart clenched. She didn't want him to break the connection. He assured her, "I'm still here."

"I love you."

He smiled into his chest. "I love you, too. I've gotta go. I'm on my way. Hold on, I'm on my way."

* * * * *

Tears rolled down her cheeks when the line went dead. She didn't want to let go, but at least she knew that the team was coming to get them. They would make it in time. Yes, they would make it in time.

She sniffed back her tears, while running a harried hand through her hair, placing the earpiece back into the tampon box and tucking it deep into the go-bag. She felt a comforting hand caress her back. She looked up to find Bibiana's warm smile.

"You owe us nothing, Dr. Lee. Thank you for everything that you are trying to do for us all," Bibiana said.

"They are coming for us. We will make it out of here, but we may have to buy ourselves a little time. If necessary, we may have to help the rescue mission along just a bit," Rayne said.

"How will we do that?" Bibiana asked.

Rayne shot her an ornery grin. "Dr. Tola ... are you prepared to have a heart attack?" she inquired of the aged man sitting at the table with Patrizia.

The little girl's eyes grew wide with fright, but the elderly doctor placed his hand over hers while sporting a curl to his weathered lips. He said, "What do you have in mind, Dr. Lee?"

"Distractions, any we can create," Rayne supplied.

* * * * *

The drive to the airbase was fast and furious. "I believe whatever is on that chip in Rayne's neck is the evidence against Justice Pérez that we're looking for," Walt said. "As soon as we get back to the copter we will make arrangement to have the chip removed at a hospital, and then feed the chip to Clark. The good news is that we don't have to babysit Chaves. Regardless, we only kill him if we absolutely have to."

"Betcha we're gonna have to kill that sonofabitch," Dan put in.

"I'm thinkin' you're right, Garrison," Jack agreed.

When they pulled into the airbase, they could see the Blackhawk waiting for them. Little rushed into the office to file a flight report, while the team gathered their weapons from the back of the SUV and made adjustments to their gear.

Little marched out of the office scowling more than usual while a young man dressed in a black suit followed close on his heels toting a large duffle bag. The man looked more like a teen fresh out of middle school rather than a full-grown adult. Stretching his hand out toward Walt, he flashed the oh too familiar CIA badge accompanied by an enthusiastic grin. He said, "I'm Agent Ellis. I'm here to retrieve any evidence you get on Justice Pérez." Lifting the duffle, he added, "I've brought my gear. I'm coming with you."

Looking him up and down, Walt chortled. "I don't think so. One—I don't have time to wait for you to gather your gear. Two—I have no intention of being the first to wipe that fresh milk from behind your ears on a dangerous mission, Agent Ellis."

Ellis puffed out his chest. "I've been trained. Yes, this would be my first mission, but I assure you—"

"You aren't qualified to assure me of diddly shit, young man. You're not coming, and that's that."

Ellis' face reddened. He glanced around at the men who made up team First Force, measuring him, except for the woman. She was immersed in whatever she was reading on her ebook. By the glowering expressions, he could see that he wasn't going anywhere—not with this group anyway. "Okay … If you insist—"

"I very much insist." With that Little nudged Casey to follow along, and the team began to make their way toward the Blackhawk waiting on the tarmac.

Finally, Ellis let out a frustrated breath. "In that case, I'll be waiting here to take Chaves into custody and to relieve you of any evidence you have."

"Good enough," Walt said over his shoulder as he grabbed his gear to follow the team out.

Ellis trailed behind him. "Time is of the essence, Mr. Wabash. Justice Pérez is to be formally nominated to the Supreme Court tomorrow morning. Any ideas what this damning evidence is?"

Letting out a beleaguered sigh, Walt said, "My niece, Dr. Rayne Lee, has a subdermal chip in her neck. We believe that whatever is on that chip is the evidence that Chaves is holding over Justice Pérez' head, and yes, it must be powerful. He has hired Hawke International to extract Chaves from Peru and bring him to the States."

"While Seamus Hawke has reported contact with the judge, no contract has been awarded to his group by Pérez. I will make arrangements for an ambulance to report here. I will accompany Dr. Lee to a hospital to have the chip removed immediately," Ellis said.

"Whatever."

Ellis nodded. "God speed, then."

Walt climbed into the helicopter behind his team. He was greeted with stone cold eyes.

Jack's tone was concise when he asked, "Why did you tell him about the chip?"

"I didn't have a choice, Jack. He asked me straight up. I couldn't play dumb and get away with it," Walt answered, his demeanor in defense mode.

The rotors slowly began to whirl until they spun like a hurricane, forcing Ellis to bow as he ran toward the building in the rotor wash. The Blackhawk lifted. The team knelt upon the floor hooking up to the repelling ropes, strapping weapons to their backs, prepping for the drop and the rescue mission ahead.

"I haven't repelled from an aircraft since Desert Storm," Walt yelled over the deafening noise from the rotors.

"It's like riding a bicycle," Jack hollered back.

"I damned well hope so," Walt muttered to himself.

What seemed like only moments, the copter was flying over the Amazon River, following the meandering curves of the murky water until Little had his sights on the rope bridge.

"We're at the drop point," he announced into his mouthpiece.

All eyes were instantly on Little, waiting for the thumbs up that he had the copter in good position for the drop. The team separated to the two doors on either side of the copter. Walt and Jack held tightly to their ropes, with their right hand above them, and the left above the hook at the small of their backs. They leaned out backward to the left side of the copter with their feet braced against the floor, while Dan and Casey leaned out the right side. They watched for Little's signal, and when his thumb flipped upward, they pushed from the edge to slid down the ropes as unerringly as a spider from its web. When they reached the ground, they quickly unhooked, and then scrambled into the jungle beneath the trees and foliage bowing and swaying violently against the rotor wash. The rope bridge rocked and bucked in the blast. The brown water churned in the river basin. Casey found herself hoping that they would not have a call to venture out onto the bridge during the mission. It looked weather beaten and insubstantial—scary beyond belief.

They watched the Blackhawk fly away through the thick canopy. Walt turned to Casey. "We'll follow you part way, and then give you twenty minutes to get into position above the waterfall. Then we're on the move." With that, he waved the team into the jungle. Guns up, they fanned out to make their way through the heavy foliage wary and alert for any and all hidden adversaries.

* * * * *

Time slowly ticked by. Rayne's stomach coiled with anxiety. She tapped her fingers on the scarred tabletop, waiting. Dr. Tola lay on the cot, dozing off and on, while Bibiana paced the tiny space. Patrizia sat across the table. Rayne noticed that the girl rarely took her eyes off her. She wondered what was going through the poor child's mind. How frightened she must've been through the entire ordeal. It would be over soon. At least Rayne was praying that it would be.

They sat in silence listening for any sounds of rescue, but the only sounds they heard were the men talking and laughing in the camp.

It was getting darker and darker in the hut. Surely Chaves would show up soon. Surely he knew that they needed light to operate. Rayne constantly pressed her fingers along her neck searching for any trace of the chip to no avail. Her spine straightened at the sound of Luis' voice bellowing beyond the thatched door. He was coming.

Bibiana stopped in her tracks. Her gaze met Rayne's, and then they looked to the doctor on the cot. He sat up to hold his chest. Rayne nodded. The door opened and Luis stepped through. Rayne was most surprised that he was alone. The two men known as Renzo and Juan who always seemed to be at his side were absent, but she had no doubt that they were very close at hand.

"It is time to remove the chip, Dr. Lee," Luis announced.

Her eyes flicked to Dr. Tola. On cue he sucked in a deep breath, wincing and clutching his chest in pain. Bibiana ran to his bedside.

"Patrizia! Water! Get some water for the doctor!" she cried out in Spanish so that Luis would understand. Luis' eyes narrowed.

Rayne leapt from her chair, grabbing her stethoscope from her duffle. "Lay back, Dr. Tola," she told him. Gasping for breath, he complied. Rayne was most impressed. She pressed the stethoscope to his chest and listened; only his heart was not beating as it should. No, he wasn't suffering the heart attack that he pretended, but it was not beating in proper rhythm. Dr. Tola needed his medication, and soon.

"What is going on?" Luis demanded.

"This man is having a heart attack," she lied. "He needs hospital care."

"Will he die?"

"It's very possible," Rayne said.

"Then I will cut the chip from your throat!" Luis bit out.

"No, you cannot," the old doctor protested, managing a weak rasp.

Patrizia could stand no more. She'd been dragged from her home. She and her mother had been threatened. She'd been forced to lie to this American woman who had so much compassion for others, and now this horrible man was going to cut her throat without any concern for what happened to her. Anger boiled inside her white-hot. Dr. Lee said that they needed distractions of any kind, and she was going to give them a big one! She grabbed the pitcher on the table, ran across the room, and smacked Luis over the head with it! Glass shattered over the floor. Luis grabbed his bloody head.

"Patrizia!" Bibiana screamed.

Luis was dazed. He fell forward. Rayne took advantage of the situation. She smacked him across the face with her duffle bag, still he managed to hold on to consciousness enough to call out, "Guards!"

The door flung open and three men stepped through with their guns drawn. Luis yelled, "You will all pay with your lives! Take the American woman to my hut, strap her to the table, I am going to cut her throat and take what I need!" He turned to Bibiana. "And then I will come here to kill you and your daughter! How could you possibly think that you could escape?"

Holding his bleeding head, he turned to the guards. "Take her now!"

They grabbed Rayne and dragged her from the hut. She kicked and yanked to slow them down. One guard grabbed her by the hair to control her head, forcing her out the door and down the steps. Luis paused at the door to toss Bibiana one last abrasive glare.

CHAPTER FIFTEEN

Through the humid night, Casey managed to make it through the jungle, climbing a steep rocky hillside, then across a short flat plain to the top of the waterfall. With her night vision goggles perched on her face, she found a solid rock to set up her rifle on a bipod and bring the camp into her sights.

All was quiet below. Only a handful of men wandered around outside the huts. She counted twelve. They were armed with Uzis slung over their shoulders. A clear confidence permeated among the group that their camp was safe, undetected by the outside world. Through her scope, she could see them joking and smoking cigarettes while sitting near a small fire. The torrent of water over the rocks made such a racket that she couldn't hear anything coming from the camp, or around her. This would work in her favor, as the men in the camp wouldn't hear her either.

Checking her watch, she figured that the team was moving in. She reported, "I count twelve men hanging around a campfire. No sign of Chaves or Rayne."

"Roger that," Walt replied.

Just then the men sitting at the fire turned quickly toward one of the huts. Three ran inside with their guns drawn, while the rest stood stiffly watching.

"Wait a minute," Casey said. "There's something going on in one of the huts. Three men just ran in."

"We've got the camp in our sights. Which hut?" Walt asked.

"Second to the right of the falls," Casey supplied. "Hold positions. Let's wait to see what happens." Sweat dribbled down her face. A bead of moisture caught her eyelash. She blinked to flick it off. The salt stung her eye, but she didn't miss the moment that the three men dragged Rayne kicking and punching from the hut. The men who remained around the fire were now entertained at the show that the American woman was putting on, and how their comrades struggled to keep her in their grip.

"They're dragging Rayne to another hut. Hold on …" she watched intently while they pushed Rayne through the door of the first hut. "She's now in the first hut with the three men, and it looks like Luis Chaves is following. Hey, he looks kinda bloody. Wonder if our girl did that."

"I wouldn't be surprised," Jack put in.

"We're on the move. Casey, you've got our six?" Walt asked.

"You betcha," she said.

* * * * *

The men shoved Rayne into a chair, tossing her duffle bag into her chest, hard. It knocked the breath from her. She coughed. Suddenly Luis Chaves' bloody hand squeezed her throat. She looked into his eyes filled with disgust and malevolence. Blood ran down the right side of his neck. Unable to breathe, she grabbed his wrist in attempt to push it away, but he squeezed all the more.

"You are as good as dead," he told her. Loosening his grip, he turned to see Renzo and Juan step through the door. With a wave of his hand, he dismissed the guards. "Renzo, go through the doctor's bag to find something to clean me up," and then tightening his grip, he turned back toward Rayne. The scowl on his mouth seething with rage, he said, "After I am bandaged, I will cut your throat to get what I need."

He let her go to allow Juan to tend him. Gasping for air, she grabbed her neck. Juan poured water into a bowl while Renzo searched Rayne's duffle, pulling out a roll of bandaging and a package of gauze. Luis flopped down in a chair across from Rayne never taking his wicked gaze from her.

Taking a handful of gauze from Renzo, Juan dipped it into the bowl, and then dabbed the back of Luis' head. He flinched, but his stare did not waver. Renzo continued to look through her bag. He pulled out a scalpel.

"You can use this to cut her," he suggested.

Luis pulled the knife from its sheath, holding it up for her to see. "No. I will cut her with this and watch her bleed to death while I look for the chip. She will feel every slice."

Finally able to breathe, Rayne straightened in her seat. She refused to show Luis the terror that rattled inside her. If the team arrived too late, at least she would die with dignity. She silently vowed that she wouldn't scream or cry when he took the knife to her. She wouldn't give him that pleasure.

Juan had to pluck out a few shards of glass from the wound. Luis' lip flicked with every probe. It took several minutes but Juan was able to get the bleeding under control and get a bandage in place.

Luis' lips curled as he fingered the bandage. Rayne's stomach clenched. His eyes locked with hers, he slowly rose to his feet. He said, "Tie her to the table."

Renzo roughly hauled her out of the chair. She managed to twist and knee him in the groin. Renzo yelped, bending over in pain. Rayne grabbed the table, and with all her might, she flipped it on its side, but Juan soon had her by the shoulders, pulling her into a tight bear hug. She twisted and struggled in his arms until Luis grabbed her by the chin. He pressed so hard that she thought her jaw would break.

Taking out his gun and holding it to her head, he said, "You have much spirit. I can see why Esteban kept you as his slave. He must have enjoyed every moment he spent between your legs. It is a shame you must die."

Juan picked the table up, while Renzo hobbled to a corner to fetch some rope. Luis said, "Now lay down on the table, Dr. Lee."

She was beaten. She had stalled for as long as she could. The team hadn't made it in time. Juan took her by the arm to help her onto the table. She lay down and closed her eyes. They stretched each arm and tied it to a leg on each side of the table, and then moved down to do the same to her ankles.

The vile feelings of complete vulnerability washed over her as she laid spread eagle on the table—helpless. She was there's to do with as they wished. She felt the cold steel of his knife caress her throat.

He pricked her.
She flinched.
He chuckled.

She felt her blood trickle down her neck onto the table.

He was toying with her like a cat plays with a chipmunk before the kill.

She could hear every breath he took. She could sense him moving around her, trying to decide where the next cut would be. Would he slice her throat or would he nick and chop at it until she begged for mercy? When he was done with her, how would he kill Bibiana and Patrizia or the old doctor? Perhaps they would be luckier than she. Perhaps the team would arrive in time to save them. She said a quick prayer for them.

Suddenly there was no movement. She could no longer sense Luis at her side. Where had he gone? She opened her eyes to find Luis, Renzo, and Juan standing perfectly still close to the door. They drew their weapons. They spoke rapidly in hushed voices.

Ever so slowly, Renzo opened a small thatched flap that covered a window to peek outside. His body lurched violently backward to the floor. His face a smatter of blood, and then the door burst open Jack stepped through with his semi-automatic to his face. Without hesitation, he shot Juan, and then turned the gun toward Luis, but he'd already had his gun trained on Rayne.

"Put down your weapon," Jack instructed in Spanish.

"I will shoot the doctor," Luis told him.

Inching his way closer, Jack said, "You are surrounded, Chaves. Put down your weapon."

"I will not!"

"*Uno* ..."

"I will shoot the doctor!" Luis insisted.

"*Dos* ..."

"I ... I ..."

"*Tres*!" Jack counted off, and then squeezed the trigger, shooting Luis in the chest. Luis dropped to his knees, and then face down to the floor. Jack added, "No take-backs."

A nanosecond later gunfire exploded outside the hut. Men yelling in Spanish erupted throughout the camp. Jack ran to the table, fumbling with the ropes to free Rayne, when his eyes fell upon her bloodied throat.

"Are you alright?" he asked.

"I'm good. It looks worse than it really is, I'm sure. What's going on out there?"

He glanced over his shoulder. "Nothing good— let's get the hell outta here."

Finally untying the last rope, he lifted Rayne from the table. Setting her aside, Jack hurried about the hut to blow out the lanterns. Taking Rayne's hand, he guided her to duck down behind the door.

Listening intently, he said, "That's definitely not friendly fire. We don't have that many operatives in the camp."

"Jack … have you got Rayne?" Walt called into his earpiece.

"Yeah. What the hell's goin' on?"

"Someone else is attacking the camp. We've got to abort. Have you got Chaves?"

"He's dead."

"We can't leave without Bibiana, Patrizia, and Dr. Tola," Rayne said.

"Where are they?" Jack asked.

"The next hut over."

Hunkered down, they listened to the volley of rapid gunfire blasting through the camp. "It's only a matter of time before we're found. Garrison, where are you?"

"One hut over. What are we waiting for? We've got Rayne, let's go!" Dan said.

"There's a woman, a child, and a doctor in that hut. We've got to get to them before these guys do," Jack explained.

"I'm on it," Dan replied.

"Walt … meet us at the edge of the jungle," Jack instructed.

"Roger that," Walt answered.

Just then the door opened. With measured steps, the shadowy shape of a gunman entered the hut with his weapon drawn. Rayne squeezed Jack's arm. He put his finger to his lips, warning her to be very quiet, very still. The gunman wore camo and military boots. He was a trained professional. He flashed a light on Renzo to find his face missing, he kicked Juan to make sure that he was dead, and then more relaxed, he made his way over to the third body on the floor, Luis Chaves. Satisfied that all three were dead, he turned to leave. Jack pumped three bullets into his chest. The gunman fell backward over the table to the floor.

Jack opened the thatched window just a bit to peek out, and then he turned to Rayne who was trying to keep it together. He ran the back of his fingers against her cheek. She leaned into the caress trying to draw as much daring from his touch as she could. He whispered, "You know that moment that you've been waiting for when you'll have to run like hell for your life?"

On a bracing breath, she said, "Yes …"

"It's here, darlin'. When we step out of this hut, you stick like glue, and run like hell right along with me."

"What about—"

"We've got to trust that Garrison's got them covered." He took her by the shoulders. "Look at me." She dragged her gaze to his, finding the strength, the resolve in his eyes that she trusted even though at this moment her fear had far outdistanced her courage. He said, "Like glue. Are you ready?"

"No, but I'm going anyway."

"That's my girl." With that he kissed the tip of her nose, and then took another peek out the window. "Hold on to the belt loops on my pants," he instructed. Crouching down, they made their way to the door. He opened it, and then grabbed her hand to run to the back of the hut and into the jungle with bullets whizzing by, breaking chunks of bark off the palm trees.

"I'm thirty feet straight ahead," Walt said.

Jack and Rayne made it to the brush that Walt crouched behind. Jack pushed Rayne into his arms. "I'm going back to help Dan. I want you to get her to the rendezvous point." Walt tried to speak, Jack told him, "Don't give me orders, Walt. Just get her the hell outta here."

Rayne reached for him, but he disappeared into the dark. She could only hear the sound of his boots beating against the undergrowth and the foliage giving way as he ran toward the kill zone. She was reaching for a phantom. Had she lost yet another man who she loved?

Rayne was torn from her thoughts when Walt grabbed her by the hand. "He'll meet up with us at the chopper. C'mon." They turned to make their escape. Rayne gasped. Walt froze. They were greeted by a tall thin man. His sweaty face was washed with black. He was wearing camo, yet his gun remained slung over his shoulder, while his hands shook uncontrollably. Walt narrowed his eyes, straining to identify the man, and then he grabbed him by the front of his shirt. "What the hell are you doing here, Ellis?"

"I … I followed. I've got my ways—I'm new, but I know shit."

"Well congratulations, asshole! You just walked into a kill zone!" Walt tossed the young agent against a palm tree. "You listen to me! You follow us back to the rendezvous point—and don't make me have to wait for you!" Ellis dropped his chin to his chest in shame. "Now!" Walt bellowed above the rapid gunfire reverberating from the nearby camp.

* * * * *

The mission had gone completely FUBAR. Casey had managed to pick off several of Chaves' men, allowing Jack, Dan, and Walt entry into their positions, but out of nowhere bullets started flying from every direction. The camp was flooded with a squad of armed men who knew exactly how to kill on the fly—professional mercenaries. She had no idea who they worked for or where they came from, but they were good—damned good.

Walt instructed her to abort her nest and head for the chopper. As quickly as possible, she gathered her rifle and stand, stuffing them into the case. When she turned she ran smack into a wall of solid muscle. She staggered backward only to be seized by a huge black man who must've weighed two hundred fifty pounds. His shoulders were as broad as a mountaintop. He was dressed in camo and she was looking down the barrel of his gun.

His deep voice boomed over the sound of the rushing water behind her. "What've we got here? A sweet little sniper. Who you workin' for, bitch?"

This was not good.

She asked, "What makes you think I'm working for anyone?"

Without warning, she felt the hot sting of the back of his wide hand. She toppled to the ground. He yanked her back to her feet. "I asked you a question, bitch. Who you with? I'll beat it right outta you."

Wiping the blood from her mouth, she looked into his unforgiving eyes. The sound of guns exploding made him flinch. He grabbed her by the front of her vest shoving her away from the waterfall. He took up her duffle, demanding, "Walk! We'll get it out of you one way or another."

The sweat from her brow pouring down over her face made the cheek where he'd hit her burn like hell fire. She trudged through the goat's track through the jungle. In the darkness he hadn't detected her earpiece. She heard Walt say, "I've got Rayne. We're almost to the copter. What is your ETA, Casey?"

She was in no position to answer. She hoped that if she couldn't figure this out for herself, the team would get the idea that she was in trouble. Her captor kept pushing her right shoulder, directing her forward, yet he appeared uncertain of their location or the direction that he should be heading. The farther they walked, the more confused he seemed to be.

"Casey ... Are you there?" Walt asked again.

The gunfire was less as the distance grew between them and the campsite. Her captor flashed his light through the jungle searching the faint path. She remembered climbing a steep hill on her way to the waterfall. It had to be nearby. She picked up the pace. The huge man had become so paranoid that he too picked up his stride. Feeling the scree beneath her feet, she stumbled. They'd arrived at the top of the hill.

She cried out, "Oh!" with that, she lunged forward, rolling down the hill and off to the side into the tall thick plant life. Quickly, she pulled out the KA Bar that she always kept strapped to her right leg. Keeping still, controlling every breath, she waited while praying that she wasn't lying next to a snake or worse. She could hear the sound of his boots shuffling over the loose rocks, slipping, hesitating, while making his way down the hill, seeking out his errant prisoner.

As he moved closer she could hear his heavy breathing until he was right next to her. He stopped. In the pale moonlight, she could see him frantically twisting from side to side, searching.

Now! She leapt from her hiding place to stab him in the calf. He cried out, bending down to clutch his wounded leg while sliding on the rocks. She rammed the knife into his back. The big man fell to the ground with a *thud* followed by a loud grunt.

Rushing passed him, riding the rolling rocks down the hill, she huffed into her mike, "I'm on my way, Walt."

"Roger that."

* * * * *

An eerie silence now blanketed the camp. The shooting had subsided. Dan made his way cautiously around the hut. Whoever had come in to take out Chaves' operation had managed in grand style. He was certain that they were searching the camp for survivors to finish off. He had no idea if the two women and the old doctor that he was going in to rescue were alive, but he had to find out.

His back against the small dwelling and his weapon poised to fire, he inched his way to the corner. Peering around the loose thatching, he could see the dark silhouettes of the opposing operatives wading through the dead bodies by firelight. Perhaps they were looking for Chaves or perhaps they were just making sure. He didn't much care— he needed to make it inside the hut undetected, and then get three people out without getting their asses shot off—no easy task.

"Dan …" he heard Jack's voice in his earpiece. "What's your position?"

"At the corner of the designated hut," he whispered.

"I'm coming up behind you."

Just then Jack emerged from the jungle to join him. Dan supplied, "I count six of them. They've cleaned out the camp, so they may move on. Cover me … I'm gonna try to get into the hut. I hope whoever they are, are still alive."

"Rayne said the woman's name is Bibiana, and the girl's name is Patrizia. There's an old man, too. I don't know his name," Jack put in.

Dan ducked down low in the shadows, while Jack took position above him at the corner, keeping his weapon trained on the men milling around the fire. Wicked slowly, Dan crept to the door of the hut, easing the door open with measured caution, slipping inside with the stealth of an apparition.

The small space was dark. It appeared empty. Were they looking in the wrong place? He hoped not, because getting to another hut could prove to be straight up fatal. To the short left was a cot. In the darkness, he could make out a figure lying on it. Keeping his gun trained on the still shape, he made his way over to find a motionless old man—his head lay off to one side, his mouth hung open. Dan couldn't see if he'd been shot to death so he placed his fingers on the old man's neck to find a pulse. His skin was cool to the touch. His pulse was nonexistent, one of the hostages that he'd been sent in to liberate was dead.

Dan scanned the room for other bodies. The dirt floor was clear. The table in the middle of the room stood undisturbed. Had the woman and the child escaped or had they been taken prisoner? He and Jack couldn't wait around much more—they had to get out. Little would have the chopper in place very soon, if he wasn't at the rendezvous point already.

"Dan …" Jack whispered in his ear. "Did you find them? They're getting ready to torch the huts."

Shit. Dan turned to leave, and then he heard a tiny gasp. He stopped, cocking his head to listen more closely. He whispered in Spanish, "I am here to help you. Dr. Lee has sent me. We must hurry or they will find us. Bibiana … Patrizia … you can trust me. Come out."

He heard a shuffle under the cot where the dead man lay, and then he saw two shadows crawl out from underneath. He hurried to reach out his hand to help the woman up, and then he gathered Patrizia in his arms. "*Soy* Dan," he told them. "I am Dan."

"*Now*, Dan … They're preoccupied torching the first hut—you're next," Jack warned in a reedy whisper.

Dan whispered to the shivering child in his arms, "I've got you, Patrizia. I'm going to get you out of here safely," and then he said to Bibiana, "Hold on to my belt loops. Keep a tight hold, and no matter what happens, stay with me. There's another man outside the hut, he will help you once we're out. *Comprende?*"

"I understand," Bibiana said in English. With shaking hands, she hooked her fingers through his belt loops. Patrizia hid her face in his shoulder, while clenching her little fingers into his shirt, gripping her legs around his torso as tightly as she could. Dan asked Jack, "Are we clear?"

"Go now, *fast*," Jack told him.

Dan whipped the thatched door open. The flames from the hut that had just been set ablaze jumped into the night sky—the heat so fierce it kissed their faces. The men surrounding it hooted and hollered their victory as it crackled, spitting sparks high into the night sky like fireworks on the Fourth of July. With Bibiana on his heels, he hurried down the stairs and around the corner of the hut, pushing Bibiana against the wall between him and Jack.

"Go with him," Dan instructed her.

Jack looped his arm through hers, taking her hand tightly in his. He whispered in Spanish, "I'm Jack. Nice to meet you. Let's go, Bibiana." With that slight warning, he darted for the jungle with Dan

313

following close behind, cradling Patrizia against his chest. Once they were twenty feet into the canopy of the jungle, they turned back to watch the huts go up in flames.

"Are you able to walk?" Jack asked Bibiana in Spanish. "We have to travel through the jungle for about four miles."

"I will be fine," she began in English. "But I don't think Patrizia can make it that far on foot."

"Don't worry about your daughter, ma'am. I've got her," Dan assured her.

"Thank you so much," Bibiana said, her voice cracked with emotion.

They had escaped. They had made it out of Luis Chaves' hellhole alive. These men had risked so much for people that they didn't know. She felt badly that Dr. Tola had died of heart failure during the attack on the camp. His heart was simply too weak to handle the overload of stress when the shooting and the yelling and the cries of death raged outside their tiny prison.

She and Patrizia had no choice but to hide under the cot where the dead doctor lay—it was their only chance at survival. When the soldiers came into the hut, they were satisfied with one dead body. Now they had been rescued before the hut where they were helplessly trapped was set on fire.

It was so much to comprehend. The past weeks had been an overwhelming ordeal. Surely she could make the four mile trip, but as she went to take the first step, she collapsed.

Without pause Jack scooped her up into his arms to carry her toward safety.

* * * * *

Gasping for breath, Rayne hugged a palm tree at the edge of the jungle. Far below the ruddy Amazon churned. Walt stood at the edge of the cliff, looking skyward for any sign of the Blackhawk's return, while Ellis clutched his hand to his knees trying to catch his breath, black sweat dripping from his forehead to the ground.

"Any word from Jack?" Rayne managed between hiccups of taking in air.

"No," Walt replied, unease filling his tone. "He'll be here. Don't worry."

Don't worry? That had to be the number one understatement of the year—possibly the century. How could she not worry? Jack and Dan had returned to the kill zone to release a woman, a child, and a very sick man. How were they going to escape with those odds? Just managing Dr. Tola through the jungle at a fast pace was mission impossible to say the least. One man would have to carry Patrizia. One would most likely have to carry the doctor, and who knew if Bibiana was strong enough to travel quickly for the three or four miles of rough terrain that she and her uncle had just traveled. Worry? She was way beyond that—she was damned near grief-stricken.

At least they knew that Casey was safe and on her way to their location. Right? Searching the edge of the dark jungle, she ran her fingers through her sweat soaked hair. They hadn't heard from Casey in over thirty minutes. She said she was on her way. Had she run into trouble? Was she okay?

Anxiety crowded her chest. She wanted to let out a scream that would rock the Andes. Lord have mercy but she wasn't cut out for this! The bushes ruffled. Rayne's spine stiffened. Her heart raced. Casey stepped into the small clearing, swiping sweat from her face with her shoulder.

"Gee-zuz, it's freakin' hot here!" Casey announced.

Rayne pushed from the tree that had been propping her forehead to rush toward Casey, throwing her arms around her to envelop her in a relieved hug. "Thank God you're okay," she cried out.

Casey hugged her back. "Back at ya, girlfriend." She looked around. "Where're Garrison and Haliday?" Her eyes fell upon the stranger staring back at her. "And who the hell is this?"

"That is a casualty we hope won't be happening. Agent Ellis, this is the First Force sniper, Casey Rhodes." Walt added, "Haliday and Garrison went back in to liberate three hostages." His brows furrowed, he asked, "Where's your weapon?"

"In the jungle somewhere. I was detained for a short time by a member of the group that attacked the camp," she explained.

"He let you go?" Walt inquired, rather bemused.

"No."

"W-what happened?" Rayne asked, not sure if she really wanted to know.

"He didn't understand the concept of a woman's wrath, and so I had to educate him," she said, taking a seat on a nearby rock. Finally having a moment to lick her wound, she pulled out a rag from her hip pocket to dab her mouth. The rag was soaked with perspiration. She winced while she tried to clean the blood from her mouth. The salty moisture only added to the burn and sting and the swelling that she could feel rising from her flesh.

Rayne knelt at her feet, taking the rag from her hand. "What have we got here?"

"I'll be okay. He swatted me a good one," Casey supplied.

Turning her head so that she could examine Casey's mouth, Rayne said, "I'll be the judge of that, *girlfriend.*"

The small group flicked their attention to the sky. They could hear the rapid whirl of the Blackhawk's rotors in the distance. Little was on his way. They wanted to be relieved, but the whole team hadn't arrived yet.

"Haliday … Garrison … what's your ETA?" Walt asked into his mouthpiece.

They waited.

No response.

"Haliday … are you there?" Walt asked.

Casey and Rayne moved closer to Walt.

Ellis shifted from one foot to the other.

Eyes to the ground, they waited.

No response.

"Garrison … can you hear me?" Walt insisted.

The Blackhawk's lights cut through the darkness—the rotors growing louder and louder.

Still no response.

Walt and Casey exchanged wary glances.

Rayne squeezed Casey's arm.

"No man left behind," Walt stated.

"We've got to go back for them," Casey agreed.

"I'm going in, too," Ellis stated.

"At this point, I may not have a choice but to let you," Walt said.

Rayne couldn't speak. She closed her eyes, only able to imagine the very worse. Tears seeped from the corners of her eyes down her dirty face.

"Honey, I'm home!" Jack called out as he eased Bibiana from his arms. Dan stepped from the jungle behind Jack, carrying Patrizia, looking relieved to find everyone present and accounted for.

For a brief second Rayne was frozen in place. She was mesmerized by the blessing that stood before her, Jack, Dan, Bibiana, and Patrizia exhausted, dirty, and dripping with sweat, but no worse for the wear. She looked passed them. Dr. Tola was not there. They didn't have to explain. She knew. He simply wasn't strong enough, but everyone else had survived and for that she had to celebrate.

Overjoyed beyond composure, she ran to the man she loved and for a brief horrifying second thought she had lost. Diving at him, she wrapped her arms around him. Her lips crashed against his. Her fingers twisted in the soft damp curls at the nape of his neck. It felt so good to touch him. It felt so good to press her body to his. He was alive. Jack was alive, unharmed, and in her loving embrace. At last, at last, everyone was safe!

Jack was first to withdraw from the kiss. He gently told her, "I'm so sorry, darlin', but the old man just didn't make it. Dan found him dead in the hut."

Touching Rayne's shoulder with her fingertips, Bibiana said, "He died during the attack. His heart gave out."

Rayne managed a withered smile. "Dr. Tola was a fine man. I'm glad I had the chance to meet him."

The torrent of wind from the Blackhawk interrupted their reunion as it descended to line up against the rim of the crag. The hatch opened.

"Just got a text from Clark. There's a medical team waiting for Rayne at the Clinica Anglo-

Americana in Lima to remove the chip," Walt yelled above the drone of the rotors and the sound of the palms' at the jungle's edge swishing in the fierce wash.

"I could'a told you that," Ellis yelled back.

"What the hell is he doing here?" Jack shouted.

"I'll explain later. Let's just get the hell outta here!" Walt told him.

Patrizia's body went rigid in Dan's arms. Her eyes were as big as cue balls and her jaw dropped open. She shook with fear at the enormous machine that was blasting them with a wind as furious as a hurricane. Dan hugged her tighter to his body, and whispered directly into her ear, "It's okay. The big bird is gonna take us to safety. Stick with me, baby girl, you're safe."

Patrizia grabbed a handful of Dan's shirt, clinging to his body for protection. Jack helped Rayne climb into the copter, and then Bibiana who was hesitant at first, but Jack flashed his wide smile accompanied with a quick wink, and she was instantly convinced that all would be just fine, and then while tossing him a grimace, Jack helped Agent Ellis aboard.

He reached for Patrizia, but she buried her face deeper into Dan's chest, unwilling to let go of the man that she had grown to trust. Jack nodded his understanding, and helped Dan aboard, and then turning to Casey, he yelled, "Last but certainly never least ..." but as he took hold of her arm to give her a lift, bullets pinged off the copter just over her shoulder.

Ducking, Jack yelled, "What the hell!"

Casey made eye contact with the enormous black man that she thought she'd killed on the hillside. His expression told the tale—it was adrenaline steeped in pure rage that was keeping him upright. He swaggered from side to side while trying to take aim at them with Casey's rifle. He managed another shot. It pinged off the Blackhawk just over their heads. Jack tackled Casey to the ground.

"Evidently, we didn't get clean away!" he exclaimed, fumbling for the Glock in his shoulder holster.

"My bad! I thought I'd killed that SOB!" Casey yelled back.

Just then two shots rang out from inside the copter. The big man lurched backward when the first hit him in the chest. He managed another step forward when the second pierced his throat. Dropping the rifle, he fell to his knees, and then to the ground.

"I think he's dead now," Jack said, looking up to see Dan standing at the hatch of the copter with a Glock in his hand. He reached down for Casey's hand to haul her aboard the Blackhawk, and then lent Jack a helping hand, too.

Walt gave Little a thumbs up, and the Blackhawk lifted away from the cliff. Jack closed the hatch and took a place on the floor next to Rayne. Utterly shattered after her two-day ordeal, Rayne fell onto his chest, finding sweet refuge. Jack wrapped his arms around her, kissing the top of her head. Feeling secure in his arms, and with the knowledge that everyone was safely aboard the copter, she dropped off to sleep.

* * * * *

One hour later ...

Little lowered the Blackhawk onto the helipad at the Clinica Anglo-Americana. Several nurses and a doctor waited with a gurney, their lab coats flying and twisting around their bodies in the rotor wash.

Dan opened the door as the copter set down and the rotors slowed. Patrizia held tight to her mother. Dan explained to them, "They are going to do a routine exam on you both to make sure you're okay and to address any dehydration issues you may have."

Patrizia looked up to him with her big brown eyes. It was the first time Dan noticed her deformity. "*Senor* Dan," she began. His lip curled in an easy smile. "Please, *Senor* Dan, come with us. I am so afraid."

"Patrizia," Bibiana began, in an almost scolding tone. "We will be fine. *Senor* Dan has done enough for us today."

"It's okay, ma'am. I can come along. I've got nothing more pressing," Dan said. Just then Little came to the hatch. He reached out his arms to help the little girl down. Patrizia cowered away from him. Dan snorted, "Don't be afraid of him. He looks mean, but he's okay."

Patrizia allowed Little to lift her from the chopper, and then he reached for Bibiana. She smiled at him, but he didn't return the favor. He lifted her effortlessly from the chopper and set her to the pavement as gently as a China doll.

"Thank you," she said, but he only nodded, and then stepped away.

The doctor rushed to the open hatch. He said in a British accent, "I'm Dr. Coyle. We need Dr. Lee …"

Jack squeezed Rayne's hand tossing her a reassuring wink, and then led her to the opening. "It'll all be over soon, and we can go home."

She sighed. "I can't wait." With that she let Dr. Coyle help her from the copter and onto the gurney. They whisked her away quickly.

Ellis hurried to follow, but Walt grabbed him by his shirt. "My niece is to be treated with the utmost dignity. There will be no interrogation, because she knows nothing about the chip. She is an innocent victim. You got that, Ellis?"

"I do, Agent Wabash."

"You'd better."

Ellis rushed to catch up to the gurney. He held the door open as the nurses pushed it inside the building. Before allowing the door to fall closed, Agent Ellis turned to nod at Walt and Jack.

CHAPTER SIXTEEN

Washington D.C.

Everything was a go. The Honorable Justice Alejandro Pérez had passed every test. He was worthy in the President's eyes to take a seat on the highest court in the land. The limousines were lined up in the driveway. The police escort patiently waited on the street in front of his home.

The first limo would be driven by Secret Service agents. The second limo driven by Grant would carry the judge and his wife to the press conference for the official announcement of his nomination. Smitty sat shotgun. The third limo followed with more Secret Service, while the police escort fell in line accordingly.

Paullina descended the stairs dressed in a conservative Navy blue suit with matching pumps, and a cream clutch. Her dark hair was pulled back in a severe bun. The foyer was lined with Secret Service agents, as was the front lawn.

Smitty lightly tapped on the judge's office door. "Justice Pérez, we are ready to depart for the White House."

The door opened. Alejandro emerged. He had been a bundle of stress for days, not leaving his office, except to sleep. The upstairs security reported that he did very little of that—until this morning around three a.m. Waiting at his usual post, Smitty heard the judge's cell phone ring from inside the office.

"*Si* …" He heard the judge say. There was a long silence until he heard the judge let out a heavy breath and state, "*Muy bien.*" It hadn't been long after the call ended that the judge came out of his office with a curl on his lips, a brandy in hand, and relief painting his expression. It was almost as if he wanted to kick up his heels and whistle a hearty tune.

For the first time since Smitty's arrival, the judge nodded at him and said, "Good night, Smith," before he climbed the stairs.

This morning, he appeared calm and confident when his gaze met his wife's, except no expression of pleasure or pride filled his face. Nonetheless, he managed a courteous, "You look lovely, Paullina. Come, we mustn't be late. Today is the day we have waited and worked toward."

Smitty was most impressed. Typically the judge spoke to his wife in Spanish, yet this morning he chose to speak freely in English before the Secret Service and lowly security staff.

"Indeed," she replied, hesitating before taking the arm he offered. Smitty had no problem recognizing that Paullina's touch was out of duty rather than affection or admiration.

Smitty and Grant escorted them to the limo, while Secret Service followed, scanning the area for any threat. Once the judge and his wife were safely inside the vehicle, the parade to Pennsylvania Avenue began. Peyton Mattock nodded at Grant as they drove by. He was trimming the rose bushes at the end of the driveway.

The ride was quiet, except for a few indignant whispers exchanged in Spanish between the judge and his wife. Gazing out the window at the monuments passing by, Smitty smiled to himself.

The pressroom was packed with reporters from every news outlet. Usually members of the Secret Service did not come into the press conferences as security scrutinized every person in attendance before they entered. But today the Secret Service was lined up along the walls, brooding and stiff in stance. Smitty and Grant were permitted to stand along the back wall as well.

Judge Pérez and Paullina stood to the side while the president made a brief comment to the press.

He too seemed to be in a brooding mood, and his stature was rigid and succinct. He turned to the judge to extend a rather cool invitation to the podium.

With his chin held high, his chest puffed out with pride, and an accomplished grin on his face, Judge Pérez stepped forward to a place next to the most powerful man in the world, but as he reached for the president's hand familiar voices filled the room ...

"You will be most pleased, Senator. The money collected by my brother-in-law in return for his protection will not only help him to gain much control of the region, but it will aid both you and I in our campaigns for our future posts," Alejandro heard his own voice echoing throughout the room like a black ghost haunting the hall.

"And if these weapons are not enough to defend his territory, what then?" Senator Billings' voice boomed.

"We continue our support until he is successful. Meanwhile, the good works that you and I are providing for the sick and poverty stricken people of the Amazon Valley will far outshine what is hidden in the medical supplies that you and Dr. Lee are taking with you."

Senator Billing's voice sounded unnerved. "What if someone discovers the weapons? What if we are stopped by customs officers? Dr. Lee knows nothing of the contents. He will not know how to answer their questions. We will be detained, arrested, and then what?"

"Dr. Lee's ignorance will be to your benefit. However, no one will stop you. I have control over all situations. You have my word," Alejandro assured.

The judge stood completely still—shell-shocked by the audio tape that continued to play on and on baring the ugly details of his dirty past dealings with the late Senator Billings.

Billings—he made this recording!

This was the evidence that Luis Chaves had against him. This is what he meant when he said that Billings had got greedy. He must've threatened Luis with the recording—what a fool! Luis made him pay with his life and other innocent lives as well. And yet he had received a phone call in the wee hours of the morning informing him of Luis' termination along with everyone in his camp. He had been assured that the huts had been burned to the ground—no one had survived the assault. He had been guaranteed that the evidence was gone along with his rancid brother-in-law.

The bright flashing from the reporter's cameras and the din of rapid questions jerked him from his cogitative state. Suddenly conscious that his hand was still extended out to the president, he looked up to realize that he was no longer there. The president had left the pressroom. A Secret Service agent took hold of the hand that dangled in the air, waiting for the moment of confirmation that he was a very big fish in a very big pond, only to have the hand jerked to his back and handcuffed to the other.

Cameras flashing in his face, cell phones held up to capture every detail of his shame, and reporters following while still calling out questions, Alejandro was led away. He heard the president's press secretary say before the door closed behind him, "This is an unfortunate turn of events. The president is regretful that Justice Pérez was involved in illegal activities to promote his and Senator Billings' careers. The president was aware of the circumstances and worked diligently with the CIA and the Secret Service to uncover this terrible scandal to keep the Supreme Court at the highest level of integrity that it has always been held to. The president will name another appointee within the week …"

* * * * *

Four weeks later …

Rayne couldn't believe how quickly the past month had flown by—it was a complete blur of preparation and activity. She had to chuckle to herself every time she had a moment to recall the marriage proposal …

Her eyes fluttered open after the short surgery to remove the chip that Dr. Tola had placed in her neck four years ago. With that sexy undeniable smile on his lips, Jack caressed her cheek. He said, "Well, welcome back, pretty woman." He brushed his lips over hers, and even though she was still in the throes of sedation, she wanted to pull him into her hospital bed and make crazy passionate love to the man she'd fallen so deeply in love with over the past year.

Instead, she licked her lips to wet them, and then in a raspy voice she said, "Life's way too short, Mr. Haliday. We've lost too much and it's time to make up for it all. Let's not waste any more time. Let's get married as soon as we get home—nothing fancy, just a simple ceremony with the people we love around us."

Clearing his throat, Jack sat straight up. "I dunno, Rayne."

What? Was he having second thoughts about their relationship? Had she somehow missed some

tiny signal that it wasn't progressing as she thought it was? Her heart practically stopped.

"I mean ..." he shrugged. "I'm kind of a sensitive person. I sort of thought that when I was proposed to that you would get down on one knee."

Her eyes widened. There she was lying in a hospital bed hooked up to a billion tubes. She shook her head. Yes, she was still a bit groggy from the anesthesia, but did he just say that he wanted her to get down on one knee?

Really?

She peeked at him askance only to find that ornery little boy smile slowly lifting his lips. He pushed his chair away from the bed, and got down on one knee, taking her hand in his.

Laying his forehead on her hand, Jack closed his eyes as if he were whispering a quiet prayer, then he gently kissed her hand and looked into her eyes. He said, "God knows how I love you, Rayne, and I'm asking you to be my wife. What do you say?"

"I say, yes. Now kiss me, you fool."

By the next day she'd been released from the hospital with instructions to take it easy for a few days. Not a chance. The team flew back to the States, while she and Jack stayed behind to get all the proper paperwork in order for Bibiana and Patrizia to make the trip with them to the United States.

Rayne contacted a friend, Dr. Linda Taylor, who was a pediatric plastic surgeon at Children's Hospital in Pittsburgh. Living in a poverty stricken area in Peru, Patrizia required quite a few inoculations before entering the States and more yet for the surgery. As soon as they returned home Rayne swung right back into doctor mode to bring Patrizia up to date with the left over inoculations before her surgery.

With all the visits to Pittsburgh, Rayne had little time to organize a wedding—even a small event. Silja was thrilled to take up the role of wedding planner. She immediately contacted Sam Shuster, who was sorry to inform her that the Presbyterian Church was booked through January, but hey, First Force Headquarters, a gorgeous Georgian style mansion, was available, and Sam, an interim pastor, was overjoyed to volunteer to perform the nuptials. He joined forces with Silja to plan Jack and Rayne's big day. Rayne was completely at ease with it all—she knew that her wedding was in very capable hands.

Yes, a month had simply whipped by, and now it was Patrizia's big day—the day of her life-changing surgery. It was three a.m. when Bibiana and Patrizia came down to the foyer from the guest rooms that they'd been occupying. Rayne, Jack, and Lil had spent time showing them around Pennsylvania—especially on the very long drives to Pittsburgh.

Lil and Patrizia played well together. Patrizia loved her new school. She blended well with the children, especially since her English was so fluent, and Lil was an attentive student to learn Spanish from her new friend. Even though there was a three-year age gape, the two girls had become instant besties—they were almost like sisters. The mansion was filled with little girls' giggles.

Rayne was quite bemused one afternoon when she looked out the window to see Little sitting under a maple tree reading a book to the girls. She paused to watch, and to keep the vision close to her heart.

Now Bibiana, or Bebe as Lil had taken to calling her, clutched Patrizia's tiny suitcase with a white-knuckle grip as she made her way to the door where Walt and Rayne waited to drive them to the hospital. They had to leave very early because it was a three-hour drive down the turnpike into Pittsburgh, and getting through the Squirrel Hill Tunnels during the morning rush could be a real trick. Patrizia needed to be checked in by six-thirty a.m.

Easing the case from Bibiana's hand, Rayne said, "Everything is going to be just fine."

Bibiana managed a weak smile. "I know this. I am just a little nervous."

"Of course you are—you're a mom. C'mon, let's be on our way. It's a long drive," Rayne urged.

Just as they were about to walk out the door, they heard a voice calling out, "Wait!" They turned to see Lil hurrying toward them. Her nightgown was wrinkled and her hair was bed-tossed. Jack followed behind with droopy eyes and looking bedraggled, yet very sexy in general—in Rayne's eyes anyway.

Lil held out the salt-water pearl necklace to Patrizia. "Take my bravery necklace with you, Pat. It helped me, and it helped Dr. Rayne. I know it'll help you, too."

Taking the necklace from her friend's hand, Patrizia smiled. "*Gracias, mi amigo.*"

Lil grinned. "That means thank you my friend in Spanish," she announced. "Pat's been teaching me."

Bibiana kissed Lil on the cheek. "And such a good friend you are."

Jack swept Lil up onto his hip and waving, they watched the SUV drive away. When it was through the gate, he asked, "Can we go back to bed now?"

Squishing his face between her hands, Lil said, "You need some serious beauty sleep."

"Ahhhh, shut up," Jack teased in his best imitation of Daffy Duck. He tossed her over his shoulder to march back to their section of the house with Lil giggling the entire way.

* * * * *

It had been a long day. Patrizia had been in surgery for four and a half hours, but when Dr. Taylor arrived in the waiting room, she was happy to report that the little girl had come through the surgery with ease, and that her new lip would be healed within a few short weeks. Bibiana crumbled into a chair, burying her face into her hands to weep with relief and joy.

"My Patrizia will have a new life because of you, Dr. Rayne," she managed through her tears. "How can we ever thank you enough?"

Rayne hugged her tightly. "Let's not worry about that at all. Patrizia will probably be out for a couple hours. Why don't we go to the hotel and get some rest, and then we can come back after a while to visit her."

Mopping her face with a tissue, Bibiana said, "Oh no, I cannot leave. I will stay here until they call me. Please, you go. I insist."

"I can stay with you—"

"No. Please, get some rest. I will have some coffee here. Just knowing that Patrizia is well and her face will be beautiful is all that I need."

"Mmmm ... okay ... Uncle Walt and I will go get some lunch from Primanti Brothers and bring it in—it's bad enough that Pat has to eat hospital food, let's not put ourselves through it too. But you must come to the hotel tonight to sleep. You'll be no good to Pat if you are exhausted. *Comprende?*"

Smiling, Bibiana nodded. Rayne kissed her on the forehead, and then she and Walt made their way down the hallway to the elevator. Pressing the button, Walt said, "I hear the wedding plans are moving right along."

"Oh yes, I'm briefed every evening."

"Yeah ... so am I—Dale is very excited," Walt said.

Favoring him with an apologetic wince, Rayne said, "Sorry, no matter how big or small, weddings are all consuming, I'm afraid. But the good news is that it's all coming together: Grant's mom is coming in from West Virginia to make the cake. She made Grant and Sil's. It was gorgeous, so Sil asked her to make ours. Jack's parents and his brother will be arriving on Friday—"

"And Dale has the flowers and the catering arrangements under control," Walt added.

Rayne snorted, "Yep, and Bill Shuster has all the official business taken care of. So we're pretty much good to go."

The elevator door opened. They waited for a nurse with a patient in a wheelchair to pass before stepping on.

"Uncle Walt ... I would like to hire Bibiana as a housekeeper. I could teach her how to assist me with patients should Smitty be unavailable," Rayne explained once they were on the elevator alone.

"Sounds like a good idea, Rayne, but where would they live? We can't move everyone into the mansion, you know," he replied.

"Of course not, but we do have an empty apartment above the garage where great grand-mother's chauffeur used to live. It's small but it has two bedrooms, and I could really use the help with the upkeep of the house. Lil is so fond of Patrizia. They're almost like sisters, and she's given Bibiana a nickname, Bebe."

Walt kept his eyes on the buttons above the door lighting up the floor numbers as they descended. He knew what Rayne was up to. She was making a play for his softer side that he carefully kept in check—divide and conquer. She was winning.

Stepping off the elevator into the lobby, he lifted a shoulder. "I suppose it could work. We've stored some of grandmother's furniture in it, but it hasn't been occupied in over twenty years, it would need some work."

"I'm sure. But I'll be moving into Jack's suite after the wedding, so they could move into my suite until the apartment is ready," Rayne eagerly suggested.

Walt smiled. His niece had a heart as big as New York City. He opened the door that led to the parking lot for Rayne to step through. "You've got this all figured out, don't you?"

"All the way down to the work visas. If they like it here in the States then we'll apply for citizenship."

Walt stopped mid-step, shaking his head. "You're just like your mother. She was all about helping others."

Rayne's lips curled in delight at her uncle's words. Arching both of her eyebrows, she cajoled, "Then … it's a go?"

"How can I say no? We'll see how much work the apartment requires as soon as we get home."

"No worries. Jack, Lil, and Smitty are already washing the walls down. Little and Dan are making sure all the plumbing is in working order, *annnd* ... Grant and Silja are out shopping for a stove and fridge," Rayne supplied, as she slipped into the passenger's seat of Walt's SUV, closing the door before he could oppose.

Rubbing the nape of his neck, Walt had to chuckle to himself. He muttered, "Yep, she's just like my little sister."

EPILOGUE

The twenty-fifth of October proved to be a spectacular day. The tapestry of gold, orange, and brilliant red set the trees a blaze under the glimmering sun. A gentle breeze plucked the leaves that were ready to resign, sending them on a whirling freefall to the ground. Rayne gazed out her bedroom window at the perfect afternoon that she and Jack would become man and wife.

She was so pleased that Jack's parents were able to attend the wedding and it was an extra blessing that Sean, Jack's younger brother, was on leave from the Navy and able to stand for Jack. It was perfect timing to say the least.

A soft knock at the door pulled her away from the window. Casey called through, "Rayne … Can we come in?"

"One moment …" Rayne hurried to the vanity to pick up a white vial that she'd laid there on a tissue. She placed it into the drawer—it had a few more minutes to go. Easing the drawer closed, she called, "Come in."

When the door opened Rayne's heart swelled at the sight before her. Lil was dressed in a darling yellow dress with lace trim at the neckline and a wide white sash tied up in a big bow behind. Between Casey and Silja they had managed to tame her hair into gently cascading curls around her face, and on her head she wore a halo of orange and yellow mums.

"Look, Dr. Rayne!" Lil burst with excitement. "I'm wearing pink lip gloss!"

The child's joy was enchanting. Rayne chuckled, "So you are! You look beautiful, Lil."

Lil's grin stretched all the way to her big brown eyes. "So do you, Dr. Rayne."

Rayne was happy that she found just the right dress for her second wedding. She wore a soft blue satin dress with a surplice neckline—a little diving, but very flattering. It was ruched at the waist with capped sleeves, the dress tapered to just above her knees. She wore her mother's pearl necklace and earrings—something old. Silja insisted that she wear a pair of her silver stilettos—Rayne agreed, and with that she had something borrowed.

While it wasn't exactly what Rayne had in mind for an autumn style for her maid-of-honor, Casey wore a cream capped sleeved sheath draped in black lace. Her long dark hair was gathered in a French twist, while a pair of diamond studded double teardrops dangled from her ears. As far as Rayne was concerned their eclectic fashion was simply fabulous.

The guest list was short but filled with people who loved and cared about them, the members of First Force, Jack's mom, dad, and brother, Dale Thomas, Bibiana, and Patrizia. Peyton Mattock finagled an invitation as well. Casey was excited—whether she was letting on or not.

"C'mon, girls," Silja said as she came into the room with camera in hand. "Gather around Rayne at her vanity. It will be a great photo."

Rayne glanced down at Casey's right leg. The KA Bar knife that the sniper kept tethered to her calf at all times was absent. She pointed out, "You removed your knife just for me? I'm flattered."

Casey snorted, "I didn't think it matched the dress very well."

Rayne, Lil, and Casey posed for several shots, and then Casey said, "Okay, I think we should give the bride some space." She shooed Silja and Lil toward the door, and then turned to Rayne. "We'll meet you at the top of the staircase for the big event in a few, okay?"

"I'll be there," Rayne said.

As soon as the door closed behind them, Rayne opened the drawer to look at the vial wrapped in a tissue, lying among her silky panties. It read—positive. Her heart leapt inside her chest. She caressed her flat tummy knowing that within a short time it would have a bump—a baby bump. She wasn't afraid of the elation that she was feeling, because she knew that it would be shared. She would tell Jack during their very short honeymoon—he would be as thrilled as she was. It was as she told him at the hospital after she'd had the chip removed—there's no time to waste.

Another knock sounded at the door.

Lil called through, "Dr. Rayne, can I talk to you for a minute?"

Closing the drawer, she said, "Of course …"

Lil hurried into the room, closing the short distance quickly to take Rayne into a big hug. She said, "I miss my mommy so much, but I'm glad you're marrying my daddy, so … can I call you Mommy Rayne instead of Dr. Rayne now?"

Rayne could barely catch her breath. So much joy and love poured into her heart. In a watery voice, she answered, "I would like that very, *very* much."

Lil kissed her on the cheek leaving a glossy lip print behind. Rayne didn't wipe it away. She wanted the kiss to go with her into the matrimonial ceremony that would launch Lil, Jack, and herself into a new life together—a life filled with love and laughter.

Rayne looked up to find a beautiful woman with brunette hair standing behind Lil. A bittersweet smile lifted her lips as she caressed the child's curls, and then her gaze met Rayne's. At first, the sight brought with it a strong sense of unease, but then, just as quickly, the feeling was replaced with knowing.

Not wanting to alarm Lil, Rayne mouthed, "Laura …"

Nodding, she brought her hand to her lips to blow Rayne a kiss, and then she was gone, leaving Rayne with a warm sensation of peace that somehow Laura was giving her blessing over the marriage, and that she felt secure in who would look after her daughter in her absence.

Rayne dragged in a ragged breath, trying to hold in grateful tears. She managed, "I love you, and I love your daddy very much. We'll be a family in just a few minutes. C'mon, walk with me to the staircase."

Hand in hand Lil and Rayne made their way down the corridor to descend the stairs and prepare for the ceremony. They all had so much to look forward to, a new family, a new start, and a new life growing inside her.

* * * * *

The foyer was bursting with the colors of autumn. The tall vintage Chinese palace vases that adorned the foyer were filled with purple, orange, and gold mums. White folding chairs were situated in the foyer facing the ornate beveled glass door for the small but jubilant group of guests. A carved podium had been borrowed from Sam Shuster's church to serve as the alter.

Twelve members from a bell choir from the same church were positioned at the top of the grand staircase. The bells echoed down the staircase filling the area with a calliope of sound as Lil carefully descended the stairs. She carried a basket filled with petals to drop once she came to the short aisle, except when she got half way down the stairs Tickles was sitting on the step meowing and batting at her ankles. Unerringly, Lil scooped up the kitten and placed her in the basket—the tiny tabby didn't take up too much room, so Lil would still be able to get to the petals. When Rayne and Casey saw the kitten sitting in the basket, they cupped their hands over their mouths to smother their laughter. Grinning, Walt shook his head at Lil's antics, and then he presented his arm to Rayne.

"Are you ready?" he asked.

"Absolutely," Rayne said, smiling.

They waited for Lil to take her seat between Grandma Dale and Jack's mother, Grandma

Marlene, and for Casey to take her place on the opposite side of Jack and Sean. Walt gave the cue and the bells fluidly switched from Cannon in C to "Here Comes the Bride." The guests stood. As Rayne made her way passed her guests, she took in the faces—the men who had not just rescued her once from the abyss of terror in the Amazonian Valley, but they'd risked their lives twice to pluck her from that hell. These were the faces of heroes.

Finally her eyes fell upon Patrizia—the daughter of the man who had tried to destroy her, and yet she rose triumphantly from the ashes, and so would his daughter. It had only been a week since her surgery, and already her face was only beginning to heal—a beautiful face was emerging from under the slight bruising. She too was about to embark on a new life with a bright future.

At last, Walt removed her hand from his arm to place it into Jack's. It felt so right the way Jack held her hand so tightly through the very short ceremony. She was so thankful that they'd found each other even though the circumstances that brought them together had been so tragic. Now they could build a new life. They could begin again—together, with Lil.

Finally, Sam Shuster asked Jack and Rayne to face their guests. They obliged. He announced, "I would like to be the first to present to you—"

"I just realized something!" Rayne interrupted her eyes wide with her sudden epiphany. "I'm now *Doc Haliday!*"

The room was silent. Everyone was staring at her like a duck had just landed smack dab on her head, and then from the back of the foyer, Little called out, "Ho-yah!"

All the guests responded with a resounding, "Ho-yah!" while Jack took his new wife, Doc Haliday, into his arms and kissed her with all the passion that they would share now and forever.

The End

*Thank you for reading **Into the Dark**. I hope you will read the next book from the First Force Series, **To the Brink** coming in 2016. Let me entice you with a short synopsis to whet your appetite ...*

TO THE BRINK

Passion ignites
between the fine line of danger and deception!

Tess thought her life would settle down after the death of her husband, Ballard Crafton. After all she'd escaped Russia with the formula to his secret serum that turns soldiers into unstoppable machines. She was certain that the Russians thought that Ballard's notes were lost in the explosion that killed him and destroyed his lab, except one man believes that Tess possesses the precious information, and he wants it for his own devious plans.

Hired assailants dog her night and day. She needs help and she needed it weeks ago. Now she turns to First Force for protection, only to find that the team is away with only one operative at First Force Headquarters holding down the fort—Dan Garrison.

How can Dan keep her safe when he isn't sure that he believes her story? How can Tess gain his trust, and how can either of them deny the underlying passion that is igniting between the fine line of deception and danger?

*Sign up for Cindy's newsletter on the homepage at her website, **www.cindymcwriter.co**m, and you will receive the first chapter of Cindy's latest book delivered directly to your inbox as a thank you!*

No worries!

Cindy does not share email addresses and she **never spams.*

Below is Jack Haliday's recipe for patty pan squash/ apple pie from chapter six. Here's to hoping that your baking experience is as sumptuous as Jack and Rayne's. Enjoy!

PATTY PAN SQUASH/APPLE PIE

Ingredients:

1 medium golden patty pan squash

1 medium granny smith apple

1 medium honey crisp apple

(Apple selections are only a suggestion, use apples of your choice)

¾ cup sugar

¼ cup brown sugar

1 tbsp. cinnamon (or to taste)

pinch of salt

1 tsp vanilla

1 egg for an egg wash

Prepared pie crust—homemade or frozen (Jack preferred frozen)

Preheat oven 375

Peel, core, and slice the patty pan squash just as you do the apples and place in a large bowl. In a small bowl combine sugar, brown sugar, cinnamon and salt. Mix well with fork and pour over apples and squash. Mix well with fork, and then add the vanilla—stir in. Pour the mixture into your pie crust, place and seal second pie crust over top—cut in vent holes. Crack an egg into a small bowl and whisk to create an egg wash. Brush the egg wash over the top crust, and then sprinkle some sugar over it to make the crust sweet, too. Bake at 375 for 55-60 minutes.

*Note: You can make the pie without the apples. That said I find that the squash enhances the flavor of the apples immensely—combined the two complement one and other very well. Mmmm ... so good!

ABOUT CINDY MCDONALD

For twenty-six years Cindy's life whirled around a song and a dance. She was a professional dancer/choreographer for most of her adult life and never gave much thought to a writing career until 2005. She often notes: Don't ask me what happened, but suddenly I felt drawn to my computer to write about things that I have experienced with my husband's Thoroughbreds and happenings at the racetrack—she muses: they are greatly exaggerated upon of course—I've never been murdered. Viola! Cindy's first book series, Unbridled, was born.

Cindy is a huge fan of romantic suspense series', and although she isn't one to make New Year's resolutions, on New Year's Day 2013 she made a commitment to write one. There are two books in the series at this time: Into the Crossfire and To the Breaking Pointe.

People are always asking Cindy: Do you miss dance? With a bitter sweet smile on her lips she tells them: Sometimes I do. I miss my students. I miss choreographing musicals, but I love writing my books, and I love sharing them with my readers.

Cindy resides on her forty-five acre Thoroughbred farm with her husband, Bill, and her Cocker Spaniel, Allister, near Pittsburgh, Pennsylvania.

For more information, book trailers, and excerpts for all of Cindy's books please visit her website:

www.cindymcwriter.com

INTO THE CROSSFIRE

BOOK #1 of the FIRST FORCE SERIES

A notorious killer leaves Jack Haliday's world in shambles.

It has been four years since ex-Navy SEAL, Jack Haliday, had an explosive run-in with a biker gang wounding their leader, Gunner. During those years Jack had acquired everything he ever wanted: a beautiful wife, an adorable daughter, and a lovely home in the suburbs— everything was just about as perfect as it could get, until Gunner returned to twist Jack's world inside-out with a vengeance that he could never have prepared for.

Now Jack has a score to settle and he's got some friends to help him do it!

Reviewers and readers love

INTO THE CROSSFIRE!

"*Into the Crossfire* is a powerful story that will leave you breathless." ~**Jersey Girl Reviews**

"If you're looking for a quick read that will get your adrenaline pumping, pick up *Into the Crossfire*."
~**Moonlight Reader Reviews**

"An ending so powerful, electric and dramatic only author Cindy McDonald can deliver it."
~**Fran Lewis Reviews**

TO THE BREAKING POINTE

BOOK #2 of the FIRST FORCE SERIES

Pushed to the Breaking Pointe!

Five years ago First Force operative, Grant Ketchum, let the ballerina of his dreams dance out of his life. Silja Ramsay returned to her birthplace, Russia, to take the position of principal dancer for the Novikov Ballet Company.

The owner and director of the ballet company, Natalia Novikov, has a dark secret: her beloved ballet company is almost broke. Natalia forces her dancers to prostitute themselves to financial contributors at exclusive after-show parties. Silja has been exempt and kept in the dark about the parties— until an American financier offers to bail the failing ballet company out. His prerequisite: Silja must become his personal companion, live in his home, and fulfill his every desire. Against her will, Silja is taken to the American's mansion, but before she goes she manages to send a text to the only man who can save her, Grant: HELP!

Now Grant is on a mission to find his lost ballerina and rescue her from this powerful man's subjugation. He will do anything to get her out alive. If they survive, will he let her chasse out of his life again?

Reviewers and readers love

TO THE BREAKING POINTE!

"Yes! This is everything a romantic suspense thriller should be!" ~ **Sara's Organized Chaos**

"I loved everything about this book!"

~**Deal Sharing Aunt**

"All the thrills of a Jason Bourne movie!"

~**Sherrie Wilson/Amazon reader**

Into the Crossfire and *To the Breaking Pointe* are the first two books of Cindy McDonald's romantic suspense series, First force, available in print or ebook at amazon. com, BAM, barnesandnoble.com and where all fine books are sold. For more information about all of Cindy's books, please visit her website:

www.cindymcwriter.com.

GET TOTALLY UNBRIDLED!
CHECK OUT CINDY McDONALD'S
UNBRIDLED SERIES:

It's really quite simple. The Unbridled Series is Thoroughbred racing steeped in murder, suspense, and a generous dose of romance—hey, what more could you ask? Available in print or ebook at amazon.com, BAM, barnesandnoble.com and where all fine books are sold.

ACCOLADES FOR CINDY McDONALD'S UNBRIDLED SERIES:

"I love this series!" ~**Wanted Readers**
"McDonald continues her dazzling writing style that keeps the reader in suspense from beginning to end."
~The Book Nerd
"I couldn't put it down. I finished the book in two days—something that I never do." ~**Socrates Book Reviews**
www.cindymcwriter.com

Be sure to sign up for Cindy's newsletter at her website, *www.cindymcwriter.com,* and you will receive the first chapter of Cindy's latest book delivered directly to your inbox as a thank you!
*Cindy does not share email addresses.